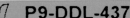

P9-DDL-437

ROBYN CARR

THE PROMISE

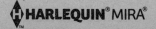

Recycling programs
for this product may
not exist in your area.

ISBN-13: 978-0-7783-1620-6

THE PROMISE

Copyright © 2014 by Robyn Carr

Printed in U.S.A.

THE PROMISE

One

Peyton Lacoumette drove slowly down the main street of Thunder Point, past all the small businesses, including the medical clinic. She drove all the way to the far end of the point where she was stopped by the ornate gates to what could only be a mansion. She could barely make out the structure behind overgrown hedges and untrimmed trees. She got out of the car to peer through the bars, but couldn't see much. If she had been with a couple of her brothers they might have wanted to scale the wall for a closer look, but that wouldn't do in a sundress and sandals.

She turned the car around and went back through the town. It looked pretty well-lived-in, but it was clean, and it was obvious from the small groups of people who had stopped to chat here and there that people were neighborly. A lot of them paused to stare at her car. It was a shiny new black Lexus and had been ridiculously expensive.

People stopping to talk happened a little less often

in cities like Portland and San Francisco and hardly ever in New York City, though she'd liked living in those cities. In Bayonne, France, it was more common, almost required that you were never in a hurry. This place appealed to her immediately, probably because it was similar to the town closest to her family's farm. Or Bayonne, for that matter. Peyton saw a woman putting buckets of long-stemmed colorful flowers in front of her shop; a man was sweeping the sidewalk in front of his store; two dogs were leashed to a lamppost at the diner's door—a spotted Great Dane and a Yorkie, sharing a pan of water. The main street appeared well scrubbed and friendly.

She parked in front of the clinic and went inside. It was noon; there were no patients waiting, and the young woman behind the counter stood up to greet her with a smile. "Hi. How can I help you today?"

"I was just passing through, wondering where the best access to the beach was?"

"Probably the marina. Or, Cooper has a beach bar on the far side of the beach, up on the hillside. There's a road to his place from Highway 101, and he has stairs down to the beach and tables on his deck. Cooper's place is the best spot in town to watch the sunset. When the sun sinks behind those big rocks in the bay, it's really beautiful. I think he gets the best part of his business from people who stop by there for something to drink or eat when they're out walking on the beach or waiting for the sunset."

"I saw the beach access from the road, but I didn't stop. There's some building going on out there...."

"That's Cooper's, too. He's building a house, and next door we're building one, too. Me and my fiancé."

"Oh, congratulations," Peyton said. "On the engagement, not the building."

The young woman laughed. "You can congratulate me on that, too. I didn't think I'd ever live in an oceanfront house."

Peyton looked around the small office. "People must be feeling pretty healthy around here today."

"This is an unusually quiet day."

"Are you the doctor or nurse?"

"Just the office manager. Dr. Grant stepped out, since there weren't any patients. Do you need to see the doctor?"

"No," Peyton said with a laugh. "It just seemed like a good place to ask about the town."

"I'm Devon McAllister." She extended a hand across the counter.

"Peyton Lacoumette, nice to meet you," she said. "I grew up on a farm up north, not too far from Portland in the Mount Hood area. I didn't even know this town existed."

"We're a little off the beaten track, and everyone seems to like it that way. There are only two ways into town—across the beach from Cooper's place or a winding road north of here from 101. That's probably how you found us—there's an exit sign. Folks around here keep threatening to take down the sign," she added with a laugh. "They won't, but some tend to like the hidden quality."

"What do most people do around here?" Peyton asked.

"Lots of fishermen, obviously. Then there are small business owners and people who work in those businesses, like me. My fiancé is the athletic director at the high school. A lot of the local population works out of town—Bandon, Coquille, North Bend."

"I drove out to the point and saw a big house or building out there. Huge."

"It's a vacant house. The stuff of legends around here—the old Morrison place. It's before my time here, but I guess the family was rich once, went bust, declared bankruptcy, and the son killed someone and went to prison. He was just a teenager. The only murder this town has ever seen, I'm told."

"Why doesn't someone do something with that place?" Peyton asked.

"I guess because it's so big—no one can afford to live in it."

"What's big?"

Devon shrugged. "Country Club big. Huge rooms, a lot of bedrooms and bathrooms, a restaurant-size kitchen, thousands of square feet on hundreds of acres right on the point. The only other building out there is the lighthouse, because that point and its twin across the bay are very rocky."

"Hmm. Sounds like a clever person could turn it into a library or boarding school or nursing home. It would be fun to see the inside," she said.

"It would. I never thought about it, but a lot of people in town have been inside that house."

"Have you lived here your whole life?" Peyton asked.

"Oh, God, no!" Devon laughed. "Only a year. I'm originally from Seattle—a city girl, really. But there's something about this town.... I like the people, but more than that, it's the feeling of the town in general. It's safe, like it hugs you. Maybe because you have to come here on purpose, it's not something you'd see from the highway and it's not a thoroughfare. I've never lived in a little town before. And then I met my fiancé and found this job, and here I am," she said, and smiled prettily.

"But who runs the office? Is there just the one doctor?"

"Just me and Dr. Grant at the moment, but he's been looking for an associate or nurse practitioner. He doesn't want a big practice, but more than one person capable of writing scripts or putting in stitches would help a lot. It's becoming a busy clinic. He's hoping to expand—we have that many patients. This town could use a twenty-four-hour urgent care, but that takes much more room and staff. He says that's something for down the road."

"And you like it?"

"I love it. I love Dr. Grant."

Peyton raised a brow and smiled. "Does the athletic director mind that you love your boss?"

Devon laughed. "Spencer loves Dr. Grant, too! This town and my job—it's perfect for us. Spencer has an eleven-year-old son, Austin. And I have a four-year-old daughter, Mercy."

"Do you like your soon-to-be stepson?" Peyton asked.

"He's a dream come true," Devon said. "Mercy worships him, and he's very good to her."

"Very lucky for you," Peyton said. "Those things can be dicey—blending families like that."

"We're very lucky, that's true."

"What if you don't find an associate?" Peyton asked.

"We'll manage," Devon said. "We make it work somehow. It's just that…well, Dr. Grant spends a lot of time helping out at other hospitals, sitting on call almost every weekend, and that's inconvenient for him. He's a very devoted family man and needs more time with his family."

"Devoted family man?" Peyton asked.

"Absolutely. Plus he volunteers with Spencer as the game doctor for the football team. This town doesn't have a lot of money, and football is very important to Thunder Point. School programs and sports are the main entertainment here, and most of the student athletes are working hard for scholarships. Spencer's last school—a big, rich Texas high school—had a certified trainer and sports medicine physical therapist. We don't have resources like that here in this little town, so it's important to recruit volunteers like Dr. Grant. I wish you could meet him."

"Devon, would you excuse me for a second? I just have to get something…."

"Sure," Devon said. "Would you like a cup of coffee?"

"No, thanks," she said, smiling over her shoulder as she walked out to her car. She came back in with a cloth briefcase. She opened it on the counter in front of Devon and pulled out a thin newspaper. "I was renting a cottage in Coos Bay for a short vacation. I happened to see this ad but didn't know anything about the town. So, I thought I'd check it out and maybe drop off a résumé."

Devon glanced at the résumé, and her mouth fell open just as her eyes became very round with surprise. "Physician's assistant? From Portland?"

"I worked for a cardiologist. I was there for three years. Very busy practice. I was hoping for something a little quieter for a while."

Devon didn't speak right away. Then she said, "So, you're not just passing through."

"Well, I could have been. I haven't officially started looking for my next job yet. I haven't sent out any résumés yet."

"Why did you leave your former practice?"

"I was replaced, but I promise you my recommendation will be excellent," she said. "Maybe you could give my résumé to Dr. Grant, and if he's interested, my cell phone number and email address are right there," she said, pointing.

"I'll do just that," Devon said. "Miss Sneaky Britches."

Peyton laughed. "Please don't be offended, Devon.

I wasn't going to leave a résumé if something about the town or the clinic or the doctor didn't feel right."

"You haven't met the doctor."

"But you love him," Peyton said. "Even your fiancé loves him."

"Who loves me?" a man asked.

Peyton looked up, and there, standing in the space that led into the back of the clinic, was a very attractive man in his late thirties. He was dressed in faded jeans and a yellow dress shirt, open at the collar, sleeves rolled up. Although he was clearly over thirty-five, he had a boyish quality to his good looks. But not to his physique—he was broad shouldered and had muscular arms and big hands. Even from where she stood, she could see a depth to his blue eyes.

Devon looked over her shoulder. "Meet Dr. Scott Grant, who obviously just snuck in the back door."

He stepped forward. "Pleasure," he said. "Miss Sneaky Britches, was it?"

"Peyton Lacoumette," she said, taking his hand. "I saw your ad. After getting to know Devon a little bit, I decided to drop off a résumé. I'm a physician's assistant."

"Is that so?" he said, taking the page, glancing at it. "I've been interviewing."

"Well, give me a call if you think I suit," she said. "I'm staying in Coos Bay for a little while—just taking a breather before summer is over."

Without looking up from her résumé, he asked, "Do you have time for a conversation now?"

"I—I guess so," she said. Then she laughed a little uncomfortably. "I didn't expect… I didn't dress for… Sure, I have time."

"Good," he said. "Come on back." And he turned that she might follow him.

Scott found himself staring down at the résumé for a long time, looking for flaws. He knew if he looked across the desk he'd see only perfection, and it unsettled him. She was only a job applicant, after all. She was very pretty, yes, but not the type he usually found himself giving a second look. His eyes were usually drawn to blondes, like his late wife. This woman had dark hair, dark eyes and a slightly olive complexion. Her hair was long and straight and looked like a sheet of silk. *Italian? Mexican? Sicilian?* Her eyes were large and her eyebrows curved in a perfect arch. She was trim—she obviously took care of herself. He noted her very nice collarbones. He almost laughed aloud. *Collarbones, Scott? Really?* He was afraid to look up. He might lean over the desk to look at her feet and ankles, not that he gave a shit about ankles. He hoped they were at least thick and weird-looking. But he knew they would not be.

"Lacoumette," he said. "Interesting name…."

"It's Basque. Originally from the south of France. Most of the Basque blood in my family is Spanish, but the name originated in the northern Basque country and has survived for generations. My parents are second-generation Americans. They have a farm near Portland." She was quiet for a moment, then cleared her throat. "Do you have any questions about my résumé, Dr. Grant?" she asked.

"You seem to have a lot of experience," he said. "This is one of the most impressive résumés I've seen."

"Twelve years," she said. "Two practices and two hospitals, plus a year at a small clinic in Bayonne, France."

"France?"

"An old clinic right in the middle of Basque territory. I wanted to see where our people came from. I'm probably related to half of them." And she smiled then, showing off a row of beautiful white teeth. She was stunning.

"What do you prefer? The private practice or the hospital?"

"For the hands-on work, the hospital wins. For compensation, I'll take private practice every time."

With her experience, Scott knew she could very likely make more money than he did, in the right place. "Did you look around? This isn't a rich practice."

"That isn't why I dropped by," she said. "Are you frowning?"

Was he glaring at her? He shook himself. "I didn't mean to do that, to be defensive," he said. "It's just that…." He took a breath. "Let me be frank. I started this clinic on a shoestring. I run it on a tight budget. Where salary is concerned, I doubt I could meet your demands."

She tilted her head and raised her eyebrows. "I don't recall making any. Yet."

He realized he didn't want her to walk out, yet he was sure he didn't have what it would take to make her stay. He folded his hands on top of the résumé and smiled at her. "What brings you to Thunder Point?"

"Just your ad," she said.

Glancing at the résumé again, he asked, "How did you see my ad in Portland? The search company?"

"No," she said with a laugh. "When I left my last job I decided to take my time looking for employment because I wasn't completely sure where I wanted to be. Plus, I didn't take much time off in the past few years. So, I took a vacation. I spent a little time with my parents, then I drove down the coast, first to Canon Beach, then Coos Bay. I just happened to be looking through the employment section—I think it was the North Bend paper. I saw your ad and had never heard of Thunder Point. I was just curious. I thought in another couple of weeks I might contact an agency. I'm more comfortable in a big city. I didn't expect this—a spontaneous interview in a little town. I was leaning toward San Francisco or Seattle...."

"Ah," he said. "You like the Pacific Northwest."

"I do, and I have family around. I was thinking it was time for a hospital," she continued. "I was not interested in another practice right now—a little cozy, if you know what I mean. And I grew up in a tiny farming community and haven't worked in a small town in years."

"There are certain advantages to a small town, a small clinic," he said. "I came from a large city to a small town as an experiment, hoping I'd take to it. It's cozy, all right—your friends are your patients and vice versa, but in the city the general practitioner is a good referral agency. In a place like Thunder Point we take care of a lot more. People aren't equipped to travel long distances to see specialists. In many cases their medical coverage is spotty. They need a good local medical team."

"And that's why you're here, to provide a good medical service? As altruistic as that?" Peyton asked.

"And because I thought it would be good for my kids. Also because the grandmothers, both widows, get a little invasive and high maintenance. I need them in smaller doses. So, that was my original motivation, but I like it here. Now, tell me why you would consider Thunder Point?"

"It's quiet," she said. "It's possible something like this could work for me for a while...."

"Awhile?" he asked.

"If you offer me a job here and if I take the offer, I'll make a commitment. And I'll keep it."

"Why did you leave your last job?" he asked.

"I was replaced," she said. "The doctor wanted to put someone else in my position."

"When I call him, is that what he'll tell me?"

"I'm not sure. He felt we had accomplished as much as we could as a team, and it was time for a change. He'll tell you my performance was excellent."

Scott thought about this for a second. "And that's what you're telling me?"

"No. That's what he'll tell you."

"And is there another story?" Scott asked.

"He's dating an RN who convinced him she could do my job. I don't know if that's true, only time will tell. Apparently they just can't get enough of each other. I suspect she didn't appreciate my continued presence in the office after they'd become an item."

"A little jealousy?" he asked.

"Or paranoia. I had no interest whatsoever in her boyfriend. That's okay, it was time for a change. Let's just clear the air on that, shall we? Before there's a lot of curiosity and conjecture—I'm interested in *work*. And I'm *not* interested in men."

Well, that cleared the air, all right. He coughed lightly. "That's very honest," he said. "No beating around the bush there." He smiled. "You're very up front about personal things."

"I don't mean to be rude—I hope that didn't seem rude—I think it's best if we're honest about issues that could be problematic. It's not something I feel like talking about, but...really, I don't need the aggravation."

He smirked. "That will greatly disappoint the single men of Thunder Point," he muttered.

"Oh, please," she said. "They'll get over it."

"I suppose. Although not without a few..."

"Few what?" she asked, frowning.

He knew it would be unprofessional to say *fantasies*. "Regrets," he said. "You'll find the cost of living in this town is low." He wrote down a number on a piece of paper and slid it toward her. "It would have to be a year at this salary."

She looked at it and gasped. "Is the cost of living *free?*"

Scott stood behind his desk. "While you consider the offer, I'll give Dr.—" he looked down "—Dr. Ramsdale a call." He extended his hand. "Thanks for taking the time to talk with me about the position."

Peyton stood and shook his offered hand. "Sure. I think this meeting was unexpected for both of us."

"It certainly was. By the way, how are you with children?"

She stiffened as if offended. "I'm the oldest of eight and consider myself to be good with kids, though I'm in no way interested in taking on childcare duties. How is that relevant to the position?"

He laughed softly and put his hands in his pockets. "It's a small town, and the people who seem to get hurt or sick the most often are the children and the elderly."

Her face relaxed. "Oh. Right. Of course. I knew that."

Scott followed Peyton to the reception area and stood by while Peyton chatted briefly with Devon. They acted like girlfriends, thanking each other for the time, saying they'd see each other again. Scott wondered what was going through Peyton's mind. Maybe she was attracted to Devon? No…he wasn't getting that vibe. It was just that Peyton was more comfortable with Devon than she had been with him.

He watched as Peyton left and climbed into the luxury car that sat right in front of the clinic.

"Wow, that's some car," Devon said.

"Uh-huh. I hope she's not making payments on it."

"Why?"

"Because on the salary I offered her, she'd have trouble. That's an LS 600. Starts at over a hundred grand."

Devon shot him a startled look. "Do you think she'll take the job?"

"Not a chance in hell," he said. Then he turned and went back to his office.

Two

Peyton went to look at the town's beach. She knew it would be unique and interesting—she'd grown up in this state, and all the beaches were so magical, so different from each other. She parked in the marina lot and walked from there. It was late June, school was out, it was warm and sunny, and people were enjoying the beach. A couple of women sat in low beach chairs on the sand under an umbrella; between them a baby played with a bucket and a few toys, and two children, about four years old, were at the water's edge. The Pacific was cold, and the children chased the waves, trying not to get too wet. There were a couple of teenage boys on paddleboards out on the bay, a couple more tossing a Frisbee around the beach. The Great Dane she'd seen in front of the diner now sat out at the edge of the dock watching the boys on the water.

It was a very clean beach, and she took off her sandals to walk. At the far end there was a flight of wooden stairs leading up to a small restaurant—Ben & Cooper's, according to the sign over the door. A few people sat out on the deck, and under the deck there were kayaks and paddleboards, obviously available to rent.

Peyton figured this beach was probably much busier on weekends. There weren't many people now—a dozen maybe. But it was two o'clock on a Wednesday afternoon, and while school might be out for the summer, most people were at work. She spotted a weathered log. It had been used as a bench before; the remnants of a fire pit, carefully surrounded by large rocks that wouldn't wash out with the tide, sat in front of it. She sat down to consider her options. *Could I hear myself think in a place like this?*

Peyton was thirty-five and single. She had a prestigious degree and a lot of experience, had a great big loving family with healthy parents, four brothers and three sisters. All of the Lacoumette siblings got along but were not all best friends. Matt got on her last nerve because he liked being the prankster of the family, Ginny annoyed the hell out of her the way she was always playing cruise director and taking control of everyone and everything, Ellie was trying to copy their parents and reproduce the nation with her five kids and counting, but Adele was her best friend, and big silent George, second oldest, still ranched on their family land and was her rock. George didn't usually have much to say, and yet when Peyton needed to talk, they had wonderful conversations. The rest of the time everyone else was talking too much.

In a family of eight children you could have sibling issues and rivalries and alliances—it was a very interesting balance, loving all of them, but definitely some better than others. She was the only one with no romantic partner, no family of her own. Well, except Matt, who was recently divorced, but that would surely be temporary—he was funny and handsome, and women loved him. But Peyton was alone. That was once by design. She couldn't wait to move away from the farm and have a life that didn't make her at least partly responsible for seven siblings. And then while the other young women her age were looking for husbands, she'd been looking for a career, travel, adventure and perhaps some great dates, but not to be tied down. She was in no hurry to have kids, if ever! Lord, she'd had enough of kids. Her first niece had arrived before she graduated from college, and the numbers were still growing. There were ten so far, and Adele, thirty now, was expecting her first. Peyton's mother, Corinne, was in heaven; her parents loved being grandparents. Her father, Paco Lacoumette, loved nothing so much as sitting at the head of a huge clan.

All Peyton had wanted was to live in a place not crowded by people, have her own bedroom, closet and bathroom. She wanted to do fun things, the kind of things her siblings with kids didn't have the time or money for—skiing, scuba diving, river rafting. She wanted to be able to spend money on clothes that wouldn't go missing from her drawers when some younger sister absconded with them; she wanted to drive a car no one had driven before her. She liked being able to watch anything she wanted on TV and reading until four in the morning if she felt like it. And she had done all that. For ten years following college, she'd lived the life she'd always dreamed of and hadn't taken it for granted for one second. She was not lonely one day of her life. And then, at just over thirty, she was finally ready to share her space again.

That's when she met The Man. Ted Ramsdale. He was so handsome he stopped her heart and took her breath away. Six-two, built like a god, dark hair, piercing blue eyes, straight white teeth. That was the first thing she'd noticed, but it was not what caused her to fall in love with him. He was a brilliant and powerful cardiologist, one of the best known and most admired in the state. He was charismatic; his success with patients had everything to do with his bedside manner. He could charm even the crankiest old man into doing everything exactly as asked. Ten minutes with a patient and Ted had them eating out of his hand. He could give courses on being a loving, giving physician. His staff would follow him anywhere; his colleagues went to him for advice. Ted always got his way, and at the same time everyone who dealt with him believed *they* had gotten *theirs*.

Just as luck would have it, Ted came with three kids. He shared custody with his ex-wife, and she wasn't exactly cooperative. They lived within a few miles of each other so the kids could spend equal time with each parent and never change schools. Getting to know Ted professionally and then personally before she met his kids, there had been nothing to prepare Peyton for the fact that Ted had no parenting skills at all. Too late, she'd learned he was totally unable to manage or discipline his own children. It was uncanny that Ted, the charming doctor, was somewhat useless as a father. When she'd first met the kids, they were aged seven, nine and twelve, and they were incorrigible. It had been a shock, really. It seemed the only people in the world Ted could not relate to were his ex-wife and their kids.

At first, Peyton had rationalized their behavior was sulky and insubordinate due to divorce issues. But, no.

For over two years she'd spent several days a week with three rude, insensitive, lazy and obnoxious tweens and teens. When she was growing up, her own parents had been firm but kind and fair, but after meeting Ted's children, her father had said, "Those three would've been taken out behind the shed a long while back." Paco, who rarely raised his voice in anger, whose worst corporal action had been a gentle cuff on the back of a son's head or a light swat on a rump, had only been half joking when he'd given Peyton his assessment. "I think I'd have to beat 'em."

For the first time in her life, Peyton had felt lonely. Ted had worked long hours and was frequently on call, his kids were horrid and abusive, and he could not seem to do anything to help. They fought with her, each other, ignored rules, were in trouble at school, and Ted was no help in any of it. Indeed, he excused them. The distance between them had grown; Ted had not only been absent, he'd been emotionally unavailable. She'd eventually realized he treated the kids like his patients—he gave them a good attentive ten minutes and then was out the door, moving on to his next challenge. He'd treated Peyton that way, too. He'd had no patience for her concerns. Peyton had tried so hard with the kids, believing if someone didn't get through to these little hellions, they were doomed to become incorrigible adults. She had given it her best shot, but she couldn't do it, couldn't stay with them any longer. Peyton had left her lover, his home, his children and, because he was her boss, left her job.

Now she needed a place to unwind and clear her head. She was desperate for her own space again… where she was never lonely. She looked out at the still bay. *I bet it's very quiet on the water,* she thought. She knew what fall and winter would be like on the coast—wet and cold and on many days it would be dark and foggy. *If I had a small house or apartment with a fireplace…*

A very pregnant woman walking across the beach from town paused in front of Peyton and gave her big belly a gentle stroking. "If I promise not to talk or wiggle around, can I share your log? I need to sit before tackling the stairs."

"By all means," Peyton said. "And you can talk. Out doing the pregnancy walk?"

The woman eased down on to the log, and instinctively Peyton reached out and grabbed her elbow, assisting. "Thank you. Yep, a long walk every day, then a little reading time on the left side for twenty minutes every couple of hours." She lifted her feet, ankles swollen. "Look at these things. Pretty soon I'll be wearing my husband's shoes."

"At the risk of seeming presumptuous, it appears that complication will be behind you soon," Peyton said.

"Very soon. I'm due in a month, and like every pregnant woman I've ever known, I'm hoping for an early debut. I'm Sarah," she said, putting out her hand.

"A pleasure," she said, taking the hand. "Peyton. Where will you do the deed?"

"North Bend. I'm told there will be plenty of time to get there. It's a first baby."

"First babies rarely come fast," Peyton said.

"You speak as one who knows?"

"I don't have children, but I am a physician's assistant. I've worked in family medicine. I looked after the occasional mother-to-be."

"Do you live around here?" Sarah asked.

"No. I grew up north of here, near Portland. But I was spending a little off-time at Coos Bay and saw an ad for a PA and decided to look around the area. Do you like it here?"

"I do," Sarah said. "I was stationed in North

Bend—Coast Guard Air Station. I decided to get out and start a new career." She grinned. "I lived in Thunder Point and commuted to North Bend, so I know the route with my eyes closed."

"Please, keep them open on the trip to the hospital," Peyton said with a laugh.

"My husband will be driving. At least that's the plan. So, where are you applying? One of the local clinics or hospitals?"

"I'd say so. I dropped off a résumé with Dr. Grant."

"Really? I heard he was looking for an assistant or associate, but that was a while ago, and I wasn't sure he had actually moved ahead on that project. We love Scott. He's a darling man. I think everyone in town loves him."

"He seemed very nice," Peyton agreed. "Devoted family man, I'm told."

Sarah gave a nod. "That would definitely describe him. Very involved in the town. Not just medically, but generally. Every town meeting or function or ball game or party, you'll find the Grants are there."

Peyton took a deep breath. "This seems like a sleepy place. Pretty peaceful."

"Most of the time," Sarah said. "That's my little brother out there. He starts college in the fall. He's teaching the taller, skinnier kid to paddleboard. It's a favorite pastime around here. That and kayaking and snorkeling, but…"

"You need a wet suit ten months of the year around here."

"You got that right," Sarah said.

"I grew up on a farm. Mount Hood was our view. Beautiful Mount Hood. I learned to ski there. Two of my brothers worked on the mountain. First in the resorts and then as ski patrol." She took another deep breath. "I like the coast, too. I like the waterfront. I worked in San Francisco for three years."

"I've lived on water my whole life," Sarah said.

"Woo-hoo!" came a girl's shout from across the bay. Three more teenagers were paddling across the still water from the marina.

"And here comes the Armada," Sarah said. "Landon's girlfriend, Eve, and a couple of other good friends from town. Paddleboarding is one of their favorite things, but I'm sure the volleyball net will go up now. If those kids aren't at work, they're at play. I'm afraid I have to get going," she said, struggling to get up from the log.

Peyton got up and extended a hand. "Time for that left-side rest?"

"Well, probably," Sarah said. "But mostly, I have to pee." Then she laughed. "I'm headed up to Cooper's. That's our place, my husband is Cooper. If you feel like a drink or snack, I'd love to treat you. I'd rather watch the kids play from up there."

"I think I'll take you up on that," Peyton said.

Peyton found herself at a table on the deck at Cooper's, nursing her bottled green tea, getting to know a few people from town. She had lifted Sarah's feet up on to a chair and said, "This won't get you out of the twenty minutes on your side, but this and plenty of water will help."

"Oh, you're darling. You must stay."

"Stay?" a big man leaning on the rail asked.

"Al," Sarah said, "meet Peyton, a physician's assistant who's considering working with Scott in town."

Al turned to her. "You'd like working with him. Scott helped me become a father."

Peyton frowned. The man was in his fifties. Stranger things had happened for older men. *But helped?* "I have to ask, helped how? Is he into infertility studies or something?"

Al laughed heartily at that. "I know I have a dumb look about me, but I'm not that dumb. No—those three down there. The kid on the board with Sarah's brother is Justin, he's seventeen. The two with the Frisbee are Kevin and Danny. They're my foster kids. I was all worried about being approved, and Scott said, let's get Sally, their mother, to appoint you as guardian—that should speed things up. Now I'm a foster father, final approval due any second."

Peyton was stunned. "You must know them quite well to sign up for that. Or you're gifted with teens?"

"Neither," he said. "I've only known them for a little while, but they're pretty amazing boys. They took care of their disabled mother at home all by themselves until she was put in a nursing home." He jutted a chin toward the bay. "We're having paddleboard lessons today. They're pricy, those boards. I'm not investing until two things are established—

one, they like it a lot and two, they're not likely to drown!" He chuckled. "Kevin and Danny have been at the water's edge a dozen times, begging Justin to come in so they can have a turn. Even though the boys can swim, sort of, I only want them out there one at a time. If one of them falls off the board, Landon is a certified lifeguard. I think this idea is going to cost me."

"Just out of curiosity, how long have you been at this foster parent thing?" Peyton asked.

"Couple of weeks," Al said. "These boys haven't had much time off. You know, kid time, because of their mother's health. I work full-time, but I don't intend to waste a day of the rest of summer—I want them to be boys for a change. They still pile in the car and go see their mom in the nursing home at least twice a week, more if they can. But I think it's important they play ball, get in the water, have some fun."

"How long did they take care of their mother?" she asked.

"Near as I can figure, about four years. And according to Scott, they did a damn fine job of it."

And I couldn't get Ted's kids to carry a dirty plate to the kitchen, Peyton thought.

Al wandered off as she was introduced to Cooper when he came on to the deck wearing a tool belt. "Aren't you due for a little rest to try to achieve ankles?" he said to his wife.

"I'm much more interested in achieving labor," she said. But she let him pull her to her feet.

"Don't be in too big a hurry," Peyton said. "You want that baby nice and plump."

"Do I?"

"Well, you want her lungs and heart nice and plump," Peyton said with a smile.

"Stay awhile, Peyton," Sarah said. "Enjoy the view. I hope I see you around."

Peyton was happy to stay awhile. This spot was calming. The group from the bay moved to the beach, erected a net and got the volleyball going. Al's three foster sons played with Sarah's brother and his friends. She met an older gentleman named Rawley who had two youngsters in tow with buckets and poles—a boy and girl. He nodded at her. "How do," he said. The kids raced off ahead of him, down the stairs.

She smiled. "Grandfather duty?"

"Sorta. That there's Cooper's boy, Austin. And my friend Devon's girl, Mercy."

"Ah, yes, I met Devon. But I thought Austin was her fiancé's son?"

And the old boy nodded. "Yep," was all he said, taking the kids down to the dock to fish.

"Well, that was clear as mud," Peyton muttered to herself.

She was almost to the bottom of her tea when another guy in a tool belt came on to the deck, followed by Al. This guy had a beer and was pretty sweaty. Al had himself a Coke and a bowl of chips and salsa. Al said, "Spencer, that's Peyton. Peyton's thinking of working in the clinic…"

"You know Devon?" he asked with a smile.

"I met her," she said. "I talked with her awhile and left my résumé."

"We're engaged." He brushed his hands off on his jeans and reached across the space between the tables to shake her hand. "I've been working on the house. We're getting married pretty soon, and there might still be some work to do, but we're going to move in the second it's livable. How do you like our town so far?"

"Quaint," she said.

He laughed. "Only on the surface. It's a tough little town."

"How is that?"

He thought for a second. "These people don't have a lot of advantages. The cost of living here is low, but there's one doctor, one lawyer, no dentists—it's a working-class town, and a large percentage of the population holds second jobs. Our teenagers carry as many credits as the teens in upscale city schools, yet most of them also work part-time. And they do well in school. We get a fair number into college."

And that would explain why Scott Grant ran on a tight budget. "Yet you like it here?"

"This was a good decision for me, coming here," Spencer said. "My last high school had a lot. It was flush with money—supplies, equipment, tutors, special programs, you name it. If the school needed it, they found a way. It was a well-heeled district. Not very many of my students had to work to get by. There were plenty of kids who held jobs, but there were more who didn't. The student parking lot was always full, and the cars weren't wrecks." He grinned again. "The Thunder Point High School lot looks very different. These people work hard to stay above water. I find it's kind of inspiring to be around a bunch of kids who don't have it that easy."

This was something Peyton had devoted a great deal of time to thinking about lately. She'd grown up on a farm, and it was a very successful farm. But they'd never been spoiled; the kids each had tons of responsibility. Everyone had worked hard, and because Paco was always worried about next year's growing season, which could be bad, no one had spent money frivolously. One early freeze could mean disaster for the pears; a terrible winter could stunt the sheep. If hand-me-downs worked, why buy new? And although her dad had hired hands on the farm, every last one of his children had had farm chores. "Work is good for the soul," he'd said. "What are you gonna learn from sleeping late? You pick pears for a few weeks, you have time to think and you have a chance to learn."

At the time, Peyton had not given her farmer father much credit for wisdom, but when she was in college she'd had classmates who'd gone out a lot or played cards in the student lounge all the time while she'd been at the library studying because she learned that you work first, then you play. She was not a recluse by any means—she had a great social life, just not a frivolous one. That beer with her friends had tasted a lot better after she'd gotten an A on a test rather than after a D. Hard training on the Lacoumette farm had served her well.

Ted's kids were overindulged, there was no question. Peyton had taken the Ramsdales back to the farm where twenty or more people would squish around a long oak table and that wasn't even the whole family. They'd yell and laugh and fight for space to say a word. It was a place where all those staying in the house would bang on the bathroom door to oust someone who seemed to be homesteading in there, where breakfast was at five in the morning. The Ramsdale kids had not been impressed. Nor had been Ted, for that matter. His oldest, fifteen-year-old Krissy, had said, "Smells kinda like shit, doesn't it?" Peyton's mother had gasped, and her father had scowled.

"That's manure," Peyton had snapped. "It's cultivating time!" Her father always said, *That smell? That's the smell of money.*

"Easy, Peyton," Ted had said. "It's not her fault she has no farm experience."

Thinking about that, she realized it might help her get her mojo back to stay in a town where the kids weren't spoiled. Her nieces and nephews were well mannered and had been taught to mind the feelings of others, but like all kids, they had their moments and got into their share of stand-offs with their parents. But they were so much better behaved than Ted's kids.

The other thing she'd realized since leaving the Ramsdale household was that she'd been without friends while she was there. She'd lost touch with her friends; the demands of Ted's practice and household had left no time. His ex-wife had never stuck to their schedule, causing changes to plans so often, requiring Peyton to take personal time to supervise the kids because Ted had to be at the hospital or on call to the ER It had seemed to Peyton it was deliberate, but Ted was insistent. "You can't take joint custody issues personally. We have to be flexible."

We? Ted didn't have to be flexible. He lived at the practice or hospital. He played golf and tennis; he said they were important professional relationships. He went to meetings out of town—he was a much sought-after presenter, given his relative notoriety within the cardiology specialty. He spent so little time with his children, Peyton was surprised he could remember their names.

Maybe she could use a little time in a town that knew about hard work. It wouldn't hurt to be around a few friendly people. She could have space again—her own bathroom, closet, TV, bookshelf. Her belongings would be safe. She could build up her armor once more so her feelings weren't hurt all the time by callous remarks and disrespect. She could figure out how she'd gotten into that mess and how to never let that happen again.

Maybe working in a clinic that ran on a tight budget would be *inspiring* in a way that Ted's rich practice hadn't been.

This little Pacific Coast village was only three hours from her parents' farm, a place she had long ago grown out of but still fled to in times of heart-ache or confusion. Maybe she could sit here for a little while and recover her lost mind and knit to-gether her frayed emotions. But at the salary of forty-thousand per year, she wouldn't live extravagantly. Her last salary had been ninety-five. But, because of her living arrangement and Ted's veritable wealth, she had saved a lot of money. In fact, she had always been careful with money and saved quite a bit, but she didn't want to spend it by volunteering in a lit-tle clinic. Unless, of course, there was a point to it.

Before finishing her tea and leaving Cooper's, she met a couple more people from town—a Realtor, the caterer who supplied Cooper's with deli items, the local sheriff's deputy and, while crossing the beach she met the Great Dane, Hamlet, who was loath to be too far from Landon, Sarah's brother, a handsome and athletic young man. The teenagers all said hello very briefly since they put their game on hold for the time it took her to pass. That enchanted her. Then she considered what a mess her life had to be for her to be that impressed by teenagers halting their ball-batting game while she passed.

It was four-thirty by the time she was parked back in front of the clinic. This time the waiting room held people—six of them. She walked up to the counter and once again, Devon stood. "Oops. I guess the doctor is busy," Peyton observed.

"He's with a patient and a few are waiting to see him, but depending on what you need, I can snag him for a minute."

"Is it always this busy, so late in the day?" Peyton asked.

"There were two appointments for after work and a few walk-ins. This isn't the case every day, but it's not uncommon. Would you like his cell number?"

"Seriously? Isn't that kind of...you know...a little too personal?"

Devon shook her head. "I think everyone in town has his cell number."

"Oh, that's scary." Patients *never* had Ted's cell number. They had to go through his service.

Peyton took a slip of paper off the counter and scribbled on it. *Three months?* "Give him this note. He has my cell number from the résumé. I'm afraid that's the only commitment I can make at this time. And I'd also need time to find somewhere to live around here. Ask him to let me know if he's interested."

Devon grinned hugely. "I'm so glad, Peyton. I have a good feeling about this. I look forward to working with you. And you might want to give this woman a call," she said, scribbling on a sticky note. "She's our local Realtor and is really good at finding hard-to-find rental property."

That coaxed a smile out of Peyton. "I met Ray Anne at Cooper's. I have her card."

"Kismet," Devon said.

Peyton thought Devon was a darling girl. She turned to go, then turned back. "Can I ask a question? I hope it's not too personal. You'll tell me if it is. I went out to Cooper's to enjoy the ocean, and I met a few people—one of them was your intended, Spencer."

"You did? Oh, good! Isn't he the most handsome, wonderful man?"

Peyton tilted her head and gave a brief nod. "He seems to be, as a matter of fact. I also met Cooper and Sarah and some old guy who didn't introduce himself."

"Rawley. He was taking Mercy fishing off the dock today."

"Yes, I saw her. And the boy, Austin, who he said was Cooper's son?"

"That's right."

"But you said he was Spencer's son," she said. "I'm just a little…"

"Cooper is his biological father. Spencer is his stepfather. Austin's mother passed away about a year ago. Spencer was the only father Austin had known, so they moved here so Cooper could be more involved. Oh, and to take the job as athletic director and coach at the high school. Some angel was definitely smiling on me."

"That explains it."

Devon laughed. "As soon as you start here, we'll get you a program."

It was five-thirty before Scott came up for air and the last person had left the clinic. He was making notes in a chart when he looked up to see Devon standing in the doorway. "I bet you're ready to get out of here," he said.

"I'm fine. Spencer and Rawley have been entertaining the kids this afternoon. But I wanted to be sure to tell you—Peyton stopped by. She left a note." She presented it to him. "She said that's all the commitment she can make at this time."

"Well, it offers some help and time to look around for someone more permanent."

"Maybe she'll like it here," Devon said.

"Don't count on it, Devon. She's sought after. She could name her price in a lot of clinics or practices. Doctors fight over PAs of her caliber and start bidding wars. I really didn't expect her to take even a temporary job here on the salary I offered her."

"Then why would she?"

"I think Thunder Point is a place holder while she decides where she's going next, for a great deal more money. And prestige."

"Why wouldn't she just go somewhere else now, then?"

"Because she's clever. She'll research, take her time, choose well, negotiate a terrific package."

"Hmph," Devon said. "You could be wrong."

"Could be," he said. "But I bet I'm not. Give her a call, will you? Tell her we'll be happy to take her offer when she's available and for the three months she suggested. Ask her if she can call with her start date when she knows it."

"I wish you'd be more positive," Devon said. "This could be perfect."

"Don't get me wrong. I'm thrilled to have someone of Peyton's experience on board," he said. "But why would anyone in their right mind go to work for less than half the salary they could receive in other practices or hospitals?"

"I don't know, Scott. You did."

"True," he said with a laugh. "I don't think our circumstances are similar. I don't want you to be too disappointed, Devon. I think she'll be great. And hard to replace. By the way, make sure she has my cell number. If she wants to call me while you're away on your honeymoon, she should call that number."

"I tried to give it to her. I got the impression she didn't want to impose...."

"Sometimes that's the only way to get my attention," he muttered. "Get going. Go find your family. If I know you, you're going to be out at that new house, tinkering around, getting it ready."

That brought a big smile to her face. "We're very close. There's flooring to put in downstairs and painting to do and endless cleanup, but we have all the walls, doors that lock, appliances that work, and we're sleeping there starting this weekend. Any work Spencer doesn't get done before football practice starts in August will wait till play-offs are over."

"Why? How many hours a day does he devote to football practice before school starts?"

Devon just laughed. "It's not the hours! Have you ever seen Spencer during football practice? He might only be out there with those teenage boys a few hours a day, but he tries like the devil to keep up with them. He can barely move afterward!"

Scott smiled. "Pride comes before the fall."

"In this case it's not pride so much as pretending to be sixteen when you're staring forty in the eye. I'll see you tomorrow, Scott. Don't stay too late."

Three

Peyton didn't expect to find adequate housing in Thunder Point; she was fully prepared to search out an apartment or duplex in a nearby town, even one as far away as North Bend. First of all, she was looking for a tailor-made lease—month to month or three months, but she couldn't commit to anything longer. Second, she no longer had her own furnishings.

"This is an amazing coincidence," Ray Anne Dysart said. "This absolutely never happens. I got a call this morning from a part-time resident. They come up here from Sacramento to get out of the summer heat—usually stay about five months, from May through September, but couldn't make it up here yet this year and looks like they won't. Health issues. They said if I could rent it for a few months to a responsible tenant, they'd appreciate it. I haven't even seen the inside. Want to have a look?"

"Sure," Peyton said.

"The daughter called. She said there might be a

few personal items left in the house—they really thought they'd be back. And the daughter can't get up here for a couple of weeks, but asked if I'd box up anything that's real personal and she'll come for it. I have no idea what that means. Let's check it out."

It was a very small two-bedroom, a duplex with a small patio with a six foot fence around it, just like many apartment complex patios. The decor was altogether too fussy for Peyton—crocheted toilet tissue cozies, driftwood accents here and there, a fishing net strung on the kitchen wall with hooks in it for oven mitts, dish towels and other paraphernalia. There were also family pictures on tables and walls, baskets holding shells and lots of seaside-themed throw pillows. But the furniture was attractive and comfortable. The place would have a welcoming air about it, once the crafty doodahs and family pictures had been removed. It was only a few blocks from the clinic—a few more to the marina and beach.

"This will do nicely," she said to Ray Anne. "I told Dr. Grant I could give him three months. Can you check with the owners about that time frame?"

"Sure. Do you have a lot of stuff to move?"

"I'm not going to move furniture for just a few months, especially since this place is nicely furnished. I have a few things I want to fetch from my brother's house where they're stored—my own linens, a couple of rugs, a few kitchen items I'm attached to. You know—creature comforts. Can we poke around closets and drawers and see what kind of things were left behind that have to be packed up?"

Peyton would buy new before admitting she had left her last address with practically nothing. She had a turntable and valuable vinyl record collection, her grandmother's lace dresser scarf that she'd tatted herself, linen placemats and matching napkins, her other grandmother's antique hand-tooled serving platters, things she wouldn't invite her sisters or sisters-in-law to use or she might not see them again. There were some old crystal wineglasses and a decanter. And she had some carefully chosen art that she'd had boxed at a gallery for storage because there had been no place for them in Ted's house.

In fact, that's about all that was left. When she'd moved in with Ted, she stored most of her furniture with George—he had room in the basement of his house. Little by little they'd gone the way of family members who needed them. Her four-poster bed was "loaned" to a niece who needed a bed; the dresser eventually made its way to the same bedroom. Her mother's antique pie safe and dry sink was being used by Ginny. "It looks so perfect in my house!" Ginny had said. Her sofa, love seat and accent tables had gone into Ted's game room where they were beaten to death by his kids. She no longer liked them and had left them behind. Her antique rolltop desk was in Adele's little apartment in San Francisco where it was being loved. Her kitchen table and chairs were with Ellie and her family; it would never be the same. She wouldn't loan the art—she knew how that worked. Although things were always "borrowed," they seemed to never be returned. They weren't thieves by any means. They were merely presumptuous relatives. And passive-aggressively forgetful.

Many of Peyton's favorite things had made their way into Ted's house—her Crock-Pot, a set of dishes and glassware, toaster oven, stainless-steel flatware, some very nice bath towels. Most of it wasn't worth packing up when it had been time to leave. In fact, she'd been on the verge of leaving, trying to make herself do it, when something that simply crushed her happened. She'd told the kids never to touch her turntable or the original vinyl record collection she kept stored in their bedroom. But then she came home from an errand, heard the sound of the original Beatles album she'd had for years coming from her bedroom. She heard it *skipping*. It was marred with a deep scratch, as were several other records…and she fell into tears. Twelve-year-old Pam had screeched, "You're just plain *stupid!* It's just a stupid record! We don't even have records anymore!" When Ted had gotten home that night, Peyton was packing a couple of suitcases and some boxes. She'd explained it was the last straw, and he'd said, "I have to agree with Pam to an extent. Leaving over a broken record is pretty stupid. I'll buy you another. I'm sure it wasn't malicious."

"It was completely malicious!" she'd said. "Everything is malicious! And there isn't another—it's a collector's item!"

"What is it you want, Peyton? Do you want me

to go drag her out of her room and force her to apologize?"

"Yes!"

"Don't be ridiculous," he had said. "Grow up."

"How can you, the most sensitive doctor I've ever worked with, be so insensitive?" she had asked.

She had packed everything she could and went to the farm. There had been things missing from her closet that she knew she'd never see again—boots, shirts, sweaters, blazers. If she could have summoned the energy, she would have searched Krissy's and Pam's rooms. She hadn't had the strength. She'd stuffed her car with everything she could and told Ted she'd be at the farm for a couple of weeks. She had a lot of vacation coming. "I'll commute to work from the farm after I take a little time to think things through, to recuperate."

"Maybe we should just make a clean break," Ted had said. "You're through with me, that's obvious. I don't see how we can work closely together after this."

"Who will do my job? Take my patients?" Peyton had asked.

He'd given her a shrug, hands in his pockets. "I'll find someone. Maybe I should just give Lindsey a chance, see what she can do."

"She's an RN," Peyton had said. "She's twenty-five. Inexperienced."

"She's ambitious. Resourceful."

And suddenly Peyton had known. How had she

never guessed? She slowly turned to him. "How long?" she'd asked.

"How long?" he'd echoed.

"You're seeing her, I can tell. How long have you been involved with her?"

"*Involved* is too strong a word. We've developed a…well, I guess it's a close friendship. You've been pushing me away. You've been hell to live with the last year. Be honest, Peyton, you know it's true. You hate it here. You don't want me anymore. I don't think we can go forward from this point. I'll give you a good recommendation."

"You *bastard*," she'd whispered. "I don't need your recommendation. I'm very well known in the medical community in Portland. *Lindsey* will need your recommendation!"

"I'll give you a generous severance," he'd said.

"Mail it to the farm," she'd said, lifting a box and carrying it out to her car.

Peyton shook herself back to the present. She smiled at Ray Anne. "I'll just get together a few things and move in, if that's all right," she said. "I'll visit with my parents overnight while I load up."

"Let's call the owner's daughter and figure out this lease right now," Ray Anne said, getting comfortable at the kitchen table and opening up her briefcase.

And it was done. Forty-eight hours later she was packing the left-behind linens and clothing and some of the owner's kitchen wares into boxes. She would store them in the second bedroom until they could be picked up. She went through the canned goods and spices and checked dates, thinning out that supply. There wasn't much for her to deal with. She got out some of her own things to use in the kitchen, hung one of her paintings and put out a few of her own family pictures. The fishnet came down. She put her precious turntable and record collection on its small display case—the only piece of furniture she'd brought—and placed it against the living room wall. And she played Johnny Mathis, *Funny Girl* and *Yentl*. She had great speakers and blasted the music, singing along with it. Singing was a Basque tradition, except mostly the men sang the folk songs. Just as well—Peyton wanted to sing with Etta James or Barbra.

Alone, in her new little duplex with her own bathroom, bookcase, garage, bedroom and kitchen, she would *dance!* She realized for the first time in a long time, she felt *safe*. And as long as she didn't think of Ted and his family, she was no longer lonely. When her thoughts drifted that way, she was reminded that she'd really, truly thought she could do it. She'd thought she could make a life with him and love his kids and somehow make a difference, even if she couldn't cajole them into loving her. Or even liking her.

Feeling like a failure was every bit as hard as feeling rejected.

Peyton had been called a perfectionist. She had never been insulted by that. She worked at things until they were absolutely as good as they could be.

How could there be anything wrong with that? With trying your hardest?

Hell to live with? she asked herself. Maybe I'm just better off alone.

Devon held up the dress she would wear for her wedding. It was an unpretentious floral sundress with a wrap for evening. She was dressing at Cooper's house because hers still smelled like paint and sawdust. They would have a little exchange of vows on Cooper's deck with about a dozen guests, toast the marriage and then Devon would kiss Mercy and Austin and leave them with Cooper and Sarah, and off they would go.

"I don't approve of the simplicity of this," Laine Carrington said. "I understand, but I so don't approve. I wanted you to have dancing, drinking, craziness, lots of food, too much to clean up and many hangovers."

Devon laughed at her best friend. "You'll get over it. This is absolutely what we want."

And so it was. There were just a few couples and Scott and Rawley. Sarah and Cooper hosted and provided champagne, Gina and Mac McCain were there, Carrie James brought the hors d'oeuvres from her deli and put out a very nice spread before the nuptials, including a beautiful, small wedding cake. Mac's aunt Lou and her husband, Joe, and Ray Anne and her boyfriend, Al, rounded out the group. Laine brought her significant other, Eric. And of course, the kids Mercy and Austin were there, being very well behaved. Devon's suitcase was packed for a little getaway and was in the back of Spencer's car

A woman named Lynette Tremain, an ordained minister from Bandon, presided. Right at seven in the evening, when the sun was beginning its downward path and before it reached its glorious moment of touching the Pacific horizon, Lynette gave a very short wedding sermon about the beauty of second chances, of rebirth and renewal since Spencer was a widower and Devon's daughter had been conceived and born in a commune. For them, this was a new start, a new life.

The vows were spoken, the kisses and congratulations bestowed, the champagne poured, and the cake was cut. Devon and Spencer stayed another hour to visit with their guests, but Spencer was very eager to whisk his bride away. Before leaving, Devon took Scott aside. "I called Peyton's cell phone and left her a voice mail, telling her I'd be out of town for a few days, and I gave her your cell phone number. I told her you thought you'd manage just fine, but if she wanted to stop by…"

"You shouldn't have done that," he said. "She might feel obligated. I managed just fine before you started working at the clinic."

"Well, that's true, except for the 'just fine' part."

"Was that an insult? Because I bought you a nice wedding gift!"

"You're wonderful with the patients, Scott. But when I started, there were months of backed-up paperwork and your files were…" She made a face. "Really, you have to stick to medicine."

"We all have our weak spots. But it wasn't that bad."

"I'll be back in five days. Just leave everything on my desk. I'll straighten it out when I get back. And if you have any questions—"

"I'm not calling you on your honeymoon!" he said.

"No, you shouldn't," she said. "But if you have any questions or if you get in a mess, you should try Peyton. She knows her way around a doctor's office."

"I don't want to impose…."

"Scott, she wants to work for you. Don't suffer in silence." Then she hugged him.

Devon then found Sarah. "Now, if anything starts up, if you feel the slightest twinge announcing the baby—you call me! We're not going to be that far away. We'll come straight back if the baby decides to come."

"I'm going to hold my knees together," Sarah said. "But only for you! There isn't a single other person on the planet I would do this for. And if I have my way, the second you're back, I'm pushing."

Devon giggled. "It'll be soon."

She found Rawley and gave him a hug. It was Rawley who'd given her refuge in Thunder Point and thus a second chance at happiness. "Thank you, for everything, Rawley. Will you help Cooper and Sarah with the kids?"

"Don't I always?" he asked.

"You always do," she said.

"I was just wonderin' one thing, chickadee. How's Thunder Point workin' out for you?"

She laughed at him and said, "It'll do. Now, I'll be back in five days, but if you need me…"

"Aw, I don't need nothin', chickadee. I just need my people settled and right with the world. What more is there?"

"Well, as it turns out, there's true love," Devon said with a laugh.

He gave a nod. "I think that coach fella is okay," he said.

"Thanks, Rawley," she said with a smile. "I'll see you in a few days."

Getting settled in a very small furnished duplex had been almost as simple as moving into a hotel room. Peyton made a run to Costco and Target for new linens and a few accessories and then spent the rest of her time getting to know the town. She'd already been to the beach and Cooper's bar, so on Saturday she went to the diner where she met Gina, who was more than happy to tell her about the town. Based on Gina's recommendation, she planned to go to Cliffhanger's for a glass of wine and a peek at the menu. She dropped by Carrie's Deli for a salad to take home and knew at once she had found the place to buy her lunches for the next three months. Carrie had a wonderful array of premade sandwiches, one-person pizzas, microwavable breakfast burritos and egg-and-sausage sandwiches. And she also had spectacular take-out dinners, from chicken parmesan to turkey lasagna—ready for the oven. "I may never have to go to the grocery store again!" Peyton exclaimed.

"Suits me fine," Carrie said. "I'm always trying new recipes. I keep menus up-to-date for the next catering job. Next week I'm doing a big batch of stuffed mushrooms—a real crowd pleaser around here."

"I'll be here!"

That night, Peyton decided to take a walk on the beach. Although it was summer, she needed her sweater; the Pacific was cold, especially at night. There were quite a few people on the beach walking dogs, strolling hand in hand, teens setting up for a campfire. She stayed close to the water's edge, keeping out of the way of others, but that didn't stop them from nodding hello. She assumed if she hadn't been walking alone, head mostly down, some of them might stop to talk.

She went all the way to the dock and sat on the edge. From there she could see the entire beach and bay, and it was a beautiful, clear night. Ordinarily she might walk up the stairs to Cooper's deck where several people sat, having just enjoyed a beautiful sunset. There were candles on the tables, and right next door, at Cooper's home, she could not mistake a few Tiki torches lighting up his deck. That was where Devon's wedding would have taken place— among the torches. She could see a few men standing around and women sitting in deck chairs; she heard their laughter over the waves. She'd stay down here, out of the way. If she sat on the deck at the bar, someone from Cooper's house might see her and wave her over. Devon had extended an invitation, though at the last minute. She didn't want to intrude. She was a newcomer here, not a part of their group of friends. Plus, she was in no mood for a wedding tonight.

After about nine months of dating Ted and working with him, frequently spending the night when he didn't have the kids, he'd asked her to move in with him. "I don't know, Ted," she had said. "Your kids haven't really warmed up to me. I don't know why—I always thought I got along well with kids."

"They're just moody," he'd said. "Kids that age are."

"It might be best just to stay as we are. I'll be happy to have dinner with you and your kids, but then I'll go home to my place. Until they're done being 'moody.'"

"You practically live with me now," he'd said. "Almost every day the kids aren't with me, you spend the night. And I love it."

She remembered fighting the idea. They didn't like her and she knew it. As it was, the minute Olivia, the ex-wife, learned that Ted had a girlfriend, the scheduling problems began. Olivia was a geologist who researched fault lines and tsunamis. She was tired of her career taking the backseat to Ted's, so she took full advantage of Peyton being available to tend them, chauffer them, even sit in on meetings at school if necessary. If Ted was to have the kids from Friday afternoon until Sunday night, Olivia found reasons to add a couple of days or just change the days altogether. She had business trips, pleasure trips she'd been deprived of for too long, extended work days.

Ted had no one to ask for help but Peyton—he had patients having heart attacks! And of course, the kids had activities and events, ranging from concerts to meets and games. Too often Ted had been tied up with patients and needed Peyton to pick up the kids, take them home, try to get them started on homework, get something together for dinner. And had they been grateful? Oh, God, no! They'd been miserable.

"I'll make it perfectly clear to the kids that this is the arrangement and they'll welcome you, treat you with respect, or they'll be in serious trouble."

Uh, right. He'd given that a little lip service and they were more careful—to be sure their father wasn't around when they hurled insults or ignored her requests. She was never quite sure if he had a lot of divorce guilt or if he was just passive-aggressive. He certainly didn't have that affliction at work; he had no problem taking an employee to task or making sure a patient had the difficult but necessary message. At the end of the day she decided, sadly, he just didn't give a shit. He had delegated. To her.

That was when she also realized, early in their live-in relationship, that Olivia wasn't willing to make any sacrifices to parent her children, either.

Peyton told herself those kids had no one. Neither of their parents really seemed to care about them.

They had very good reasons for having little time—they were both successful. But the kids… Those bad kids. No role models, no loving parents, just caretakers like Peyton. It was beyond sad. No wonder they were so ill behaved.

When she'd moved in, Nicholas had been eight, Pamela had been ten, Krissy had been thirteen. She had asked herself so often how she had lasted over two years under the same roof with them. Her first year with Ted, she'd helped with the kids but hadn't moved in. The third year, the last year, had been miserable because she was at the end of her rope with the kids *and* Ted. But that second year? There had been respites every week when Olivia took the kids and Peyton's work life and home life was calm and serene. On those days she'd reexamined her love for Ted and believed without a doubt that if not for the kids and their lack of discipline and respect, she could be very happy with the man. He was strong and affectionate and generous. And he loved her so much—he said so all the time. It took almost a whole year for her to figure out that his schedule was much better when it was only Peyton and not his children cluttering up his life.

At first her parents had doubted the situation was as severe as she described it. "Oh, honey," her mother had said, "it can't be that bad. What are they but kids! They're not very old. You have your boundaries, make sure they know your limits, reinforce. We had eight, and our household was sometimes loud and messy, but we managed just fine."

Then she'd taken Ted and the kids to the farm. Pam hadn't wanted to tour the farm or orchard, so she'd gone upstairs to the bedroom she was sharing with Krissy and closed herself in the room with her iPad. Krissy wasn't about to eat the dinner she was served. Pam didn't enjoy gathering eggs with Peyton so she threw them on the ground and laughed like a hyena at the splatter. Nicholas switched the channel on the TV, and when he was told it was Gramp's choice now because he'd put in a long day, he pitched a fit. When told there weren't televisions in every bedroom, he threw himself on the floor and screamed until he was blue, and Ted had had to carry him outside. Krissy kicked the dog, Pam threw a cat out of her way. Nicholas deliberately tipped his milk over on the table because he didn't like milk with meals—he wanted Coke. There was no Coke at the farm. No Coke, no TVs, no private bathrooms, no entertainment and Ted felt *trapped.* Ted, who didn't own a pair of blue jeans. He lowered his voice to say to Peyton, "We'll have to leave early. My kids are not farm kids."

"I don't think this is going to work with your man, Peyton," her mother had said later.

"Because of his kids?" she'd stupidly asked.

"No, darling little Babette. Because of his disability. The poor man appears to be blind and deaf. That's going to present problems."

So for almost three years they'd fought a lot, made love on days off from the monsters, fought some more, and the weeks—so busy Peyton could barely think—ran together until she'd realized she'd been with him for almost three years, was almost thirty-five, and nothing had improved. In fact, it had been getting worse by the day.

Then she'd found pot in Krissy's backpack. The bag was sitting on a kitchen chair, the zipper open, the drugs clearly visible. Peyton went ballistic; she confiscated it and called Ted home from work. The fireworks were nuclear. Krissy accused Peyton of searching her personal property, insisted she was holding it for a friend she wouldn't name. Ted was furious to be called away from his practice for a "minor" problem like that. "Come on, Peyton, like you didn't come into contact with a little weed when you were a teenager!"

Oh. My. God! Peyton knew her father would have killed her! But Ted wouldn't even agree to ground Krissy. "You're going to be sorry," she had told him. "That girl is on a bad journey, and it's going to get worse. She's not even remorseful. She blames *me!*"

Peyton had lasted about two more months.

No wonder she was determined not to work for a single father again. She knew not all kids were terrible, but she was not up to working her ass off as a PA and taking on parenting duties after work. Scott Grant, devoted family man, was obviously happily married and wouldn't be imposing in that way.

A couple, holding hands, came cautiously down the stairs from Cooper's house to the beach. Wedding guests. The woman was a pretty blonde, carrying her heeled slippers, and he was a tall man with dark red hair and kept his arm around her waist. They walked about twenty feet and stopped. He lifted her chin and kissed her deeply.

That was hard to see, Peyton thought. Fresh from her breakup, it wasn't easy. She wanted to be loved; she was willing to give a lot to a relationship. She had tried so hard.

On Sunday, before she was completely settled in Thunder Point, Peyton called a friend from Ted's office—their triage nurse, Amy. She hadn't talked to her since her abrupt departure three weeks before, and Amy had been her closest work friend.

"I'm taking a position in a very small clinic in a very small town. It will give me time to think about my next job. I made a three month commitment, and during the next three months, I'll put out some feelers, try to decide where I want to be. It isn't going to be in Portland, Amy. I don't want to run into Ted and his new assistant."

"You should know—they came out. They're a couple. It's all huggy-huggy, kissy-touchy. They're officially dating."

Peyton sighed. "It's like they couldn't wait for me to leave."

"You were gone an hour," Amy said, disgust in her voice.

"He's twenty years older than she is."

"He needs a babysitter," Amy said. "In the end he might need a sitter for her. My advice? Don't look back."

Peyton texted Ted and told him she had not yet seen the severance check and gave him the address for Scott's clinic and asked him to send it there. Posthaste. She didn't need it, but by damn, she was going to push for it. No one had given Ted more than she had. Fortunately, she had saved enough of her income over the past several years to emerge debt free and with a healthy savings account. She could get on with her life.

Alone.

Monday morning at around ten, Peyton dropped by the clinic. She hadn't given Scott a starting date, but she had nothing to do to settle into her little space, so she might as well see if he needed her. She had noticed Devon wore scrubs and tennis shoes, perfectly appropriate for clinic personnel. But Scott had been wearing jeans, so she opted for nice jeans and a starched blouse. While it was definitely sandal weather, she wore closed-toed shoes with a heel. She'd soon find out if scrubs were more practical.

"I wasn't expecting you until next week," he said.

"I know, but Devon called and said she'd be away and if I could spare the time…"

"I can manage if you have things to do, Peyton," he said.

She really didn't want him to know how pathetic her life looked, that she had almost nothing to move into her little duplex. "I'm fine. There's not much to do to get acclimated, and I wanted to give you at least a few hours today in case you got busy."

"If you're sure, we'll think of it as orientation. It won't take any time at all before you know where everything is. Over the weekend I made room for you in my office. You can use my desk whenever I'm not using it, but I added a small, portable but very sturdy folding table and desk chair and brought a laptop from home in case—"

"I have my own laptop," she said. "Do you have wireless so I can get online? Ten years ago I carted around boxes of books but now…"

"I know. We've come a long way, haven't we? I subscribe to a medical link service. I'll give you the password. Everything from a Physician's Desk Reference to very classy pictures of rashes and warts."

She laughed in spite of herself. "See a lot of those, do you?"

"It's not that there are a lot. I have trouble telling them all apart! There's a white lab coat in the back if you want to save your blouse from…from the many vagaries of our profession."

Orientation was comprised of more than learning Scott's system, where the supplies were kept and figuring out the appointment calendar. It was also meeting the people. In a small-town clinic, she learned, you served the neighborhood. There was Mrs. Rodriquez's diabetes, Lynn Bishop's prenatal visits, Bob Flannigan's arthritis, Crawford Downy Sr.'s high blood pressure and elevated cholesterol, and his wife's onset of acid reflux. There was Mrs. Bledsoe's Parkinson's—beautifully controlled at the moment, Tara Redding's asthma, Frank Samson's chronic back spasms, a strained and perhaps torn rotator cuff from one of the fishermen down at the marina, a few referrals and a couple of blood draws. The clinic was busy all day, and whether Scott would admit it or not, Peyton knew he would have had trouble keeping up without her. For the two of them, it wasn't overwhelming, but there was no downtime. She administered some antibiotic, put in a few stitches, applied an ice pack and caught up on some charting. She thought she was home free until the nine-month-old with a fever she had balanced on her hip threw up on her.

"Feel better?" she asked the infant.

The baby flashed a wide, adorable, toothless smile, causing Scott to laugh so hard, he bent over.

"I keep a couple of spare shirts in my closet," Scott said, still laughing. "I'll get you one."

Peyton finished the day in Scott's shirt, but it had been such a good day that she didn't mind a bit. With hardly any training at all, they had worked together exceptionally well. "I guess I'll either wear the lab coat or add a couple of my own shirts to the closet," she said.

"Choice of clothing is entirely up to you. Devon likes the scrubs for comfort, and it keeps her costs down. Some days I just throw on scrubs, but those are usually the days I'm scheduled at one of the hospitals. I don't have many patients to see on rounds, but if I can give them a few hours in their clinic or ER, it helps."

"They let you have a schedule that gives them just a few hours?"

"It's all I have," he said. "Plus, I'm pretty cheap." And then he grinned.

She was caught on that smile, momentarily mesmerized. There was no veneer, no cover. He was completely accessible, maybe a little vulnerable. On that very first day she understood, *He's not about money or image; he's all about being a good health care provider.* That's all it took—one day and that engaging smile and she knew, Scott was the real deal. A good man. Good to the bone. He was welcoming. Warm and giving and talented. And that was why the clinic was working. His patients clearly loved and trusted him. They depended on him thoroughly; they dropped in whether ill or well, just to update him on the latest news, and not just about their health.

Realizing this was almost a blow, given where she came from. Ted was the kind of man who could knock you off your feet, reel you in, get you to do anything he asked. Ted had articles written about him; he contributed on television medical news stories. Scott wanted to take care of his people. He was more embracing, anxious to give you something you needed. Ted was a Lamborghini; Scott was a Jeep. Ted was all flash, while Scott was unpretentious and solid. There was no hidden agenda here. And while she might've started the day thinking it was a three-month gig to give her a chance to live simply and get her head together, she quickly saw it as a good idea, an opportunity to learn about small-town medicine from a master. And the other shock was she found the Jeep far sexier than the Lamborghini.

Her second day in the clinic was much the same as the first, busy all day, and she already felt at home.

"It might go a little easier on me if you weren't so damn efficient and personable," Scott said. "If you were klutzy, lazy and annoying, I wouldn't mind giving you up in three months."

She laughed at him and said, "There's another reason I can't stay longer," she said. "It's not just the money, although you have to admit…"

"I'll be the first to admit it's not nearly what you deserve," he said. "It's just what the clinic can bear. So, what else is going on?"

"My youngest sister is having her first baby, and I promised to be with her. She's the sister I'm closest to and she's in San Francisco."

"Auntie Peyton," he said with that warm, loving smile. "Well, if that's all it is, we can always work out time off. Family comes first."

Don't be too nice to me, don't make me want to be here. I really can't afford to trust a man again too soon, she thought.

And then, at three in the afternoon of that second day, there was a red flag. It was almost as if it was delivered on request. Gina's daughter, Ashley, brought Scott's children to the clinic. "Scott, I checked with everyone, even my mom, to see if anyone could babysit for a couple of hours, and I'm sorry, there's no one. We're covered for tomorrow till five, but now I have to go to work at the diner."

"Don't worry, Ashley. Not a problem. They can watch their movies or color in the break room for a couple of hours," Scott said.

"Are you sure? There's always Cooper or Rawley—I didn't try them because they have Devon and Spencer's kids."

"They probably have their hands full. This is okay." He bent down to kiss them each on their foreheads.

Ashley handed over a couple of backpacks, one pink and girlie, one camouflage and oh, so manly. "You're loaded up with books, Kindles with their movies, crayons, special cups, bags of fruit chewies…."

"Thanks, Ash. You've been a big help. Ashley, this is Peyton, our new physician's assistant. Peyton, meet Gina's daughter, Ashley James."

Peyton put out her hand. "Nice to meet you."

"I heard about you. My mom mentioned meeting you. Welcome. I hope you'll like it here."

"I already like it here," Peyton said.

"I'm off to the diner. My mom has to get out of there on time—the younger kids have lessons and stuff, and Mac is on duty until dinnertime."

As Ashley headed out the door, Scott introduced the kids. "This is Jenny, and this is Will, four and five years old. Will starts kindergarten in the fall."

Peyton crouched. "How do you do," she said, smiling. They were simply beautiful children, Jenny with her long, curling brown hair and Will trying to act so grown up, one strap of his backpack slung over his shoulder. "Where's Mommy today? Working?"

"Mommy lives in heaven," Jenny said.

Peyton almost fell flat on her ass. She had to put a hand down to steady herself enough to rise to her full height. She was stricken. She looked at Scott, shaking her head. "I'm so sorry," she said softly.

He held up a hand. "Not a problem, Peyton. Let me get the kids settled in the break room, and I'll explain."

She actually had to sit down. Her knees wobbled slightly.

He was back in no time. "Well, I don't know how you made it a whole week in Thunder Point without knowing that, but to be honest, I'm relieved. I guess that means they don't all talk about me as the lonely widower as often as I thought they did."

She shook her head, but couldn't seem to close her mouth. She cleared her throat. "A devoted family man," she said weakly. "With a mother-in-law?"

"I am devoted, and my wife might be deceased, but my mother-in-law is going to be dancing on my grave," he said. "I lost Serena immediately following Jenny's birth. She was on life support for a while. She wouldn't have liked that, but Serena was an organ donor and…well, I'm glad now. She wasn't in pain, and I really didn't want Jenny to grow up associating her birthday with her mother's death. I was widowed four years ago. I have a nanny. Au pair. Babysitter. Right arm. Gabriella is twenty now and has been with me here in Thunder Point the past year. She's been managing the house and kids with my assistance and going to school, but her mother was diagnosed with breast cancer. She's going to be fine, but Gabriella wanted to be with her and left kind of suddenly. I think she just got scared. Understandable. Usually Devon and I, both single parents, could help each other out when things came up, but I'd shut the clinic before I'd call her on her honeymoon...."

"Devon is no longer a single parent," Peyton said.

"I doubt that will change anything. Mercy and Austin are as comfortable at my house as they are at home." He laughed. "Austin has two families as it is—talk about a flexible kid."

"But what if you're called to the hospital?" Peyton asked.

"I'm not on call. I had to cancel when Gabriella left."

"Does this sort of thing happen a lot?" she asked, tilting her head toward the break room. "Kids in the office?"

"Only once in the past year. They're very well behaved, but I don't want them here as a habit. For obvious reasons..."

"Sick people, being one?"

"And the sheer distraction, not to mention a million questions."

There was a sudden loud *whoop-whoop-whoop* from outside, and Peyton whirled to see Mac in the sheriff's deputy's SUV roar down the street with lights and sirens. And right behind him another deputy followed, also lit up. Behind them, the wrecker from the service station was moving pretty fast, lights revolving.

"Wow," she said.

"That doesn't look good. I've only seen Mac all lit up once since I moved here. I've never seen Mac and the other deputy both tear out of town like that."

Right then his cell phone rang, and Peyton had a sinking feeling. It matched the look on Scott's face. He pulled out his phone.

"Scott Grant," he said; then he listened. He nodded to the phone. "Hold on," he said. He looked at Peyton. "The perfect storm," he said to her. "Bus accident just off 101 near Bandon. Church camp bus— full of kids. All area medical and rescue has been called."

She didn't even have to think about it. "Go."

"On my way," he said into the phone. He pocketed it. "The clinic keys and keys to my house are in the top desk drawer. You can close the clinic. Put up a sign—closed for emergency. You can take the kids to my house—plenty of food and toys."

"I don't know where you live!"

"Well, everyone else does. Just ask someone."

"I don't have safety seats!"

"It's three blocks, Peyton. We walk from my house to the beach all the time." Then he dashed into the break room to tell his children goodbye. She heard him say, "When I get home, I want Peyton to tell me you're the best children in the world."

"Oh, God," she whispered to herself. "This isn't happening to me."

Four

There were a few patients scheduled, and Peyton thought she might be just turning them away with the excuse that the doctor had an emergency, and since she was new, she didn't want to presume to take over their treatment. But six people stopped by and didn't expect to keep their appointments—they only wondered what she had heard about the accident. One of them was Carrie from the deli next door, and she was kind enough to give Peyton directions to Scott's house.

She sat at the table in the break room for a little while, making sure the kids were comfortable with her before taking them home. "Well, I suppose we should lock up the clinic and head to your house. Want to show me the way?" she asked.

"Follow me," Will said, backpack slung over one shoulder.

She shoved her directions into her pocket and, holding Jenny's hand, followed. Will went up the walk to a small house with a nice little flower bed in the front. He waited by the door until she could unlock it for them. Then, inside they went, dropping backpacks in the foyer.

"First, we have a snack," Will said.

"What kind of a snack?" Peyton asked.

Jenny went to the pantry and got out some Goldfish crackers. "We have our own dish," she instructed. "Then we play. Then we have dinner. Then we have a bath. Then ice cream."

"Wow, that sounds like a very busy schedule. And sounds like you're almost ready to take care of yourselves. Want to show me the dish you want for the fishies?"

Jenny was happy to do that. She pulled the step stool over to the counter, climbed up and opened a cupboard that revealed some bright-colored plastic plates and bowls.

"Do you have kids?" Jenny asked.

"Nope. But I come from a very big family, and I have lots of brothers, sisters, nieces and nephews. Lots," Peyton replied.

"Like five?"

Peyton laughed. "More like twenty-five."

Jenny looked quite impressed.

The very first thing to put Peyton a little more at ease was Scott's house. It was quite nice but very ordinary and on the small side. She looked around a little bit. There was nothing uppity or fancy here. There was a kitchen with nook, small dining room, living room, master with bath, second bath and two more bedrooms. Right away she was pretty sure Scott would never say the words, *I have an image to maintain, Peyton.*

"Where does the babysitter stay?" she asked Jenny.

"Gabby has the *whole* downstairs!" Jenny said.

"We're not allowed down there—it's *hers!*" Will said. "She has her own TV!"

"I suppose she should," Peyton said. "She probably has things to watch that you wouldn't like that much."

"And she has a boyfriend! Charles. They kiss!" Jenny said.

Peyton laughed. "You might have a boyfriend someday, you know."

"No, I don't like boys. Except Daddy and Will. *Sometimes* Will."

"And what does Daddy say about that? As if I don't know."

"He says, good."

Will lost interest in the conversation when it veered into boys and kissing. He went to his backpack for his Kindle and held it up while he snacked, watching some downloaded movie or cartoon. During this time, Jenny informed Peyton that they could have pizza for dinner because that's what they did when there was no cooking. Gabby had to visit her mother, so Daddy was cooking, but not too much. Peyton was shown where to find the frozen pizzas and ice cream. Peyton was fully capable of that but wondered if Scott might be home before then. While

Jenny was conducting her kitchen tour, Will left the room. He returned quickly, his arms laden with blankets, some dragging along the floor.

"Excuse me, sir," Peyton said. "What's going on there?"

"It's for a fort."

"Where?"

"There," he said, indicating the dining room table.

"Where did you get the blankets?" she asked.

"From the closet floor. They're fort blankets, not bed blankets. They're too dirty for the bed, Gabby said."

"I see. So I guess Daddy allows this?"

"Sometimes he gets in it with us, if he doesn't have a book or a phone call," Will explained.

Peyton stepped closer to the dining room to watch the construction of the fort, which was accomplished with all the precision of experienced builders. Heavy books held the blankets on top of the table, chairs were turned around to make more space underneath, one blanket on the floor, a couple of pillows inside.

"And what do you do in there?" she asked.

Will shrugged and just pressed on. "Take stuff in there."

"Sometimes we have ice cream in there," Jenny added. "Or movies. And games and books and stuff. But not paints or clay or Play-Doh."

"I can see how that would be a problem," Peyton said. "I'll be in the living room."

The kids disappeared inside, and she was very grateful for that. She wanted to turn on the TV, see if there was any coverage of this wreck. It wouldn't be good to turn on the news and have the kids hear anything shocking or scary since their father was there. But she wanted to know any available details. She was not optimistic there would be much news as this was a very small town, and it was an accident off the main roads.

But, ah! In the age of smartphones there was amateur footage already sent to news stations. And it looked god-awful. A blue school bus was on its side halfway off the road, back emergency door gaping open and lots of emergency vehicles all around. There were other vehicles scattered around, but she couldn't tell if they'd been involved. A Coast Guard helicopter was taking off, presumably airlifting a patient or patients—USCG provided emergency services to the local area. The scene looked chaotic and terrifying, but the broadcaster said that even though there were thirty-seven children on board and many injuries, there was only one fatality, the bus driver.

The group had been en route to a church camp along the river; they'd come from the north part of the state. There were young camp counselors among the group, and one young lady with a bandage on her forehead was interviewed. "We were skidding and spinning and hitting other cars, and then all of a sudden the bus just flipped over. All the kids were tossed everywhere, and we landed on top of each other in a big pile. No one knows what happened."

The newscaster said that while it was as yet unconfirmed, it was possible the accident was caused by the driver suffering a medical episode.

Indeed, news film showed two cars and a truck that looked damaged, and it was reported that area hospitals were preparing for injured. And, typical of a small town, curious about everything, the police were now managing crowd control.

"Looks like pizza for dinner," she muttered to herself.

Scott called Mac's cell from the car. "I got the call. I'm going to come by the scene to help first responders with triage before continuing on to the hospital."

"Can't hurt. They're calling F.D. from Douglas County and Coast Guard is en route."

"Any details on injuries or fatalities?"

"A lot of kids have evacuated the bus already, some helped out by motorists. Watch the road and park behind emergency vehicles."

Scott approached cautiously and pulled off the road behind the tow truck. As he was jogging with medical bag in hand, he passed Eric Gentry, who waited just outside his tow truck. Right beyond Eric and the wrecker was a paramedic rescue unit and behind that, an ambulance. Fortunately, he knew the fire captain. No pleasantries were exchanged. "I want you on that medic unit over there and treat who you can. We'll transport the ones who can't be treated here," the captain said.

"Gotcha," Scott replied.

It was sheer pandemonium, but Scott could see

a gathering of young children standing around the medical unit, some of them holding compresses to their heads or limbs. Mac was setting out flares along the road ahead, closing it off. It was an ominous sight, a blue church bus on its side, glass all over the road.

"What have we got?" Scott asked the medic.

"So far it looks like a lot of minor injuries in need of follow-up like X-rays, head CTs, stitches. A couple of fractures we'll have Coast Guard transport via airlift, and the ambulance can transport our worst casualties, the worst lacerations or contusions. Most of these kids exited the bus on their own, but there are a couple coming out on backboards."

"The driver?" Scott asked.

"Deceased. The coroner is on his way."

"Let's get patching and transporting," Scott said.

A second and third fire department showed up, and working together, they began lowering the population of injured at the scene of the accident. The accident was upgraded to a fatal, given the driver, and the state police fatal team was soon collecting data, measuring, taking pictures. There was only one adult supervisor for this large group, a youth pastor, but she was only slightly banged up and held the master list of all the children's names and contact information. She worked with emergency personnel to keep track of the kids being transported and their destinations. Luckily, there were enough teenage camp counselors present to accompany groups of younger children to various area hospitals. It took close to two hours to send ambulances with four, five or even six kids to local hospitals. Scott followed the third group to the Bandon ER It was going to take hours for parents and guardians to fetch them since they were all from out of town. It looked as if only a few had to be hospitalized overnight for fractures, and they were taken to Eugene's county hospital.

The ER was so chaotic, Scott didn't have time to call Peyton, but he took a moment to text her that he was tied up and asked if she was doing all right. She texted back immediately. At your house, pizza for dinner, all is well. He spoke to a number of parents, frantically en route to Coos County, and tried to allay their fears as well as he could.

"That could've been horrible," he said to one of the RNs he knew well. "There could've been dozens of little bodies all over the road and down the hill."

She shuddered. "I know. Even though it was mostly cuts and bruises, I don't think I'll sleep tonight," she said.

"Me, either," he agreed.

Throughout the evening, between pizza, games of Candy Land, baths and getting ready for bed, Peyton flipped on the news from time to time just to catch any updates on the accident. They were still showing the original footage, and the reports remained the same. The authorities hadn't confirmed it, but it seemed that the bus driver, a fifty-seven-year-old woman, had suffered a stroke or heart attack, causing her to lose control of the bus. And the children, some thirty-seven of them, all survived.

But what a terrible, tragic mess.

Here at Scott's home, doing the one thing she swore she would not be coerced into doing ever again, Peyton was babysitting for the boss. She wasn't going to tell him she didn't really mind. In fact, had Ted's kids been even half as polite and well behaved as these two little ones, she might still be in Portland. There were so many simple chores that went so smoothly with Jenny and Will. Like brushing out Jenny's long hair. "Use that," Jenny said, pointing to the anti-tangle spray in Scott's bathroom. And then she sat still and quiet, even sighing from time to time. This had never happened with Ted's kids; his girls wouldn't let her help them with anything. She had so wanted to brush their hair, take them shopping, cook with them, help decorate their bedrooms, watch girl movies with them, but they'd held her at arm's length. She'd soon learned never to compliment their clothing or hairstyles or she'd never see them look that nice again.

Scott's kids ate their pizza slices at the table and carried their dishes to the sink. *Really? At four and five?* Peyton wasn't sure what came next. "Should I get your bath ready?" she asked.

Jenny nodded, but Will said, "I take a shower in Dad's shower." *Ah, so manly.*

"Try not to make a big mess, please," Peyton asked nicely. And he didn't. He even hung up his towel and put his dirty clothes in the hamper.

Oh, I was so arrogant, she thought. She had known Ted's trio of kids were tough, but she thought she could manage them, whip them into shape. It was not as though she was without experience, both personally and professionally. And she had failed completely. Not only couldn't she keep her relationship with Ted alive, but to her horror, the kids had seemed to deteriorate, growing ever worse in their behavior. Their scrapes with their teachers increased, their sass to her became worse than ever, even their grades dropped as if she'd done more harm than good. They weren't going to turn out well. In fact, she feared what kind of people they might become.

"One last game of Candy Land?" she asked the squeaky clean kids.

"Yay! One more!"

And then it was quiet time. They wanted to "camp" with their Kindles and crawled under the table. "Peyton, you can come in, too, if you want."

"Think I can fit?"

"You have to make yourself small. And be careful about your head," Jenny said.

"What the heck," she said. Down on all fours, she crawled into the tent, ducking her head for the wooden braces where the leaf fit. "Just for a little while. I should put the tent away before your daddy gets home."

"It's okay. It doesn't make Daddy mad," Will said.

"He's a very good daddy," Peyton said, once inside. Will and Jenny slid apart, putting her in the middle. "Very nice," she said. "You can live in here."

"We have a real tent," Will informed her.

"For camping?" she asked.

"Uh-huh. We camp in the backyard, but pretty soon we're going to camp on the beach before it gets too cold. You can come, too, if you want to."

"That is so sweet," she said, carefully lying down on her back between the two of them, her feet sticking out of the tent. "Sadly, I will be busy that day. So, now what do we do?"

"We watch," Jenny said.

She held up her small screen to share with Peyton while Will was not so charitable. He rolled on to his side, his back curled against Peyton, watching his screen privately. She snuck a peak to make sure it wasn't inappropriate; he was into dragons, it appeared. "Well, I guess I'll watch with you. What's this?"

"Up," Jenny said. "It's about balloons."

Indeed. A balloon salesman who had a very satisfactory life selling them, married to a happy wife, growing older gracefully if not completely fulfilled since he missed out on some adventures. But he was mostly content. And then his wife died!

"He's going to cry now," Jenny pointed out.

"I think *I'm* going to cry," Peyton said.

Jenny turned toward her and gently stroked her cheek with her small hand, turning her beautiful big brown eyes up at Peyton. "It's okay. I'm right here."

Oh, God! Did she really hear right? She's four!

Stop, Peyton, stop! Do not fall in love with these children! They belong to the boss! Another package deal that didn't work out, that would hurt way too much. She didn't even have a whole heart left after what Ted and his children put her through.

"Now he'll make his house fly and be happy and fun."

"That Disney," Peyton said. "They take no prisoners." And she sniffed.

Scott felt terrible about imposing on Peyton. It was criminal! She was new in town, had come in to the clinic ahead of schedule just to help out and try to cover for Devon, and what had he done? Not only worked her to a full-time schedule, but gone off on an emergency that sucked up over eight hours. It was after midnight, and there was still confusion and commotion at the hospital, banged-up children sleeping on cots, couches, chairs and gurneys.

Of course, had he not thoroughly checked out her résumé, talked to former employers and observed her with children in the clinic, he might not have dared. He absolutely believed he could trust her with his children.

He crept quietly into the house, the kitchen light was on as well as a living-room light. The TV was off, and there was no one on the couch, but there was a fort in the dining room. And out of the fort stuck two grown-up feet.

He laughed to himself.

He crouched down and shook her foot. "Peyton," he whispered.

She sat up with a start and bashed her head into

the dining room table. She went back down with a thud.

"Shit. Peyton. Peyton. Are you knocked out?" Scott said. And then, for lack of a better idea, he grabbed her ankles and pulled her out from under the dining room table. Her eyes were open, her black hair streaming out behind her, and she was glaring at him. "Damn, I'm sorry! It's that table-leaf insert, it hangs down a—" He squinted at her. "Um, we might need a little ice there."

"I'll be fine," she said tartly.

"You fell asleep in the fort. Happens to me all the time." He rubbed a spot on his forehead. "So does that."

"What time is it?" she asked.

"It's almost one. I'm so sorry, this never should have happened. I don't take advantage of people like that, I swear. I extended babysitting to Devon long before I asked her to help me. But then I had Gabby's help. And, man, all in one week, Gabby has to leave, Devon gets married, you start working for the clinic and a church camp bus holding thirty-seven kids wrecks." He shook his head. "If that ever happens again, I'm moving...."

She started to get up. He held out a hand to help. "I want to hear about it. All of it..." she said.

"It's so late."

"I know. And you're so tired. But seriously, I saw little snippets of news, and I want to know what it was like. What you found when you got there, what you did, how you helped...because I was thinking, if you had had a babysitter, I could've gone. I've only been involved in a couple of emergencies like that, but it really got my motor running."

He grinned at her. "I should've known. An excitement junkie. I've had too much coffee to sleep right away, anyway," he said, heading for the kitchen table. "Was there any video?"

"The same one, over and over—bus on its side, a couple of banged-up cars, enough kids to start a small school."

"It was a miracle there were no serious injuries. Only two broken bones and they were transported to Eugene. Cuts and scrapes and bruises." He got out his cell phone and brought up the pictures. It was common practice since his residency, taking pictures of injuries to refer to afterward. "That's going to need a plastic surgeon referral, but I did the best I could on the stitches. That wicked hematoma earned a head CT and overnight in the hospital. Go ahead, look through them. All parents were notified, and by the time I left, most of the kids had been united with their parents. That's a wide-awake nightmare— send your kids off to camp and get that kind of phone call." He shook his head. "How were mine?"

"Perfect," she said. "Very well behaved."

"I probably owe most of that to Gabriella. Such a gentle soul, but she's firm."

"They're almost abnormally good," Peyton said.

He just laughed. "Oh, they have their moments. Especially Will. I didn't know when we named him that it was short for Willful."

"He was a little prince."

"I told him he wouldn't get to camp on the beach if I heard one complaint."

"He is very excited about that. He invited me to join you."

"Oh?" Scott asked.

She yawned. "Unfortunately, I'm busy."

"We haven't picked a day yet."

"Whatever day you pick, I'm busy." She stood. "I'm heading out."

Scott stood, too. "You can have Jenny's bed. The sheets are clean. She's been in my bed every night since clean sheet day."

"That's generous, but, no. I have a date with my toothbrush."

"I have a new toothbrush, Peyton. It's late."

"Going home, Scott. I'm not friendly in the morning."

He pulled his keys out of his pocket and handed them to her. "Take my car. Bring it to the clinic sometime tomorrow. And don't feel obligated to show up to work if you can use the rest—this is bonus time, anyway."

"I'll be there," she said. "I'll drive your car to the clinic and take mine home from there. You have an extra car key, don't you?"

He nodded. He couldn't help but smile at her. Damn she was beautiful. Too bad about that not-interested-in-men thing because she really rocked a pair of jeans. Her legs were long, her ass so round and firm. He suddenly knew how women felt, the women who asked why were all the really good ones gay?

"Your car will be safe parked at the clinic, next to the sheriff's office."

"I'm not worried about the car, Peyton. And thanks a million, really. I promise that isn't going to be a habit—it's not in your job description to baby-sit for me. Devon will be home day after tomorrow."

"Babysitting isn't a commitment I can make, but this was an emergency. A rare emergency. And your kids are enjoyable. I don't feel taken advantage of."

Scott wasn't surprised that Peyton was a trouper. She was at the clinic at eight in the morning, and she seemed to be in a cheerier mood.

"Well, good morning," she said to him. "Where are the kids today? In the break room?"

He shook his head. "Ashley has the whole day free for me. She's not working at the diner or the deli today. I think she gave me one of her few free days, but she's hungry for money and happy about the work. She might walk them down to the beach later. If she does, I'm sure she'll drop by to let me know. Some of her friends might be down there. They all work, but when they're done, they gather, and it's usually at the diner or the beach."

"Have you heard from your sitter?"

"She called, yes," he said. "Her mom is doing well—no lymph involvement. Still, they're waiting for a chemo decision and schedule. She's going to stay with her mom until they have more information.

I expected that. Thank God it's summer. Between Devon, Ashley and Mac's daughter Eve, I should be covered."

"I bet you're tired today," she said, tossing her purse under the counter.

"I'm okay. I'm used to catching sleep when I can. But I'll tell you what I didn't catch—breakfast. Cover for me here while I run across the street? There aren't any appointments until nine."

"Sure," she said.

"The kids were lazy this morning. They were just waking up when Ashley got to the house. I was just about to call Gina and ask her to meet me in the middle of the street with an omelet to go."

She laughed at him. "Take your time. I've got it."

"You seem pretty well rested," he observed.

"I had a nap in the fort," she said with a shrug.

He grinned at her. "And a slight concussion."

"I should've negotiated for hazardous duty pay," she said, smiling gently.

"Can I bring you back anything?"

"Yeah. If they have something kind of glazed, a sticky bun or donut or something not healthy. I have a little bit of a sweet tooth."

"I'll see what I can round up," he said.

There was still a small breakfast crowd at the diner, though the majority of their clientele was very early, and the rush was usually completely exhausted by nine. Scott took the stool that had become his and asked Gina for his usual.

"Let's see—three-egg omelet with cheddar and bacon and some potatoes?"

"And coffee."

She slid the ticket through the serving window to Stu and poured Scott some coffee. "Late night?" she asked.

Of course, Gina would know what went on since Mac was her husband. "It was a mess of people, but we got real lucky. Only a couple of serious injuries. I have to find out what church that is—thirty-seven kids, bounced around a bus, and they not only survived, we didn't have any critical injuries."

"Well, except the driver," she said.

"Poor woman. My money is on a heart attack."

"And Peyton had your kids?"

He nodded. "I feel terrible about that. We hardly know each other. There was no one to call. If it hadn't been an emergency of that magnitude, I would never have done that. I wouldn't have asked. But…"

"I doubt that'll happen again, Scott. You've been here a year—when was the last time we had something that big?"

"I was called out one night when a bunch of drunk teenagers had a brawl and split some lips and skulls. But there were seven of them, and that was madness enough."

"She must be a very good sport," Gina said. A bell dinged, and she reached behind her to deliver Scott's breakfast.

"She is that," he said. "And she has a very sassy wit—easy to get used to, although Peyton and Devon in the same office could be overwhelming." He put a forkful of eggs in his mouth.

"And she's beautiful," Gina said.

He nodded, swallowed. "No kidding," he said.

"Maybe your luck is changing."

"How so?" he asked.

"Scott, you've been ready for years now. But the right woman hasn't appeared. Now you have, right under your nose, a beautiful, funny, talented, *single* woman. Maybe this one will work out."

"Not likely," he said. *Not since she's playing for the girl's team.* "She made it very clear, she's not interested in men. And she'd only give me a three-month commitment. That's understandable—a little clinic like mine doesn't pay well, and she can use this time to find her next position for more than twice the salary. Nah, my luck is the same. Don't you have a pretty cousin somewhere you can introduce me to?"

"No," she said with a laugh. "Listen, lots of women say that they don't want to date. Could be anything—just coming off a breakup, frustration with the way things haven't worked out in the dating world, some reason we'd never think of…."

That's for sure, he thought.

"When I was frustrated with Mac not noticing me as a datable woman, a romantic partner, I was so furious I swore off men. Be patient. The right opportunity might present itself."

"Um-hmm," he muttered, eating his breakfast. "I think I took you out to dinner a couple of times during your moratorium on men. Timing is everything."

She smiled at him. "Sorry that didn't work out, Scott."

"No, you're not," he said.

"No, I'm not. I say we give Peyton time to settle in and then reevaluate."

"Gina, I say we face facts." *And too bad about the jeans,* he thought. *But, damn!*

Five

Devon and Spencer weren't due back until Thursday, but on Wednesday afternoon they pulled into the garage of their beachfront home. They dropped their bags inside the door of the house and went directly to Cooper's.

"Hey, the bride and groom are back!" Cooper said. "Don't you have another day of freedom?"

"I missed the kids," Devon said.

"She missed the *house,*" Spencer corrected.

"Well, I've never had a house before!" Devon said. "And there's still a lot to do before football practice starts, and I no longer have a husband."

"She brought me back to work," Spencer said. "I don't know what's harder on my back—football or construction."

"But we're so close…." She flushed a little. "And I *did* miss the kids," she said.

But to Devon this house meant security, for maybe the first time in her life. She'd been raised by a woman known as Aunt Mary, but she was really the day-care provider Devon had been left with when her mother died. She didn't realize Mary couldn't leave her a house to live in until after her death when Devon was a very young woman. The years since had been hand-to-mouth, until she'd met and fallen in love with Spencer. Once Spencer understood how uncertain and unstable her life had been, he thought the best thing he could do for her, for both of them, was to own a piece of property, protected and secure. Devon loved him so much for understanding, for helping to provide. And she'd made a promise to him. "I'm going to make it the most loving home you've ever known."

"All you have to do to accomplish that is live in it with me," Spencer had said.

Cooper grinned at them. "I'll help out while I can, but I think pretty soon Sarah is going to have chores for me."

"How is she doing?" Devon asked.

"She's laying down right now. She has heartburn, water retention and gas. I had no idea how sexy pregnancy was." Everyone laughed at him. "Your kids are down there with the real babysitter."

Down on the dock Rawley was fishing with Mercy and Austin.

"I'd better go tell them we're back," she said.

"Let 'em fish," Spencer said. "They'll figure it out pretty soon and come up here. Cooper's going to give me a beer." He looked at his watch. "I have at least a few more hours of honeymoon left."

"Is that Ashley with Scott's kids down there by the water?" Devon asked.

"Uh, yeah," Cooper said. "It's been kind of exciting around here. Let me get that beer and I'll tell you all about it. A wine, Devon?"

"That would be wonderful. What's going on?"

Cooper sat with them on the deck and explained that Gabriella had left suddenly because her mother needed her, the bus accident being the big talk around town, Peyton helping out in the clinic and Ashley babysitting—the story as he knew it. It was only a few minutes before Mercy was up the stairs and on her mother's lap, a few more minutes before Scott was walking across the beach at the end of his work day to check on his kids. He came up to the deck to have a beer, and Rawley and Austin joined them. And then Sarah appeared, looking a little sleep rumpled.

"And here's Mrs. Cooper with her big bump and bed head," Cooper said.

"I couldn't sleep," she said. And then with a muffled groan, she bent over slightly, and water spilled down her legs.

Cooper jumped to his feet with a horrified look on his face.

"Oops," Sarah said. "Maybe that wasn't gas."

"Mommy," Mercy said. "Sarah had a accident."

With a very large grin, Sarah said, "I'm going to have ankles again."

"That's not all you're going to have, Sarah," Scott put in.

* * *

Peyton enjoyed the pace of the Thunder Point clinic, especially once Devon was back managing the schedule and paperwork. It ran very smoothly. A three-person clinic with appointments spaced to give the practitioners the opportunity to handle the walk-ins, to take time for lunch and breaks, even to arrive late or leave early, was so easy on the nerves. Scott was able to spend some time at the ER or Bandon clinic, which supplemented his income. Now that Peyton was on board, that moonlighting didn't rob him of time with his kids. They had it worked out so that the bulk of their appointments fell when both Peyton and Scott were available to see patients, and with Devon's expertise in scheduling, they were at the clinic together at least twenty hours a week.

A couple of very low-stress weeks zipped by. Peyton even took a long Fourth of July weekend with her family at the farm.

Peyton happened to be standing at Devon's desk one weekday afternoon when Al Michel brought in one of his foster sons. The boy was pale as a ghost, slightly bent at the waist, and he was holding a bowl. "Oh, boy," Peyton said. "Who is this, Al?"

"This is Kevin, and he's feeling really terrible."

"That bowl was a dead giveaway. Come on back. Let's figure it out."

"I heard there was a bug going around," Al said, following them to the exam room. "I had to pry him off the bed to bring him in to see you."

"Can you make it up on the exam table, Kevin?" she asked him.

He took his time, but he made it.

"Ordinarily I'd put you in a gown, but if you'll just loosen your jeans, that should be enough. Lay down for me. And tell me where the pain is."

"Right about here," he said, indicating his lower abdomen just south of his belly button. "But I been throwing up, and I think it's just sore."

She pressed down, and when she let up, he winced.

"Al, can you take Kevin's shoes off, please? Socks can stay on." While Al was doing that, Peyton took the boy's temperature. Then she swatted the bottom of his feet, and again, he winced. "When did this start?"

"Early this morning, but it's getting worse," Kevin said.

"Did it come on suddenly?"

"Sort of, yeah. Like food poisoning—I had that once. It's like one minute you're fine, and all of a sudden you're dying...."

She smiled at him and ran a hand over his sweaty brow. "Stay down for me, Kevin. I'll be right back."

She stuck her head in Scott's office. "I've got a hot appy. Hundred and one temp, extreme tenderness, vomiting. Want to weigh in and decide where to send him?"

Scott was on his feet instantly. When a practitioner made that call so fast, it could be real hot. He already knew after just a couple of weeks of working with Peyton that she wasn't indecisive—when she was sure, she was right. She certainly didn't lack confidence. He walked in to the exam room. "Hey, Kev," he said, right before starting to torture him, pressing, poking. Kevin winced and moaned. Scott felt his hot, damp brow. "So, Al, we think this is appendicitis. I want you to take Kevin up to Pacific Hospital in North Bend. I'll call ahead and make sure there's a surgeon available."

"Is this an emergency?" Al asked.

"It certainly could be. That's not my call, that's the surgeon's call, but we don't mess around with appendicitis. That's why I want him to see Kevin right away. I have a feeling this is going straight to the operating room."

"I should go scoop up the boys," Al said. "They don't like to be separated, especially when something big is going down. You can understand."

"I'll go see to the boys. I'll tell them what's going on and make sure they get up to North Bend if there's going to be an operation. There could be some waiting around while someone decides. They're going to want some blood work to confirm. Or, it could move fast. Want me to explain to Eric you're not going in to work?"

"Well, when it rains, it pours. Eric and Laine left town for a few days, and I'm in charge. I have the station and the tow business. Norm is my backup— could you let him know he'll have to stay late? He can call Manny if necessary. We'll just hope no one needs a tow. Justin is at the station, and Danny's at home right now. I told them I wanted to make a quick trip to your office to make sure Kevin just had a bug."

"Al, I don't want an operation," Kevin said, a little tremor in the twelve-year-old's voice.

"Don't be nervous," Peyton said. "It's an easy operation, as long as they get to it quickly. Once they get that appendix out, you're going to feel so much better. But you have to get to the ER right away. No time to waste."

"Everything is going to be fine, Al," Scott said. "I'll make a couple of calls, all right? I'll make sure they're expecting you. No screwing around, no stopping for any reason. Get going."

"Thanks, Doc. Tell Justin I'll call him as soon as I get to the hospital, as soon as I know something." Al worked Kevin's shoes back on while Kevin fastened his jeans. Then Al pulled the boy to a sitting position, and rather than helping him down from the exam table, he lifted him in his arms. "Let's not jiggle it around," he said with a nervous smile. "Hang on to that bowl."

Al was out the door quickly. Scott pulled out his phone and called the hospital ER They had a surgeon there on another case, and they would keep him another thirty minutes to meet Al and Kevin. Scott requested a call-back from the doctor. Then he slid the phone into his pocket and looked at Peyton. "I have a feeling that was a good call."

"That one was easy. His symptoms aren't vague. If we're wrong, they're going to take out a healthy appendix. But I guarantee his white count is going to cooperate with the diagnosis."

"I'm sure you're right." He walked out to Devon's desk. "Do I have anything now?"

"Mrs. Bledsoe's check—the usual."

"I can take that, Scott," Peyton said.

"Then I'm going to walk down to Lucky's and talk to Norm and Justin, fill them in on what's happening with Kevin. I won't be long."

"Everyone has your cell phone number, you deliver messages and even offer transportation to family members," Peyton said. "An all-service physician."

He just smiled at her. "All-service," he said. "Here's the thing. If the doctor was a long way from here, like in another town instead of down the street, a person might want to wait to see if they started to feel better. When people feel sick or hurt, not only do they not want to be any trouble, they don't want to go to any trouble. And while they're giving it another hour, the appendix can blow or that numb left arm can turn into a myocardial infarction. But if their doctor is around the corner…" He paused and gave a meaningful shrug.

"I've never looked at it that way," she said.

"Why would you? The cities you've worked in had urgent care facilities or ERs on every corner. There wasn't a doctor here for years. When 911 responded, they had to take the patient to Bandon or North Bend. Now there's someone they can call. I'm not the salvation of the town, by any means. I'm just willing, that's all. I'll be back in fifteen minutes. And thanks, Peyton. That was great work!"

He went out the door, and Peyton watched his departure. She leaned a hip against Devon's desk.

"He is, too, the salvation of the town," Devon said. "Have you ever known a guy like that? That responsive? That genuine?"

"Yeah," Peyton said. "Hank on *Royal Pains*." When Devon shot her a questioning look, she said, "It's a TV show. In other words, fiction." She thought for a minute. "The doctors I worked with have all been excellent physicians and good men and women, but they protected their time and God forbid give a patient a cell phone number. It's too invasive."

"Well, you won't be expected to do that, Peyton. Scott will handle that."

"Be sure to warn his next wife, Devon. Tell her what she's getting into. Being married to a doctor is hard enough."

"I'll do that," she said with a laugh. "Want to walk across the beach with me when we're done here? Have something to drink at Cooper's?"

"I'd like that," she said. "Know what I'd love? A little peek at your new house."

"As long as you remember—it's a work in progress. But we're close! So close!"

Before closing up the clinic, Devon and Peyton learned from Scott that Kevin was being prepped for surgery. Knowing that Scott would want to drive to North Bend to check on his patient, Devon took his kids off Ashley's hands. "They like to play with Mercy," she explained. "And they love the beach."

"I won't be late," Scott promised.

"Don't worry about it. I'll give everyone dinner, and if you're not back by bedtime, they can stay the night. We're doing sleeping bags this week—they'll love it."

They went to Devon's house so Peyton could have a tour, and she was immediately in love with it. From the beach, one walked up a wooden staircase to the deck and entered the great room through the double doors. Everything on the main level was finished and furnished—great room, large kitchen, dining room, wide foyer, master bedroom and second bedroom. There was also a driveway and two-car garage on that level—everything a family needed, and it was lovely. The view from the great room, dining room and deck was spectacular. Devon pointed to a staircase to a loft that she explained was Spencer's office—nice and spacious, but only one room. It was the downstairs that was still unfinished, which one could access from an inside staircase or a stone path and stairs that rose up the hill from the beachfront.

Devon left Jenny and Will in the great room in front of the TV while she showed Peyton the lower level. It was such a practical arrangement—two large bedrooms with bathrooms separated by a game room. Windows from the game room gave a view of the beach and ocean. There was a smaller deck. "High tide isn't ever going to be a problem," Devon said. "But in a tsunami warning, we'll have to evacuate and pray."

They continued the tour. "This is for the kids," Devon explained. "I thought Mercy would want to be upstairs with us, where she's been sleeping, but as it turns out, she can't wait to move down here. She wants to be a big kid like Austin. I wonder where they are?"

They walked into one of the bedrooms and saw the remnants of wall texturing supplies and drop cloths. "Well, I can see how Spencer spent his day, but I have no idea where he is."

Peyton looked around. "It's wonderful! There's not so much left to do. It's bare, but ready."

"Painting, papering, a wall unit to be installed for the TV, games, books and things, carpeting, all the final touches. Furnishing. We're waiting for a couple of built-in desks for the kids' rooms. Between us we had just enough to furnish most of the upstairs, so we've had to order furniture. But we're almost there. We'll be done before football practice starts," Devon said.

When they went upstairs, Jenny and Will were gone. Devon put her hands on her hips. "Now where are they? I can't seem to keep track of anyone!" She walked out on the deck to look down toward the dock to see if they might all be out there with Rawley or Landon, fishing. Instead, she saw everyone next door on Cooper's deck.

Spencer waved to her, signaling for her to come over.

Devon's eyes lit up. "I think Summer is outside. Wait till you see her."

"Oh," Peyton said. "I'll just…"

"You'll just come with me!" Devon grabbed her hand and pulled her back inside and out the front door, right next door and into Cooper and Sarah's front door. Everyone was out on the deck. Cooper and Spencer were laughing about something, Austin was hanging out with them. The baby was in a big Cadillac of a stroller with a Great Dane standing guard and three little faces peering into it. Sarah was relaxing on a lounge.

"How are you feeling?" Devon asked, going to her and giving her cheek a buss.

"Like I never had a baby," she said. "Until I look in the mirror."

"You look wonderful! How's she doing?"

But rather than answering, Sarah smiled and said, "Well, hello, Peyton! Nice to see you again!"

"I hope I'm not intruding," she said. "I came home with Devon to see her new house."

"Of course not. We've had quite a few drop-ins. And we're all feeling fine," she said. "A miracle, because I think I had the longest labor in the history of the world!"

"How long?" Peyton asked.

"Like twelve hours or something! It was brutal!"

Peyton and Devon exchanged glances and smiles.

"Oh, what? I suppose that's considered average or something! Well, I was not impressed. And I'll have you know that I've been trained by the Coast Guard. I am fit, strong and—"

"It wasn't quite twelve hours," Cooper said.

"Yes, it was," she replied. "What was it, then?"

"Slightly less, like six. But it looked pretty awful at times," he said. "I could tell you weren't having fun. But then, when it was over—it was just *over*. Wow. I've never seen anything like that! Nothing but smiles and giggles. Just like that."

"I should have let you do it," she said.

Devon shooed the kids away from the stroller, so Peyton could get a better look. There in the stroller bed, fast asleep with her little hands balled up, wearing a pink onesie, was Summer Cooper. She had a cap of dark brown hair, her mother's color. Her cheeks were rosy with health, her little mouth bright pink and heart-shaped.

Peyton smiled at Sarah. "It was worth it—the labor. She's absolutely beautiful."

Sarah glowed. "She is, isn't she?"

"Wait till you see these," Cooper said proudly. He pulled apart the receiving blanket and showed off her feet. "Have you ever seen feet that big on a baby?"

"They're pretty remarkable," Peyton said.

Hamlet, the Great Dane, moaned. Then he moaned again and nosed the stroller.

"All right, all right," Cooper said. He rewrapped the baby, gently picked her up and held her at Ham's level. Ham gently sniffed her, then he looked up at Cooper. His tail wagged. "That's going to have to hold you for a while," Cooper said. And the dog visibly relaxed as Cooper moved to put Summer back in the bed of the stroller. "Ham hasn't left her side since she came home. He can barely manage enough time to relieve himself."

"Cooper, may I?" Peyton asked.

"Sure, of course," he said. "She's very nice to hold. Sarah says we probably hold her too much."

Peyton reached for the baby. "There's no such thing." She brought the baby against her and instinctively her lips and nose went against that little cap of brown hair.

"You're awfully good at that," Sarah said.

"I'm a professional," Peyton said. "I have seven siblings. I held my first baby when I was two. Very big extended family. There have been many since."

"I'm surprised you don't have one of your own," someone said.

She laughed. "Maybe that's why I don't...."

But her heart gave a tug. She hadn't been in a hurry to have children, but now she was starting to feel something was missing from her life. Lots of things were missing. She began to hum to the baby without even realizing it. She swayed with little two-week-old Summer in her arms. She wanted more. She wanted a good, strong, faithful man, a child of her own, a family, a future, a life beyond her life. It almost caused her eyes to tear. She kissed the baby's head, and when she looked up, everyone was staring at her. She laughed uncomfortably. "Sorry. I got a little lost there for a second."

"She'll do that to you," Sarah said. "You're a natural."

"Call on me anytime your arms need a rest," she said.

"You can expect a call at around 2:00 a.m.," Cooper said.

Ham was soon sitting very close to Peyton, giving the little pink bundle an occasional sniff. While Peyton and Devon visited with Sarah for a little while, Ham wasn't the only interesting thing they observed. Austin was in and out of the house, and everywhere he went, Will was on his tail, asking questions, trying to share a bag of pretzels, acting goofy. After about three or four trips on to the deck and back into the house, Devon leaned toward Peyton and explained. "Will has a man-crush on Austin."

"And the Great Dane has an Alpha dog attachment to Summer," Peyton added.

"Big-time. Well, Sarah, I'm getting the kids out of here. You're probably kind of sick of them by now," Devon said.

"Actually, I think I'm having an adrenaline rush, but I don't want to use it cooking for a bunch of kids. Will you invite Austin over?"

"Sure," Devon said with a laugh. "Spencer and I will throw some food at them. Peyton, will you join us for dinner? It won't be fancy, and it could be loud."

"That's very sweet, but I think I'll call it a day. Let you get your family settled."

Peyton walked back to the clinic where her car was parked. She had some stuffed peppers from Carrie's deli at home in the freezer. She could heat up a nice big one and park in front of the TV with it.

But she sat in her car and texted Scott. Any news on Kevin?

Surgery went well. He's in recovery and will be in his room in a half hour.

She looked at her watch. Just under four hours since she'd seen him in the clinic. That indicated he went quickly into a surgery that was under two hours in length, a very good sign. She started her car and instead of going to her little duplex where a stuffed pepper waited for her, she drove out of town and headed to North Bend.

Six

It wasn't routine for Peyton to visit her patients in the hospital. She had, of course, if she was concerned or had a patient with whom she'd developed a close relationship. Rounds were more a function of the physicians, not their assistants. But she wanted to see how Kevin and his family were getting along. Al, this single man in his fifties, taking on three teenage boys even though he had major responsibilities to his employer, just plain intrigued her. Though she didn't know him well, she didn't think she'd met a more likable man in a long time.

She was given the room number, and when she went to the second floor, she saw Scott just exiting the room. "Well, Peyton! I didn't know you were coming up here."

"Last-minute decision," she said. "How's he doing?"

"He's a little goofy," Scott said. "But he's in good shape. I'm sure he'll be discharged in a day, maybe two. And he's going to sleep very well tonight! Al and the other boys were here when he came out of recovery. I just sent them on their way—I think they're convinced he's all right and won't be much company tonight. He has plenty of people to wait on him if he needs anything."

"Aw, I was hoping to see Al. Is he doing all right with his youngest just out of surgery?"

"Holding up fine," Scott said. "It went like clockwork. Have you eaten?"

"No, but I have one of Carrie's stuffed peppers in the freezer at home."

"Save it. I'll buy you dinner. Then I have to pick up the kids. Devon fed them and has them parked in front of a movie, and I'm hungry. What country do you feel like—Japan, Italy, Mexico or some good old Pacific ocean fare?"

"You don't have to do that, Scott…."

"I should have done it a couple of weeks ago! I'd be glad for the company. I could manage some nachos and a big fat burrito. I'm not on call tonight, and I'm in the mood for a cold beer. Want to follow me? I know a great little place."

"All right. Are you sure?"

"I'm sure. I'm starving!"

Twenty minutes later they were seated in a small but crowded Mexican restaurant, with a beer each and separated by a bowl of chips and salsa.

"So, you have the weekend off?" she asked Scott.

"More or less. I'm on call to the hospital Saturday night and Sunday night, but that doesn't mean they'll need me. For that matter, I've been called to North Bend when they need help, even when I'm not on call. It's rare for me to say no, but I like it better when I'm being paid to sit at home."

"But what do you do with the kids? Especially now with your babysitter out of town?"

"Devon and I have an arrangement. Mercy is at my house a lot, too. When Spencer's teaching and coaching and Devon is working at the clinic, Mercy has been at my house with my kids and Gabriella. I have her overnight now and then, so Spencer and Devon can have time alone. And now we're going to have to figure out a few things, because Gabby is coming back next week, but she's decided to move back home at the end of summer to go to college in Washington state so she can be closer to her mom. I think that cancer scare got to her."

"I can imagine," Peyton said. "What are you going to do?"

He gave a shrug. "Devon and I have been talking about it. We're thinking about day care, but there's no day care in town. We'll also have to find a babysitter to share during clinic hours. After clinic hours, we'll share the load, just like now. It really does take a village, especially in my case. We're going to barely blink, and the girls will start public school—just another year. Then it's going to get even more complicated...."

Oh, yes, she thought. *After-school clubs, sports, lessons, friends to hang out with or invite over.*

And needs—needing rides or clothes or supplies or equipment. "You have no idea," she said.

"You speak as one who knows," he said.

"I'm the oldest of eight, remember? I have ten nieces and nephews with number eleven due soon. Plus, Dr. Ramsdale was a single father of three, and there were times he had to ask office staff to pick them up or chauffer them."

"I hope you understand, I really don't intend to do that to you. That last time was a big emergency, Devon on her honeymoon…"

"I appreciate that, but I didn't complain, did I? I understand extreme circumstances. And you know what? I enjoyed your children. They're very entertaining. And they're nice, Scott."

"Will miracles never cease," he said, just as their dinners arrived—a big burrito for him, a taco salad for her. "What was it like growing up with all those brothers and sisters?" he asked.

"It was a circus," she said, spearing some of her salad. "Try to imagine feeding ten on an easy day. Not only were there occasionally friends to add to the lot, but there were aunts, uncles and cousins, mostly from Oregon and some from California. It's a big family. My mother doesn't own a platter or bowl that won't hold enough food for an army. Towels were washed daily, there were so many. By the time we could spell *cat* or *dog,* we were taking out trash, helping in the garden, picking pears, doing kitchen chores and learning to operate the washer and dryer. If you can drive a tractor, you can wash clothes. The week was divided—two kids per day got the washer and dryer. If you didn't perform laundry on your day, you were outta luck. We bartered to throw a favorite pair of jeans in with someone else's load. My dad used to say we learned to dance by waiting for a turn in the bathroom. No one had their own room, and we were pretty exited if there were only two sharing a room. Oh, by the time some of us left for school or work or the military, the younger ones had their own rooms for a few years, the spoiled brats. It was crazy."

"Good crazy?" he asked.

"Depends on your perspective. There were feuds and fights sometimes. We lived in a big old farmhouse, and there was barely a quiet corner to study in, but if we didn't get A's, we were toast. My parents were very strict. They had to be. But my mom—she was amazing. *Is* amazing. She tried to find special one-on-one time for each of us. There were too many of us to have a lot of that. My folks worked to the bone every day, so when it came time for games, recitals, concerts, plays and all that stuff, they were spread pretty thin—they couldn't show up for everything. My dad got up at four every morning and put in fourteen-hour days. My mom ran a farmhouse and garden and eight kids, and she was out of bed to give my dad breakfast every morning and had a solid dinner on the table every night. We were all at Mass every Sunday morning. That was non-negotiable. Since the pope had everything to do with them having eight kids, we were, by God, spilling out prayers every Sunday."

She saw that he was looking at her in sheer wonder. She smiled at him. "Your burrito will get cold."

"I'm fascinated. I have one sister and a widowed, overprotective, possessive mother. My sister, Nancy, and I refer to her as The Mother. When I moved to Thunder Point, leaving my mother to focus on my sister rather than her poor, widowed son, my sister threatened to sue me."

Peyton laughed.

"When a person grows up in a big family, does that make one want a big family?" he asked, finally diving into that burrito.

"Are you kidding? All I wanted was my own room! And travel, freedom and independence. When I was a teenager, if I got a new sweater or great pair of boots—bought by me, of course, from babysitting money—I had to hide them or I'd see them on a sister! They're scavengers!" She played with her salad and thought briefly of Ted's kids. They hadn't been terribly different except for two things she had come to view as important—remorse and reciprocation. Ted's kids, unlike her sisters, were proprietary. They had a sense of entitlement.

"But I will say this—being raised on a large working farm in a big family, there's no opportunity to develop laziness or become self-centered. And my parents couldn't have chaos—the whole operation would collapse. So there was a real low tolerance for irresponsible, rude or selfish behavior. You're mad at your brother? Get over it! You don't love your sister today? Act like you love her! I mean, we were human—there were issues all the time. We really were regular kids. But we learned to keep it under the radar. My parents weren't inclined to look the other way when someone was mean or spiteful or, God forbid, disrespectful. The Basque are a passionate people, but respect for family is high on the list of requirements. If you want to live," she added with a grin. "And yet," she said somberly, reflecting again on Ted's kids, "my father rarely raised his voice. In anger, that is. When my uncles were around or when the family worked or celebrated together, you could hear my father's voice booming from acres away. And my mother had a Mother Superior voice that brooked no argument, but I can count on one hand the number of times I heard her yell."

"You're close to your family," he said.

"I couldn't wait to get off the farm. And now, when exhaustion or indecision or disappointment consumes me, I run to the farm."

"Because it's peaceful?" Scott asked.

That made her laugh. "You have no idea how many things can disrupt a farm or a ranch. Agricultural problems, pests, drought, floods, freezes. Issues with the stock— My brother manages the sheep on the other side of the property, and they're kind of delicate. Breeding, sheering and lambing are major events. No, a farm isn't necessarily peaceful—there's always something. A lot like emergency medicine, it takes a steady hand. And to be a good farmer, you have to be at peace with nature, with the land, and you have to have profound faith. I don't go back there for a peaceful rest," she said with a laugh. "The second my dad sees me, he says, 'Get her a basket. She must be here to pick pears, gather eggs or thin the garden.' But then, I'll eat like I haven't eaten in months and months. Tapas and marmitako and chowder *el punto*—fresh and hearty. All washed down with a crisp, white *Txacoli*—a fruity white wine. White because the Basque have been fishermen for many generations and most traditional Basque food is from the sea. Or lamb—lots of lamb. For the red beans and braised meat, *Rioja,* the Spanish red. The Basque know how to handle a grape. My uncle Sal has a vineyard—he's a genius with a grape! And then we always have a dense, thick bread to soak up the beefy sauce." Her eyes closed as she nearly smelled the beans, potatoes, lamb stews, chowder. "I don't think my mother has opened a can in her life."

She slowly opened her eyes and found, once again, she had Scott's full attention. She noticed, not for the first time, that he could listen with his eyes. There was nothing remarkable about the shape or color, but the way he looked at people caused everyone to trust him. *She* trusted him.

"I think I drooled right there," he said.

She laughed. "If you turn out to be my friend, maybe I'll take you to the farm someday."

He took a bite of his burrito before responding. "I envy you, Peyton. Not many people enjoy that richness of tradition, the specialty of it, the uniqueness. I'm just white bread—a mixture of about ten different cultures that no one clung to and have become so watered down by now there's probably not a single family recipe in the family. Tell me something—did your brothers and sisters marry in the Basque community?"

She shook her head. "Only two. George, a committed Basque sheep herder, found himself a Basque wife, but she's not an old-world domestic. They have two children, and she's a physical therapist who drives all the way to Oregon City four days a week where she's the director of a therapy facility. She can throw together a hell of a lamb stew, though," she said, laughing. "And Adele, baby sister, was determined *not* to marry in the culture, and then she accidentally fell for a restaurateur from San Francisco. Now, that's where you want to eat if you like Basque cuisine. They're the ones due to have their first child soon. I will be there for that!"

"I would love to meet your family someday," he said, his voice soft.

"I don't think I have time for a lot of kids, but I want what my parents have. I don't recall one single time they weren't on the same team. My father never vetoed a decision made by my mother or vice versa. If Papa disciplined one of us, my mother upheld it to the letter. They were always the first up in the morning, and I woke to the sounds of them talking about things, planning the schedule, maybe arguing a little, getting everything straight before the start of the day. Same at night, their low voices in their bedroom." She laughed. "And he still embarrasses her by grabbing her and kissing her in front of everyone. They're over sixty and completely devoted to each other. They're very good friends. They're partners. I want that. I doubt I'll ever find it, but I want it."

Peyton was unlike any woman Scott had ever known. Smart, funny, wise and, oh, so beautiful. Exotic and sexy and just plain hot. She was so different from his wife. Serena had been a small pale blonde, petite except for her feet and sometimes frail-looking, even when she put on weight. Peyton was tall and sturdy and strong. Rosy-cheeked, tan skin and of robust health. And he couldn't recall ever knowing a woman whose hair he wanted to stroke, to lie in, to bury his face in. And yet, she was completely unavailable to him.

"You seem to be sensible and well grounded," he said. "I'm surprised you don't have a partner."

"Well," she said slowly, as if trying to decide whether or not to share. "I was in a relationship. I'm afraid it was a bitter breakup and one of the reasons I needed a change. I don't think I want to go back to Portland, where we had so many friends. Even though that was convenient for visiting my parents."

"I'm sorry, Peyton. Are you okay?"

"I'm okay," she said with a shrug. "I should've known. I'm not usually naive. There were so many warning signs that we weren't compatible, and I somehow managed to ignore them all. But let's not go there. I take all the blame—I wasn't paying attention. Or something." She flushed a little, laughed in embarrassment and lifted her glass. "Gotta love a little beer. I didn't mean to say even that much."

"Don't be embarrassed," he said. "If you ever want to talk about it, I'm a good listener."

"What's your excuse?" she asked pointedly. "Your wife's been gone awhile now."

"Well, my lunch counter shrink, Gina, said that even though I might want to move on, it was obvious I wasn't ready."

"Oh?"

"I took Gina out a couple of times before she and Mac were engaged. According to her, I talked about my deceased wife the whole time. Through two dinners."

"Oh," she said. "Yeah, I suppose a little bit of that goes a long way if you're trying to date someone."

"So I'm told…"

"Well, you've hardly said a word to me. If fact, you were so quiet about her that I thought you were married, not widowed."

"I didn't intend that, either," he said.

"Well, knock yourself out. Tell me all about her. You're not going to damage our relationship."

He thought about it and realized the urge to talk about Serena was not as strong. Not that he didn't think about her. He did. He just didn't feel a burning need to tell Peyton all the details. But he didn't want to seem rude. "We were together a long time," he said. "We started dating in high school. We were each other's first loves. She was with me all through college and med school and residency. We'd waited a long time to start a family, both of us working. She was a CPA who worked with a big firm. We planned that she would one day manage my practice. So, finally we had Will, and it was so effortless, we decided to do it again right away. She died right after Jenny's birth. An autopsy revealed SAH."

"Subarachnoid hemorrhage."

"Rare, but not unheard of. It must have been an aneurysm lying in wait, and no one knew."

"I'm so very sorry, Scott," Peyton said.

"Thank you. I think I've gotten my life together pretty well since then. A couple of years ago I did a study of areas in the Pacific Northwest that were underserved, visited about twenty small towns, two little kids along for the ride. Serena and I loved California—I studied at Stanford. We never talked about small towns, but here I was a single father and I had to decide where to raise my kids because I couldn't possibly know if I'd ever again meet a woman I was that compatible with. We could finish each other's sentences. But Thunder Point, with no doctor's office or clinic, reminded me of a small Astoria, a pretty town, a place where I could work and keep tabs on two kids. I think it was a good choice." Then he smiled and added, "But it's not going to make me rich."

She tilted her head. "How fond are you of riches?"

"Not that much. I'm fond of having enough. Do you know if you go to any of the local farmer's markets around here you're going to get the most amazing fruits and vegetables? At harvest it's mind-blowing." Then he laughed at himself. "Listen to me brag about that to a farmer's daughter! And if you get friendly with some of the fishermen and crabbers, they'll hold back some catch after they've been to fisheries and markets along the coast. I stitched up a fisherman's hand not too long ago, and I'm still getting fish." He grinned, "Devon had to put her head between her knees while I put in the stitches."

"She's a fainter?" Peyton asked with a smile.

"She didn't go down, but she's not the right person to hold a bloody hand for you while you sew."

"I'll remember that."

"So, have you been to Astoria?"

"I have, and I love it there. I think you're right—Thunder Point is like a little Astoria. Pretty. Not as rich, though."

"Far from rich. These people are simple, hardworking folks. There's some wealth around, but it doesn't stand out. I think Cliff from Cliffhanger's is pretty well fixed, and there might be a few others, but mostly middle class or struggling to get to middle class."

"Will your kids get everything they need here?" Peyton asked.

"I believe they will. Education is a priority in this town. Lots of Thunder Point kids get scholarships and not just athletic scholarships. The teachers are dedicated and talented. It's friendly. Crime is almost nonexistent. And now there's good medical care."

"And what about a second wife for the town doctor?" she asked with a lift of one brow.

"Well, I'll be honest—I'd like that. I liked being half of a couple. But that looks pretty doubtful. There aren't many single women hanging around, and I'm kept a little too busy for the hunt. But that's all right, I guess. I like my life and I'm needed here. I think from the first day I chose pre-med, I wanted to be needed. I wanted to have the thing that helped."

"Hmm. Maybe you wanted to be admired," she suggested.

"Maybe. What did the last doctor you worked for want? What drove him?"

She didn't even have to think about it. "To be the best. Best in the world. Universe. He created an image he had to uphold. He talked about it a lot— his image. He wanted to be the difference between life and death."

"Well, I don't want that. I'd prefer my patients not be near death. I just want to put in some good stitches, prescribe the right medicine, give sound advice. If someone wants to admire me for that, I'll take it. I'm pretty uncomplicated. I'm a simple guy. That's probably why I'm here. I'm hoping I'm the right guy for the job."

Peyton would have named Scott the best guy for any job. She liked him so much. On her drive home she tried to remember feeling that way about Ted— *liking* him. What was clear in her memory—she had been *dazzled* by him. The way he practiced, the success he had with his patients, it was simply phenomenal. It was almost like the crush she'd had on a charismatic chemistry professor in college—the coeds followed him like puppies, he was so commanding and sexy. And Ted was so goddamn handsome it was surprising he didn't *cause* heart attacks. When he'd looked at her, she began to melt right down to her lady parts! It had been very hard for her to maintain her professionalism in his presence during those first, early days of working in his office. She believed she had, but it had been a challenge. He seemed to walk about six inches off the floor. Ted hadn't made her warm, he'd made her *sizzle!*

Ironically, sex hadn't been a big deal with them. Ted wasn't as sexually driven as she was, not by a stretch. He'd been kind and accommodating, and she'd had no complaints. Their sex life had been… adequate. But because Ted was so masterful in every other way, she'd assumed it was her. Lacking in some way.

Ted had caused her to feel oddly off-balance, though it was sometimes very subtle. Being off-balance had her struggling to make sure everything was all right with him, with her, with them. She'd filled his periods of silence with questions, ignored his small tantrums, recognized the need to reinforce his confidence in her. And he'd rewarded her with material things. Throw three kids and a demanding ex-wife into the mix, and the result was Peyton's loss of confidence and erosion of her self-esteem, but a collection of a few nice baubles.

She had been extremely attracted to Ted, but she didn't think she liked him much. And she had been stunned to come to the conclusion he didn't like her that much. At some point, she'd realized Ted liked himself better than anyone else. She hadn't quite trusted him. "I think we should make a clean break, Peyton. You haven't loved me for a long time."

Oh, God, she thought. Ted had been right. She'd felt her love for him seeping away like a slow leak for so long. She'd kept trying to stick her finger in the dam, to build a partnership between them, to save the kids before it was too late, but it kept leaking, leaking, leaking until there was almost nothing left. They hadn't had sex for months before she left. They'd barely had a cordial conversation. He was right—she'd frozen him out, and Ted needed to be adored, admired, loved.

No wonder. No wonder all of it.

In Scott's small clinic she felt competent. Trusted. In balance. She didn't sense a hidden agenda and wasn't afraid of an emotional collapse. This was a complete accident—this town, this job—but as it turned out, this was going to be a good place to get leveled out and remember exactly who she was and what she wanted from life.

Still, she was going home to her little duplex after her lovely dinner with Scott and planned to do some damage to a gallon of Ben & Jerry's.

Carrie's deli wasn't open on Sundays. Sometimes she did a little cooking at home, if the spirit moved her, but she usually tried to observe a day of rest. On this particular Sunday, she decided to take her little beach-mobile across the beach to Cooper's to get their food order for the week. She had called ahead, and Rawley was working because the baby was still new and Cooper was spending less time at the bar.

The place was pretty crowded—typical of a sunny Sunday afternoon in the summer. The tables on the deck were full, there were folks sitting on low beach chairs on the sand, kayakers and paddleboards on the water. Carrie said hello to those she knew and went into the bar. Landon was sweeping up sand and dirt, which made Rawley the only adult present and therefore standing behind the bar.

"Landon, how's that little niece of yours?" Carrie asked.

"Loud," he said. "And she pukes a lot."

"Oh, dear."

"Sarah says it's normal. Glad I don't remember being a baby."

She laughed at him and jumped up on a stool in front of Rawley. "How are you doing, Uncle Rawley?" she asked with a smile.

"Kinda hard to believe Cooper had anything to do with Summer, she's that pretty," he said.

"You aren't getting overworked, are you?"

"Nah. I like being here. I just ain't much for a lot of people, but this bunch seems to know that. They don't ask me a lot of questions."

Carrie pulled her menu out of her pocket and unfolded it. "Are you up to making an order for the week, or should I pester Cooper for it?"

"No big deal, I'll do it. Let's have a look. Prolly be all the same stuff."

"I marked the usual items, but do look it over, Rawley. I'm trying a few new things. I have a cold barbecued chicken breast, sliced really thin, on a bed of greens with Chinese noodles, and it's great. And bite-size crab rolls served with garlic edamame—a good plate. And I have some cold, seasoned asparagus spears wrapped in provolone and prosciutto with sliced tomatoes on the side—to die for."

"Sounds like something you should swat."

She laughed in spite of herself. "All the usual sandwiches, pizzas, wraps, egg muffins and breakfast burritos."

He checked off some items, then turned the page toward her. "You can pick one to try out here, see how it does. Only one experiment a week, Miss Carrie."

She checked off the asparagus dish. "Business is good," she observed. "And something smells good."

He jutted his chin over his shoulder. At the end of the bar he had set up a little slow cooker station. Two slow cookers, buns, condiments. "I been trying something new. Fresh barbecue and franks. It's been moving pretty good."

"Great idea," she said. "I can tell you how to make ribs in the Crock-Pot if you're interested."

"I wouldn't mind it for the family, but it's too big a mess in here with the customers. We have enough trouble with barbecue and franks. Can't imagine what these folks could do with ribs...."

"Thank you, Jesus," Landon, the cleaner-upper muttered.

She let Rawley buy her an iced tea, visited for a while, asked Landon about the baby again and then, having been encouraged by Landon, walked next door to Cooper's house. She tapped lightly on the door, and Sarah let her in. "What are the chances of a little peek?" Carrie asked.

"Excellent, she's awake. Cooper is changing her, and I'm getting her bottle ready. Come in."

"Cooper is changing her?" Carrie asked.

"It's his turn," Sarah said. "Sit down at the table while I get this ready."

"Where's Austin?"

"He's next door, painting with Spencer."

Cooper walked into the kitchen, the baby on his shoulder and Ham close by his side.

"I see you have protection," Carrie observed.

"Every step we take with the baby. Ham might think he's the father. He hasn't left her side. We have to beg him to go for a walk," Cooper said. "Would you like to do the honors?"

"I would love that!"

After a nice visit, Carrie took her little beach-mobile back to the town and her deli. She wasn't planning to work today, but she liked to get things set up for the week. She had to be very well organized—cooking was done in the morning, selling was done from lunchtime till six. She put her list from Rawley in the book and looked at her weekly planner. First thing Monday morning she was going to make some beef kabobs, a large pan of lasagna and some chicken and rice—her deli nuke-able dinners. People were busy these days, many of them working two jobs, and fast meals were in demand. It was a convenience for working people to stop by on their way home to grab a prepared dinner. They often picked up one of her salads or even a sandwich for the next day's lunch at the same time. Catering was a good business, but the deli items sold over the counter— that was her bread and butter.

She set up her step stool and climbed to reach the large lasagna pan on the top shelf, and she nearly had it free of the pans stacked inside of it when the stool wobbled. Her hands were holding up pans, so they wouldn't fall off the shelf, and she lost her balance. To prevent herself from falling like a giant oak, her left leg stepped off the third step of the stool. Her foot went one way, her hips went the other, she heard a *pop,* and she went down. Flat on her ass. Buried in pans.

At least they were aluminum, she thought. If they'd been cast iron, she'd be dead. As it was, the only injury seemed to be to her right buttock. *Lord.*

When she tried to stand, her left leg wouldn't hold her. Her knee buckled, and she almost went down again. The pain was excruciating. She could barely put weight on it. At least she no longer felt the pain of her butt.

In great discomfort, she stacked the fallen pans

on the counter in a somewhat organized manner and limped out the front door. She locked up the deli and drove herself home.

Her day of rest would be enforced.

Seven

When Peyton walked into the clinic on Monday morning, Devon was already behind her desk and working at the computer.

"I should've known I wouldn't beat you," she said.

"I got an early start," Devon said. "I listened to the messages. Carrie James needs to see someone—she says she wrecked her knee. It's painful and very swollen."

"Give her a call, will you, Devon? Tell her we're open for business. Is Scott coming in?"

"As far as I know," she said. "Did you have a nice weekend?"

"Uh-huh," she said, picking up the schedule and glancing over the names. "Sat on the beach and read for a while, went exploring around the inland towns, had a three-way." Then she grinned. "Me, Ben & Jerry. It was fabulous."

"Whew," Devon said, dialing the phone. "I thought I was about to learn a few things."

"From me? Not likely."

Twenty minutes later Peyton was looking at Carrie's knee. "Wow. I think *wrecked* is the operative word." She manipulated it a bit to the patient's discomfort. "My money is on a meniscus tear, maybe some ACL damage, but you're going to need an MRI to be sure."

"I've had trouble with my knees before, but this seems really bad. I take pride in the fact that these problems are usually experienced by athletes, but then my work is just as challenging, if not so competitive," Carrie said.

"How'd you do it?"

Carrie explained her fall off the step stool, twisting her knee painfully, landing buried in pots.

"Ouch. Did you hurt anything else?"

"I have a nasty bruise on my butt and upper thigh. It doesn't hurt, but it is in the shape of Florida." She turned wide eyes up to Peyton. "What am I going to do? It hurts like the devil. I've had my knees and ankles swell before, but this is terrible. It looks just plain scary."

"You can get beyond this, but Carrie—you can't stand in that deli kitchen for ten hours a day on this knee. You're going to have to rest it."

Carrie got an angry look in her eyes. "It's how I pay the bills."

"I assumed so. I'm sorry, but this injury has to be dealt with, and we'll have to get an orthopedist involved. But in the meantime, I can help with the pain."

She was shaking her head. "I don't want to take a lot of drugs. I don't like the way they make me feel."

"I understand. I think we might try an injection in the knee. I haven't done a lot of that, but I bet Scott has." She looked at her watch. "He's probably here by now."

"Injection?"

"Steroid. Cortisone. Sometimes it works wonders and can last for weeks." Peyton leaned close. "You still have to heal it. Rest it and heal it."

"I don't know how I'll manage."

"Get past that panicked voice telling you you're doomed, and think about a plan. I know you have help in the deli kitchen from time to time. You might have to cut a few things, like the fabulous dinner meals. Oh, I would grieve that! You might have to make do with part-time help for a few weeks. It wouldn't be the worst thing that could happen. You're very fit, young, healthy, strong...."

"I'm sixty-one!"

Peyton smiled. "And a powerful woman. My mom is sixty-two, had eight children and works a farm with my dad. She's like you—she works hard, and her fitness is enviable. But hard work takes its toll sometimes, and for my mom, her back gives her trouble now and then. Holding her down is nearly impossible, but it's the only thing that works. You have to heal the knee. Let me go see if Scott is in."

Scott came into the exam room right away. "So, you want to try the cortisone injection?" he asked.

"If you think it'll help," Carrie said.

"Can you get yourself over to Bandon for an X-ray? I'd really like a film to be sure the injection is in the perfect site. And even though we're going to treat this injury conservatively and get you back on your feet, I'd like to set you up with an orthopedist, get an MRI to be sure of the extent of the damage and get his recommendation. We can do that when you're getting around a little better."

"Okay," she said, clearly dispirited.

"Listen, if you're having trouble moving around or driving, I can take an hour off and drive you over there," Peyton said.

"I'll manage," Carrie said, shifting to get off the exam table.

"Hold on," Peyton said. "Let me wrap that knee for support. Devon will call the hospital and arrange for your X-ray. Be sure to bring the films back with you and we'll get that shot. Before you leave, I'm going to have you take an ibuprofen, and regular doses of that along with ice packs and elevation should get this swelling down."

"I need it healed before noon," Carrie said, her voice very grumpy.

"I know," Peyton agreed. "Unfortunately this time it's up to the knee...."

Peyton had a very busy afternoon in the clinic. Right after Carrie had returned with her X-ray film and received her injection, Scott took off to spend a few hours in the Pacific Hospital ER Before he left, Peyton stole a moment of his time in his office. "By the way, thanks again for dinner last Friday night. I enjoyed that," she said.

"So did I. Think you're going to let me be your friend?" he asked, his tone teasing.

"I think so. But I'm still leaving after three months."

"You're a hard sell," he said. "But I understand."

"You need an X-ray in here," she said. "You need quite a few things."

"I'll need money first," he said. And then he cut out for the day.

Devon stuck her head into the office to say good-bye. "Need anything before I go?"

"Nothing at all. I'm going to stay a little while and finish charting, but I won't be too long."

"I'll lock the front door. You get the lights. See you in the morning."

It took the better part of an hour to get nearly caught up, and Peyton found herself wondering what she should do for dinner. Since she couldn't avail herself of one of Carrie's premade dinners, she thought she might just wander down to the marina and treat herself to a nice dinner at Cliffhanger's. She'd only been in there once since moving here, and just for a glass of wine. But she had looked at the menu and had seen a few good possibilities. She looked at her watch; it was nearly six.

Her cell phone chirped, and she looked at the number. She smiled as she picked up for her friend, Amy, the triage nurse in Ted's practice. Amy was about Carrie's age, a seasoned, sixtyish cardiac care nurse who was worth her weight in gold to any heart doctor. Amy had taught Peyton as much as Ted had. And Amy had been her only confidante while she was going through her worst trials with Ted. "Well, hello, my dear," Peyton said. "How are you?"

"I'm not the happiest right now, Peyton," Amy said. "I have to do something I find very distasteful."

"Is that so? What's the matter?"

"Are you done with work? Are you alone?" Amy asked.

"I stayed late to finish some charting, but I'm the only one here. I'm just about ready to leave."

"I want you to hear this from me because you're going to hear it eventually. Ted and Lindsey are officially engaged."

Peyton felt as though the wind had been knocked out of her. In fact, the news threw her back in the chair. When she found her voice, all she could say was, "That took hold awfully quickly. Last I heard, they were barely dating."

"That's what I thought," Amy said. "As far as I knew, it was a few weeks ago they started dating. Lindsey made sure everyone in the office knew of her status."

Ted was forty-two—a seventeen-year age difference. Men did that sort of thing all the time. In their three years together, Peyton had not been engaged to Ted. Of course, he'd talked about making it official. She had been the one with major concerns about that, given his tumultuous home life. "I bet she's in heaven," Peyton said.

"She's pregnant," Amy informed her, taking a deep and shaky breath.

Peyton was really speechless now. The last thing Ted needed was another child to virtually ignore. But he probably needed a babysitter more. "Well, they certainly didn't waste any time…"

"Three months pregnant," Amy added.

"God."

"I'm afraid so, Peyton. I'm sorry. I hate to tell you but I knew that eventually…"

"He's a dog," she whispered. "I've been out of his house for less than six weeks!"

"I know. He's a dog. He's also my boss," Amy said.

Peyton sighed, lowering her head to her hand. "I learned as I was leaving that Ted had been seeing her while I was still in his life. It was a blow—the one thing I didn't expect, yet probably should have. I fooled myself that it had been very recent but… You know I won't say anything. In fact, I will say nothing to him, ever again. You must believe me, Amy, I had absolutely no idea they were involved until the day I left. I wouldn't have stayed with him a day past knowing he was cheating."

"I know, Peyton."

And then something occurred to her, and it was very painful. "Did everyone else know? Were they the talk of the office while I was working my ass off in the practice and taking care of his family and sleeping with him at the home we shared? *Were they?*"

"There was some chatter about flirting going on, but I didn't actually hear anything substantial. You know I would have told you, horrible though that would have been for both of us. I saw her flirting, and I warned her that was unprofessional and might not go the way she hoped."

Peyton gave a hollow laugh. "Shows what you know."

"I'm appalled," Amy said, "Appalled and angry and embarrassed for him. And if I had a daughter who acted like that, it would be hard not to slap her."

"I can hardly criticize," Peyton said. "I flirted with him. I hope I kept it well away from our working environment, but I don't know—I was very taken with him. Though, to my knowledge, he wasn't committed elsewhere at the time. Ted has a lot of faults, but I never suspected him of cheating. And I'm having a hard time believing he's fool enough to get someone pregnant."

"I know. Me, too," Amy said. "Sometimes he's a little hard to take, but he has admirable qualities or I wouldn't have worked with him for so long. Listen, I know it doesn't feel so at the moment, but I think you're lucky things didn't work out for you with Ted. He has shown his true colors."

"Makes one a bit curious, doesn't it?" Peyton asked. "What if I had wanted to stay? To try again? Would he have come to me to explain about this new baby on the way? Or would he have told me it was time for me to go? Because I left him. And not because I suspected him of cheating."

"I can't even speculate. But he's in his forties, saddled with some very large alimony and child support, three intolerable kids whom he seems to avoid, though they spend the majority of their time in his home, and I can't imagine him with another one. I think she tricked him. I think she planned it. She's a silly little thing. And lazy."

"This explains so much," Peyton said. "When I told Ted I couldn't live in his house anymore, he dismissed me from the practice. He mentioned giving Lindsey my job, and that's when I knew. Up to that moment I thought my biggest problem was how to handle his children. I never suspected another woman. Do you suppose there were more?"

"I never suspected anyone, Peyton," Amy said. "But I find this horrifying. You're better off."

Dear Amy, Peyton thought. She was quiet for a moment. "My mother would call it a lesson hard learned. She always said those were the most enduring lessons. What a fool I am."

"Oh, please," Amy said. "He's an unfaithful ass and you call yourself the fool?"

"Don't women usually know?"

"Not always. Obviously!"

"You're just biased."

"I'm sorry this happened, Peyton," she said. "And I believe he's going to regret this. He can't replace you, you know. And he surely can't replace you with *her!*"

As much as Peyton wished to hear Amy rant about the injustice of it all, the nastiness of Ted and Lindsey's behavior, she had to end the call so she could think. She was so grateful to be alone, but then Amy was smart enough to know it was likely after hours in the clinic. She had asked before unleashing this bit of news. And all Peyton could think was, *I must have been blind, deaf and stupid!*

Her eyes burned, and she felt the tears come, though she wished she wouldn't cry over him. She was done with him, after all. Once he'd severed their relationship and told her he was moving on, that he had started something with this pert young nurse, she was done. But pregnant? Engaged? She'd been completely unprepared for that. What she had learned to expect was that Ted would replace her because he had needs—he needed a woman, he needed a housemate, he needed a babysitter, he needed an assistant.

And Peyton needed three years of her life back. Three years of her life during which she had accomplished nothing and at a very high cost.

The past year with Ted had been so difficult. So much arguing between them that even their brief respites from his children were not a comfort or rejuvenation. Had he just come from a hot session with his pretty young nurse that night he'd found her crying in their bedroom because his kids had deleted her entire recorded season of *Homeland?* Just because they didn't like *Homeland* and wanted space for their own recorded shows. That night Ted, tired and sweaty from a long day, had been unsympathetic. "Listen to yourself, Peyton. You're upset about a television show. Just buy the goddamn series on DVD! They're children. Can't you be the adult for once?" The same man who wouldn't allow his kids to set foot in his office, touch his computer or move his books. The same man who threatened them with unimaginable punishments if they dared to screw around with his golf clubs or leave a fingerprint on his Lamborghini.

She laid her head down and sobbed as she wondered how many people she had worked with knew Ted was doing Lindsey right in front of her. She felt so humiliated. The idea of Lindsey being next, even immediately next, she could somehow deal with that. But the idea that he had chosen Lindsey long before he'd dispensed with her… How many women had he needed to massage his formidable ego?

What is wrong with me? she wondered. *How could I fall for someone like that? How could I kid myself for so long? Why was I there for so long? What the hell did I think was going to happen?*

Scott had a good afternoon in the ER, not too busy, never boring. He stopped at the clinic to pick up a new prescription pad for his medical bag and parked behind the shops, next to the back door. He unlocked it, let himself in and heard a sound. Maybe someone talking in one of the exam rooms. *Could it be a patient, a late in the day walk in?*

He went to his office to get the pad, and there, sitting at his desk, her head down on her arms, was Peyton. Sobbing.

"Hey, hey," he said, going to her. "Peyton, hey."

She raised her head, and her eyes were red and

swollen, her cheeks wet, her lips fat and her nose pink. *Oh, boy,* he thought. She'd been at it awhile. "Come on, honey," he said, sitting on the edge of the desk, gently stroking her back. "What can I do?"

She shook her head vigorously and muttered something unintelligible that made her cry some more. She put her head back down on her folded arms and had at it.

Scott grabbed the tissues from his desktop and pulled out a couple. "Come on, Peyton," he urged, trying to lift her chin to look at her. "You can cry some more after you tell me what happened."

She sobbed, hiccupped, shook her head and grabbed the tissues out of his hand. She wiped her face, blew her nose and tried to talk. "He…he…he…" And she fell into her sobs again. "So humiliated… So hurt…."

At a total loss as to what he should do next, Scott slid off the desk. With one knee on the floor to be at her level, he turned her toward him, wrapped his arms around her and stroked her back. She turned in his arms and, resting her head on his shoulder, she let it all out. "It's okay," he said softly. "I'm right here."

She sniffed a little and slowly lifted her head, backing away a little bit. "That's…that's where she gets it."

"Huh?" he asked.

She was gasping a little bit from the sobs. "Jenny. She says that, you know." She wiped her eyes and nose. "You must say that to her."

He just smiled. "Maybe I do…I don't know. Peyton, do you want to talk about it?"

She pursed her lips. "I don't know…."

Scott rose and pulled the other desk chair over, closely, facing her. "You can trust me."

"Oh, I know that. Don't ask me how," she said, another hiccup escaping. "I know I can trust you. It's just that…I feel so *stupid!*"

He chuckled and shook his head.

"That's funny?" she demanded.

"You're proud," he said. "Something hurt you, and you think you should have known, been ready, figured it out before it happened. You're smart and you're proud."

"Well, so what? That's what I want to be—smart and proud!"

"I know, kiddo," he said. "But what happened to make you cry?"

She sucked in a deep breath. "After the breakup, I…well, I got a call from a friend. I left Portland six weeks ago. I lived with him for almost three years, I left six weeks ago, not on the best of terms, of course. But he is already engaged. To a twenty-five-year-old nurse who is *three months pregnant!* While I'm torturing myself over whether to stay or go, while I'm working my ass off in his practice and racing home to stand guard over the world's most malicious teenagers, he's fucking some little nurse on the side. The arrogant bastard was cheating on me! Using me to run his practice and his home!" And then she started to cry again. She blubbered, and Scott caught a few words. "Just grow up, Peyton! Who's the adult here…. What is it you want from me? Don't I give you enough? Don't you live here rent-free?"

Scott was thunderstruck. He just stared at her in a stupor. When she finally calmed down enough to make eye contact, there was only one thing Scott could say. *"Him?"*

She sighed wearily. "Ted Ramsdale, the cardiologist I worked for. We were together for almost three years. For over two we lived together. He shared custody of three kids. Three mean, rude, obnoxious, lazy kids. I'm sure if you asked him their birthdays he'd have to consult his calendar. I know for a fact his ex-wife used to text or email him to tell him it was time to buy a birthday gift. Which he would ask me to go pick up and wrap!"

Scott ran a hand through his errant hair. "The cardiologist?"

"Yeah, well I've never done anything like that before. In fact, I would not have taken this job if I'd known you were single. Especially a single father!"

He laughed. He realized it might've sounded a little like a gleeful giggle, so he quickly cleared his throat.

Peyton lowered her gaze. "It's very embarrassing. I should've known…."

"Why? Why should you have known?" Scott asked.

"Because there were signs. He's beautiful, for one thing, and he knew it. Women used to sway as he passed by. He's not just striking, he's stun-.

ning. Movie-star handsome. Once you get to know him you can see—he *preens.* He's demanding. He's manipulative and he's in love with himself. It's all about Ted. He takes care of Ted first. He wasn't getting taken care of by me too well the last year we were together, so he got himself a stand-in because Ted likes love and attention, but more than that he needs to be worshipped." She started to cry again, but softly. "The rat bastard. He was cheating on me, and he still asked me to take care of his kids! He needed a babysitter! Or a warden!"

"He," Scott said again.

"What?" she demanded through tears.

"What?" he repeated.

"Why do you keep saying that. *He.*"

"Oh. Um. Not important," he said.

"Yes, it is. Why?"

"Well, because I was under the impression… That is, I thought your relationship was with… I thought it was a woman you were involved with."

"A *woman?*" she asked, reddened eyes suddenly round.

"Based on things you said, you know…."

Suddenly, as if enraged, she slugged him right in the solar plexus. "You think I'm a lesbian?"

He backed away a little bit, rubbing his chest with his knuckles. "I thought that's what you were telling me! Not interested in men, et cetera!"

She was still frowning, but it seemed from wonder rather than fury. "You think the only reason a woman wouldn't be interested in men is if she's a lesbian?"

"Hey, I was wrong, apparently! I just…"

"Made stupid assumptions. Why didn't you just *ask* me? Jeez, you are not as smart as you look!"

"Clearly," he said, still rubbing his chest.

A noise escaped from her, and she crumpled on to her folded arms again, literally wailing.

"Hey, look, I'm sorry, all right? I meant no offense. I mean, it wouldn't matter to me, not in any way. Except in the way that it puts you off-limits, not just technically, but… Come on, Peyton, I'm sorry. Come on!"

She lifted her head, and there were tears on her cheeks again, but not from crying. She was laughing hysterically. Her smile was huge. She wiped at her eyes again and shook her head. "You're such an idiot."

He frowned at her. "Get it out of your system and be done with it. I made a mistake. I didn't do it on purpose. And I didn't mean to offend you."

"I wasn't offended," she said, giving her nose a good blow. "I was shocked! And now I'm wondering what kind of vibe I give off."

"It wasn't a vibe. It was what you said— I thought you were laying it out there. Establishing boundaries. 'Before there's a lot of curiosity or conjecture,' you said. That sounds like you're saying, 'Before anyone wonders why men don't interest me….etc, etc.' To tell the truth, I was pretty shocked, too."

"Well, let's establish a couple of things, then. One, I'm straight. And two, the last thing I need right now is a man!"

"Understood," he said. "Tell me about Ted."

"Actually, I think I'll go home and microwave a Lean Cuisine since Carrie is temporarily out of service. I'll have an injection of white wine and make a call or two to my intimates to vent. Because see, leaving him, his house, his practice, his life—it was upsetting. Depressing. I was very sad and troubled and a little confused, though I thought I knew what went wrong with us. But I hadn't had a good cry. Not until I heard he got someone pregnant before we officially broke up. That really brought me to my knees. And not because I'm not ready to let go of Ted. Ted can go screw himself. But because I've worked in a number of hospitals and practices and I know— there aren't very many secrets. While Ted was fooling around with that young nurse, people knew. And they were either laughing or pitying me. And that hurts." She sighed and closed up her laptop. "Pride."

"You sure you don't want to talk about it? Because I'd be glad to make you dinner, and while the kids are in the dining room table tent, we could talk over a glass or two of wine. Or…we could take our wine into the tent…."

She laughed at him. "As tempting as that is…I'm going home to run through my rituals that I use to get over myself. And I'll see you in the morning."

"You're not afraid to trust me, are you?" he asked before he could stop himself.

She shook her head. "No, Scott. We'll talk about it someday. Just not today."

She packed up her laptop, purse and lunch tote,

and he watched her leave. She turned at the office door. "Sorry for the meltdown. I thought I was alone."

"You were alone, Peyton. I hadn't planned to come back. I'll lock up."

"Thanks," she said. And then she was gone.

Hmm, not true love, eh? he thought. *Well, that's encouraging.*

Eight

Carrie James didn't need a referral to an orthopedist. She already had one. Dr. Todd in North Bend had treated her before for the same problem. Her knees often gave her some trouble. Since she had to rest the knee for a couple of days, the deli was closed, and she waited while Dr. Todd made arrangements for her to get an MRI.

Fortunately, Carrie had some deli stock prepared, and with some help from her daughter and granddaughter, she could take a couple of days off. She kept her leg elevated, took an anti-inflammatory, iced her knee religiously and about forty-eight hours after seeing the doctor, the cortisone kicked in and the pain subsided a great deal. The swelling was much improved. Dr. Todd thought it would be a good idea to scope the knee and repair the meniscus, something Carrie didn't want to do unless it became absolutely necessary. First she'd try to heal it, even if it meant wearing an Ace bandage for the next year.

Carrie thought about the conversation she'd had with Peyton just this morning. "I understand your reluctance, and it does look a lot better," Peyton had said. "But, Carrie, if you go back to your grueling schedule and take this knee for granted, you're going to quickly be right back where you started. Tell Gina and Ashley you need their help right now."

"They're happy to help all they can," she'd said. "They're great at making wraps, salad plates and sandwiches, but neither of them is much of a cook."

"Even with your supervision?"

"I'm afraid not," she'd said. "I'll just have to get by with my deli stock, take at least a few weeks off from the heavy cooking and baking and pass along the wedding I'm scheduled to cater to one of my competitors in Bandon. I hate doing that. Brides are so easily upset by changes. And their mothers are positively psychotic."

"What did Dr. Todd say about the knee?" Peyton had asked.

"Not a lot," Carrie had said. "He was busy sharpening his knives."

"He wants to scope it, doesn't he?"

"Yes. At least. I'm going to have to be very careful because if I see him again, he's going to recommend a total knee replacement. I'm over sixty, and I'm afraid I've been hard on my knees."

"Well, yes, be very careful because even though you're feeling better, you know how these knee injuries go. One minute you're standing, and suddenly, without warning, you're on the ground. You don't want to hurt anything else." Then Peyton had smiled. "Too bad my mom has a farm and ten grandchildren—she loves to cook. Your seaside deli might take on a slightly Basque appearance, however."

"I would kill for some of her recipes," Carrie had confided.

"Ah, that's like asking for the Holy Grail. Family food is pretty sacred in Basque tradition. Next time I'm home for a big meal, I'll bring you some things to taste."

For a few days Ashley helped Carrie in the mornings, and when Gina was finished in the diner, she came over and helped in the afternoon. Carrie's best friend, Lou McCain, did her shopping for her a couple of times. Of course, they were all more than happy to help, but Carrie was watching the money like a miser. Her sales were instantly down because she had to eliminate the dinners. And worse than that, she hated not being completely independent.

She was sitting at her desk in the deli, going over her ledgers on the computer yet again, when the door opened and in came Rawley Goode. "Well, hello, Rawley. Didn't Ashley deliver your order?"

"Sure she did," he said. "All taken care of. I had some time, so I came over to see what you need done."

"Need done?"

"I'm sure there's a good bit of chores that go hard on that knee. Trash? Clean up? Move things around? Deliveries? And I'm a fair cook, long as someone either tells me what to do or gives me real careful instructions."

"Rawley, I can't accept your help. You're a customer!"

"Every one of your neighbors is a customer sometimes."

"Besides, I can't just let people in to cook and bake...."

"I can bake, I used to make my dad sugar-free deserts. Not easy, neither. Then I made 'em for Mercy when they stayed with me. Got so she liked 'em, too."

"Listen, it's a business. It's licensed. Before a person can prepare food, he has to—"

Rawley pulled out his wallet and opened it. "Has to have one of these?" he asked, showing her his food handler's card. "Why, Miss Carrie, did you think Cooper and me were just hoping no one would ever stop by and ask? Even Sarah and Landon have their cards. I went to the health department for mine when Ben was still alive, but now you get it off the computer. Simple as pie. Now, why don't I start by emptying trash and checking the dishwasher? Then, if you're inclined, why don't you tell me how to make something? Start with something easy. I'm partial to your meat loaf."

"Rawley..."

"Cooper's got the store out there at the beach. Landon's got cleanup and boat and board rentals."

Carrie shifted her weight. Just standing for a few minutes bothered her. "Did Ashley say something about me needing help?"

"No, ma'am. She did mention that she made most of the wraps and sandwiches, but some of your other stuff would just have to wait on your knee. It got me thinking… One plate of those crab balls and Cooper might give me a bonus. Now what say we get started?"

She just shook her head in wonder. "Of all the people in the world I might expect to come to my aid, you are certainly the last, Mr. Goode."

"Now that doesn't speak well of me at all, Miss James."

It took Peyton a few days to get her head together after the news of Ted's engagement and pending fatherhood. Her struggle didn't show, especially at the clinic. Other than a quick, "How are you doing?" from Scott, nothing was said. After a few days, she felt less obsessive, though she thought it might take her years to think back on her time with Ted and the way it ended without feeling hurt and resentment. But that's what people dealt with. Relationships could be real messy—one of her brothers was divorced, and he was still pretty pissed off about it, though it looked as if he was better off.

That's all she wanted at the moment—for it to look as if she was okay. She knew her deeper emotions were bound to catch up. Eventually.

Scott, she had to grudgingly admit, had been a real find in every way. Not only had he given her a nice place to work, to rest while she got her life back together, but he'd been very supportive. He was a nice guy, there was no question. He wasn't like Ted, not in any way. He was good-looking and sexy, but Scott didn't seem to know it. His shoulders and forearms spoke of strength, yet he handled little old ladies and small children with such gentle care. His smile could be mesmerizing while his eyes drew a person closer. And he had a very cute butt in those jeans. But most of all, if you were with Scott, whether as a coworker, patient or friend, you felt secure.

And never mind all that—it was his integrity that Peyton appreciated. She was very grateful for that. She believed they were going to be very good friends.

She had been eavesdropping in the clinic and figured out that Scott was camping on the beach with the kids tonight. The July night was warm and clear with a cool breeze off the water. Scott's sitter had been back in town for a few days, so in the morning she would take the kids and Scott could go to work. She had heard him explaining it to Devon. "I'd better get this camping trip over with. Will won't shut up about it."

Peyton packed up a thermos and cups in a beach tote, parked at the marina and walked across the beach to the site where a small, yellow tent was pitched. The tent was glowing from a dim light inside. There was still a bit of a fire, and as far as she could tell, there were no other people on the beach. He was close to the hill just below Devon's house, and there was a light on outside Devon's lower floor.

As she drew closer she could just make out Scott sitting right outside the tent's zippered opening. He was cross-legged on a towel beside the fire. "Ahoy," she said quietly, drawing near.

"I thought that was you," he said. "What are you doing out here so late?"

"It's only nine-thirty. Are they already asleep?"

"Out cold. I ran them around the beach for a while, took them for a bathroom stop at Devon's and bedded them down." He reached over to the small cooler next to him. On top was something wrapped in foil. "S'more?"

She knelt in the sand on the other side of his fire. "I believe I will. Was that dinner?"

"First, hot dogs, then s'mores. My stomach is roiling," he said.

"Did you put an open can of beans on the coals? Because that's real camping."

"That's all I'd need, right?"

"What's lighting that tent?"

"Battery operated night-light. The last thing I need is some clown in a dune buggy mowing us down in the night. That's why we're out here on a Thursday night instead of the weekend. Less competition."

"I brought you some hot chocolate," she said, passing him the beach bag.

"I don't suppose it has a little brandy in it?"

"I'm afraid not. Are you going to need a little something to get to sleep?"

"I think I'll be napping with one eye open. The

other thing I'm not in favor of is a kid wandering into the water."

"Did Devon leave the light on for you?"

He nodded and poured himself a cup of hot chocolate. "Half the fun of camping is peeing behind a rock or bush, but if we have any larger issues, her door is unlocked." He sipped the hot drink. "This is great, Peyton. Really nice of you." He reached back, pulled a log off a pile and tossed it on the embers.

"You're a very good sport," she told him. "This is the sort of thing they'll always remember."

"Me, too," he said. "What kinds of things from your childhood stand out?"

She chuckled a little. "Come on, I grew up on a farm—it's a playground twenty-four hours a day. While my folks didn't get to all the school events, just about every class party for every kid was held on the farm. My dad buried potatoes and ears of corn with hot coals, there was barbecue and homemade ice cream. And there was nookie in the loft."

"Is that so?" he asked with a laugh.

"During sheep shearing a lot of extended family came to stay—lots of cousins. Lots of food. All the women cooked nonstop while the men sheared. Shearing was closely followed by some butchering. It was like a holiday."

"Did your father have a lot of sheep?"

"While I was growing up there were fruit trees, vegetables, mostly potatoes, and a nice flock of sheep. My oldest brother, George, took over the sheep and grew the herd. Now it's an even bigger circus. Kids tend to smuggle lambs into the house, treat them like puppies or kittens—it's a rancher's undoing. There's other livestock, but mostly for personal use and consumption, not for commercial farming. We have chickens, a few cows and horses, three llamas—rude, spitting llamas. Dogs and cats. Every once in a while a stray animal shows up. There was a Clydesdale without a home when I was very young. He lived with us for years. We butchered the occasional calf. We grow some chickens for dinner and the eggs are plentiful. It was a menagerie, but my dad is serious about the pears and potatoes, and George is the king of sheep. In fact, if you don't have anything major going on this weekend, I'd like to go to the farm for a couple of nights."

"You're not on call or anything," he said.

"If you need me I'll put it off a week," she offered.

"Nah, go ahead. Gabby is back, and Devon is going to be around if there's an emergency."

"I'll bring you some great stew and bread."

"I would love that. So, you're feeling better about things? Or is part of getting better going home to the farm?"

She laughed softly. "Sometimes it is, but my sister Adele will be at the farm for a week or so. Her husband will be with her for a couple of days, but as I mentioned, he has a restaurant in San Francisco—he's afraid to leave it for a minute. But Adele is in her eighth month, and she's due during the harvest which means Mama won't be able to go to her then.

I'll stand in for Mama. That's why it's so important for me to be there."

"So you're doing better," he said.

"Do I seem better?" she asked.

"You seem a long way from your condition when I found you…you know."

"Crying like a fool?"

"I wouldn't have put it that way," he said. "You were understandably upset."

"When I was a girl, I had the usual number of disappointments and broken hearts. I liked to go up into the hayloft for hours to work things out in my head, to map out my emotional journey. My papa always said my biggest problem was that I wanted everything perfect and didn't allow that other people might have plans that weren't exactly like mine. I might need a little time in the loft. When I started dating Ted I thought we were perfect for each other. We had a shared vocation, he had kids and I'm great with kids. I might not have been looking at the right things…."

"Like loving him?" Scott asked.

She swirled her hot chocolate and laughed. "Someone like me might think it's love when all it really is is appearances. But I'm a lot better, thanks. On one hand, that bad news gave me just the kick in the ass I needed to really move on. To stop hoping he'd come to his senses and see that I was the perfect woman for him. I wanted to be done with that whole situation, but I admit, it was hard letting go. It is no longer hard. What's hard is that I now doubt my instincts about men. About people. I've always been able to read people—I could smell a phony, a liar. I knew when I was being played. I also knew when I'd found someone real, someone wonderful. Now I wonder if my radar is all screwed up."

"Just practice it for a while, Peyton," he said. "Turn your radar on and test it here and there. I bet you'll find that even though you slipped off the rails once, it was just once. I see you with people every day. You're good. You're genuine. You know how to talk to them. You know what to ask and what to say, and they're drawn to you. I think you're going to be okay."

"I hope so, Scott. I grieve the time I gave Ted and his kids. I put my life and my desires on hold to try to meet their needs. I—"

Scott was looking beyond her, and she turned to see what he was looking at. There were lights on the bay, fairly close to the big rocks that rose out of the water.

"Boats?" she asked.

He shook his head. "Teenagers. Probably Landon, Eve, Ashley and Frank. They wear headgear like miner's hats with lights on them, kneel or lay on their bellies on their boards and peer down into the water. They see amazing things down there in the dark of night. Huge fish. Dolphins. Frank claims to have seen a shark—hardly unheard of, but not too common in this inlet. Ashley told me it's better than snorkeling, it's like boarding on the top of an aquarium.

But they don't dare go very far out. The occasional boat comes motoring in, headed to the marina."

"I would love to do that," she said, a little breathless with wonder. She'd never heard of this.

"I'm sure you can get that group to take you out." He shrugged. "Maybe I'll go with you. I have yet to try it."

"Let's do that," she said, a little excitedly. "Do you paddleboard?"

He shook his head. "There's never been time."

"Well, you have a PA now, let's make time!" Then she turned to watch the lights on the water. In the quiet they could hear the occasional talking or laughing. There wasn't much of a moon, but it lit a path along the water. It was so peaceful, watching the lights glide along the water accompanied by a teenager's laugh. Peyton had turned toward the water, watching, and eventually her eyes adjusted away from the firelight, and she could vaguely make out the shapes on the paddleboards—two standing, one kneeling, one sitting. Then there was a splash— one standing, one kneeling, one sitting. And there was laughter, louder than before. She shivered at the thought of being in the water.

A jacket suddenly fell around her. She glanced over her shoulder to see Scott sitting just behind her. "Thank you," she said softly.

He squeezed her arms. He took her cup of hot chocolate out of her hands and put it aside. Then he pulled her back so she was sitting in the V of his legs, held in his arms. She turned and looked up into his eyes, which had grown darker.

"Peyton, I'm not married and you're not a lesbian. Think of the possibilities."

A laugh burst out of her. "That is the worst pick-up line I've ever heard!"

"I guess I'm not good at that sort of thing," he said, but he held on to her.

Peyton thought he was adorable. And he was the genuine one. He didn't have lines because he'd never needed them. He made her laugh and want to kiss him. She gave his cheek a little stroke with her fingertips. "Being slick isn't the best thing, Scott. Or so I've come to learn." She sat up again and found her cup. "Can I have a little more?"

If Peyton was tired, it was her own fault. She had stayed up talking on the beach with Scott till nearly one in the morning. Neither of them could seem to shut it off, this getting to know each other with the assistance of a little cocoa and a few more s'mores. There was something about the exchange of information in the quiet, in the dark, over the red-gold flames of a campfire, that was just irresistible. They talked about school, childhood experiences, friends, college, travels, everything. She knew he had proposed to his wife while they were stuck in a traffic jam on the Golden Gate bridge when he was only twenty. Serena had been visiting him at Stanford over spring break, and he'd begged her to finish her term at Washington State and then transfer to be with him while he finished pre-med. They were married before medical school, and Serena had worked to support them. He'd said that for all the talk about how much work marriage was supposed to be, Scott found that life was infinitely easier with a partner.

That was something Peyton had always believed must be true, or at least should be true. Even with eight kids, it seemed to have been the ideal for her parents.

When he'd finally convinced her it was time to get some sleep, he'd watched her walk across the beach to the lone vehicle parked in the marina lot. When she'd gotten to work the next morning, he was already there. After a busy morning Scott had asked, "Are you still planning to drive up to the farm today?"

"After work," she'd said.

"You've got a couple of appointments after two today," he said. "I'll cover them. You get yourself some strong coffee and head out of here early, get the driving done before you start to fall asleep."

"Don't worry, I love to drive."

"I'd love it, too, if I were driving your car," he'd said with a laugh.

"It was my consolation prize to myself. A parting gift, if you will."

And Scott, who now knew as much about her as she could comfortably share, had laughed and said, "I think I'd like to break up with Ted."

"It came from me, a shallow and materialistic way to soothe my injured pride," she'd corrected.

"Ah. That makes sense. Is it working?"

She'd grinned. "It helped at first," she had replied, though the thing that was helping the most was her growing affection for her new boss. Was that a red flag she saw flapping in the breeze?

He'd told her to get going and to drive safely.

As she approached the Lacoumette farm, her spirits were rising. When she saw Adele sitting on the porch, waiting for her, her smile radiated. She jumped out of the car and raced up the porch steps to wrap her arms around her sister.

"You feel good," Peyton said. "I think the baby kicked."

"She won't stop kicking for five minutes," Adele said with a laugh. "I got us some tea. Don't go inside yet. Mama is in the last stages of dinner. It's crazy in the kitchen. I want to know how you're doing."

Peyton was happy to sit on the porch awhile. "Who's coming to dinner tonight?"

"Not too many," Adele said. "George, Lori and the kids, Matt's here but he won't stick around long after dinner, but tomorrow night—look out. There will be a bunch of Lacoumettes. How are you? Since you heard from Amy about Ted?"

"Better than when I called you. You haven't told Mama about Ted and his nurse, have you?"

"Are you kidding me? And have her go to San Francisco and run through the Basque boarding houses in search of a proper husband for you? How catastrophic would that be?" Peyton knew that back in the old days, Basque men trolled the boarding houses where young single immigrant girls often worked. Some men traveled all the way back to their old village to pick out a bride. Arranged marriages and the use of matchmakers was not unheard of, even today. "Mama is upset about you and Ted, however," Adele went on. "She's happy it didn't work out but angry at the way he treated you, the way his bratty kids treated you. She's worried about you."

"She shouldn't worry," Peyton said. "I'm pretty tough. Plus, I think I'm in a good place right now."

"Geographically or emotionally?"

"Both, really. Thunder Point seems to be a good little town, and the clinic is very small and surprisingly efficient. There are only three of us and one treatment room and two small exam rooms. I share an office with the doctor. I've been in bigger RVs, but it's working and the people in Thunder Point use it all the time. I think they're so happy to have a doctor in town."

"What's he like? The doctor?"

"Adele, he's McDreamy. Very dedicated, and spread very thin. He keeps an ER schedule at a local hospital at least two days a week and sits on call most weekends—he says that's what's keeping the lights on. But he's pretty confident he's within months of the clinic supporting itself. I'm thinking of trying some grant writing before I leave—that clinic should qualify for assistance. He serves a lot of Medicare patients and folks on state-funded programs. He also volunteers as team doctor for the local high school, which can't afford certified trainers or medics. This guy, Scott? He wants to make a difference."

Adele was making a face. "Didn't Ted want to make a difference?"

Peyton nodded. "Indeed he did," she admitted. "Ted wanted power—the power over life and death. It brought him great satisfaction. He also wanted to make lots of money. It was his due. A person who routinely works hard and saves lives should make a good living, yes? Ted is brilliant, treats his patients very well and thoroughly enjoys his place in the world. He's also arrogant, selfish, inconsiderate and, as I've learned, unfaithful. All that being said, if I had a serious heart condition, I'd get an appointment with Ted. Despite his shortcomings there is one thing I know he won't do—he won't fail as a cardiologist. I know, because I've worked with him, for him. He's meticulous. He's driven. He wants to make a difference…for himself. I'll observe the Thunder Point clinic for a while longer, but I think Scott wants to make a difference for the town, for the patients, for his kids. I could be wrong, but that's what I think."

Adele smiled. "You like him."

"God help me," she admitted.

"You like him a lot."

Peyton sighed and took a sip of her tea. "You'll like him, too. He has a generous spirit. A strong moral compass. If the babysitter called him and said his kids were impossible, he wouldn't ignore it or make excuses. He wants them to grow up strong and good."

"Would you date him?"

"I think it's a very bad idea to date a single father, especially a doctor I'm working for. The last time I did that came at such a price! There's too much at stake. There's only one small problem. I'm starting to get a crush on him. He's so wonderful.... But, no, I'm not going to date him." She sighed. "I hope."

Adele smiled. "And I was never going to date a Basque man, especially one with a restaurant. Famous last words."

"Why *did* you date him?" Peyton asked.

"I don't know. I couldn't help it. I was putting together his ads so we spent some time working together, and I couldn't resist him. He asked me if he married me, would I do his ad copy for free and I said, no, absolutely not. Mama said, 'That one you should marry.' I said that would *never* happen. And it didn't...for three more months."

"Mama is afraid for people who don't get married," Peyton said. "She can only see the world one way—in pairs. I'm a huge disappointment to her."

"I think she's proudest of you, but be warned—she's going to live to be a hundred, and she will never give up. She's very close to engaging a matchmaker, and she will see you married."

"She'd better come up with some new material, then. Single doctors with children are off the table. Or at least they should be."

"But you like him," Adele said with a smile.

"Not that much," Peyton said. But she liked him so much that she looked forward to work after the weekend with her family. And she hadn't kissed him yet, but she knew she was going to. She wouldn't dare tell Adele. Adele might start rooting for him, and all she was considering was a possible kiss. Because he was so lovely. And hot.

And then she was going to run for her life!

Nine

The first time Peyton had taken to the hayloft to escape and be alone, she was six years old. No one knew where she was or how long she'd been missing. The younger children were napping, Papa was in the orchard, Mama was in the garden and kitchen. When the little ones were waking, it was noticed that Peyton was nowhere to be found.

While her mother searched in and around the house, Paco and some of his hands were searching the orchard, fields, outbuildings, corrals and the water holes and streams on their property. Although they called to her, she hadn't heard them. By the time she climbed down from the loft she'd been gone a couple of hours. She had straw in her hair. Everyone associated with the Lacoumette farm came running at the sound of the bell. Mama was on her knees, holding Peyton close. "Peyton, what were you doing up there?"

"Just working things out," she said clearly as if it made all the sense in the world.

In a loud and busy household, almost each one of them had a place they escaped to when they needed a little quiet space to think or hide. George liked the pasture, Matt climbed the pear trees, Ginny hid in the cellar, Sal liked to sit on the ground in the front yard, hiding behind the large trunk of a very old tree.

On her weekend visit Peyton disappeared to the loft. She lay on her back, hands behind her head, one ankle balanced on her raised knee, and thought things through. *Would it be wrong to let him kiss me? Because he wants to and I wouldn't mind. And it doesn't mean I want to move in with him and take care of his children, right? If I don't let that happen too soon, it should be all right. I'm still planning to leave, to live somewhere else, to start my life over... I think. But while I'm taking a leave from my career to do a little community service, I could do with a little love. God knows, it's been a long dry spell. I will even help him find someone good to replace me and not some trashy little twenty-five-year-old. Of course, a true friend would hook him up with a girlfriend, since I'm not interested in being anyone's girlfriend...though I might be ready in a couple of months....*

It took roughly two hours to come up with something of an agenda. She'd been in his clinic for a month, she would let herself be kissed. They could be social, go out together sometimes, but it would be rare since he was so busy. She would do a few things for the clinic, things that would help him after she left. She would enjoy those sweet kids, but she would not become their nanny. And she might even stay in touch with him because he was, if anything, excellent friend material.

Except, the crush factor was beginning to influence her into thinking maybe she could start over right where she was. If the crush got stronger…

When she went back into the kitchen, her mother kissed her cheeks and pulled a little straw from her hair. "Did you get everything worked out?" her mother asked.

"I don't think so," Peyton said with a smile. "Well, one thing is worked out. I was right to leave Portland."

Sometimes visiting the family farm exhausted Peyton, sometimes it rejuvenated her. This particular visit felt very good. It helped to see Adele so healthy and happy. Since it was not shearing, harvest or Christmas, the homestead wasn't overflowing with family, so it wasn't as chaotic as it could be. They used Skype to chat with her brother Sal, currently serving on a Navy destroyer. Twenty-four-year-old baby brother, Mike, called home from grad school; the phone was passed around to a dozen family members.

She was able to have some time to talk with her father on the porch, just the two of them. "You're more yourself than you've been in a long time," he said.

"I am?" she asked.

"It seems like," he said. "You ever hear from any of those folks? Ted and his tribe?"

"No," she said. "Ted has moved on, and the kids were very happy to see me go."

He squeezed her hand. "I'm sorry, Peyton. Ever since I pulled you squalling from your mama's body, I've known you to work hard and honest and do your best no matter how rough the job."

She laughed at him. "Thank you, Papa, but you didn't deliver me."

"Might as well have. You surely made your presence felt around here. I could hear you in the barn!"

"Now, Mama says that little Mike was the loudest and most trouble. That's how I remember it."

"Oh, Mike. He thought he was something special from the first breath he took. The Pope himself sent your mother a letter to say there were finally enough Lacoumettes in the world."

"The Pope? Well, I always wondered why you and Mama didn't try to squeak out a few more...."

"She swears it was the Pope who wrote. She was getting a little cranky," he said. "What's your life like now, my little bird?" Her father was always careful not to call the kids little lambs, as their days were definitely numbered.

"It's good," she said automatically.

"In what ways is it good?" he wanted to know.

The images that came to mind that described her current happiness were so unusual, she wasn't sure she could explain. A Great Dane who followed a newborn, begging for a chance to sniff her. A teenage football star who took the time to teach a bunch of foster kids to paddleboard. A four-year-old who said, "It's okay. I'm right here." A conversation on the beach over a fire that stretched out till the wee hours, strong arms around her the whole time. A little clinic where folks stopped by to talk as often as they sought medical help. A little diner where the food was passable, the gossip rich and the camaraderie binding.

"It's a nice little place," she said to her father. "The people are very friendly."

"You saying that fancy car didn't make you happy?" he asked, raising one salt-and-pepper brow.

"It drives like a dream," she said, laughter in her voice.

"You mean it doesn't drive itself? Does it make a lot of little cars?"

She laughed at him. Paco Lacoumette would never spend good money on something as frivolous as a fancy car. "It hasn't made any little cars yet," she said.

"Keep an eye open," he advised. "For what that piece of tin costs, she's gonna whelp soon, make you a proud mama."

He was a riot. She'd never tell him she regretted spending so much on a car and that she wasn't even sure why she had. She kissed Paco's weathered old farmer's cheek. "I have to speak to Mama, see if I can help in the kitchen."

There was already plenty of help in the kitchen. Her sister-in-law Lori, Adele and her mama were hard at work in a hot, sweaty kitchen. But Mama was in her element—she loved having a houseful. There would only be nine for dinner—a small group. So Peyton didn't feel too guilty asking a favor.

"Mama, my new Thunder Point friends don't have much experience with Basque cuisine. If you have extra from tonight that you can spare or any freezer dishes you can part with, I'd love to take some back with me. One of my friends is a deli chef, and she's especially curious."

"Is that so?" Mama asked, not looking at her.

"Only if it's convenient. I could borrow a cooler or thermal carrier and take it home with me tomorrow. Fresh. Just if there's enough."

Her mother turned and looked at her. "There is always enough food, Peyton. Not enough of other things sometimes, but of food there is never a shortage. I can spare some for your friends to taste."

"No oxtail or tongue, Mama," she said. "They're beginners." Then she smiled somewhat timidly. Her mother's home was the only place she was ever visited by timidity.

Her mother crouched to pull a roasting pan from the shelf beneath the work island in her big kitchen and handed it to Peyton. She pulled a knife from the rack and said, "Fine. Kill a chicken."

"Oh, Mama, can't George?"

"I think George is busy in the barn, and I understood you to say you wanted something Basque for you friends—not too ethnic or exotic."

"Okay," she said. "But I've always hated killing chickens! And I think you're taking advantage of me."

"Always, my little Babette," Mama said. And then she smiled.

In the end Peyton packed up a couple of large take-home boxes that would do a restaurant proud. Mama pulled out all the stops—she was clearly showing off. Lamb-and-spinach-stuffed mushroom tapas, *lomo* and sautéed shrimp, tomato-and-garlic soup, creamy red potatoes, red beans and chorizo, mussels and rice, chicken basquaise, lamb shanks in stew, bread and two bottles of Rioja. "You are so brilliant, Mama," Peyton said.

"And where did you think you got all your big brains? From that old farmer?" She threw back her head and laughed.

"You and Papa are in love every day," Peyton said.

"And on the days we're not, he behaves better."

That comment almost sent Peyton back to the hayloft.

When Peyton stopped for gas on her way back to Thunder Point on Sunday she called Carrie and Scott and asked if she could drop off a little Basque treat on her way home, and of course, both of them were thrilled. She went to Carrie's house first. Lou McCain let her in and led Peyton into some kind of gathering in the kitchen. Rawley Goode stood at the stove, Ray Anne sat at the table with Carrie, who had her leg elevated on a kitchen chair. Peyton put her offering on the table and asked, "What have I interrupted?"

"Just a hen party, Peyton. Do you know Rawley?" Carrie asked.

He turned from the stove and looked at her rather critically. "We seen each other around. And in case you're wonderin', I ain't no hen."

All of the women laughed, and Peyton noticed they were having wine, cheese and crackers.

"Hi, Rawley. What are you working on?" Peyton asked.

"Rawley's been helping me with the cooking since I wrecked my knee," Carrie answered for him. "The girls and I try to get together for a glass of wine every week if we can."

"And your knee?" Peyton asked.

"Much better. It gets a little sore and swollen when I'm standing a lot, but I'm watching it and taking it real easy, thanks to Rawley."

"I beg your pardon," Lou said. "Didn't you get a little help from your other friends? We've all been making wraps and sandwiches, grocery shopping, offered to take the August wedding job since we're experienced servers. We've done it at some of the most notorious parties in Thunder Point. We need supervision, of course, but we've been helping!"

Rawley turned from the stove where he was casually stirring some kind of sauce and said, "I think the lady was talking about the natural talent."

Again they all laughed.

"What's in the box, Peyton?" Carrie asked.

"Oh, right... I was momentarily distracted. My mother packed up some samples of her best offer-

house. And while she was driving there she asked herself why she had set this up—going to Carrie's first and then Scott's. Was it because she hoped to spend more time with him? How foolish, especially since she was going to see him every day this week. And really, wasn't this a bad idea, liking him as she did, wanting to be with him whenever she could?

She tried reminding herself she could end up in the same position she had been in with Tod—his forgotten paramour and the manager of his household and family while he was pursuing things he found infinitely more rewarding. It wasn't quite working. She knew Scott wasn't that kind of man. But she thought it would be very wise to move as slowly as possible. To that end, she left her car running as she took her box of food containers to the door. It was identical to the box she had left with Carrie, a fine collection of her mother's best.

Scott opened the door wearing a fitted T-shirt and pair of sweat pants. He'd apparently taken a day off from shaving, and sweet baby Jesus, did he look delicious. "Peyton, hi! Here, let me take that. When you said you had a treat I didn't expect... Come inside."

She shifted the box into his arms and said, "I... ah...I really can't stay...."

And they came running. Yelling. "Peyton! Peyton!" Jenny and Will attached themselves to her legs, hugging her so hard she dropped to one knee to gather them in. "You're here! You came!"

Oh, God. She hoped Scott wouldn't see that tears

sparked in her eyes. They liked her? They were happy to see her?

"I can show you a movie," Jenny said.

"We can have one on the TV, all of us," Will said. "We can have popcorn and ice cream because we ate a good dinner!"

"Or we can have a tent! You can come in it!"

"Do you want popcorn and ice cream?" Will asked.

"We can play Candy Land in the tent!"

She looked up. Scott had put aside the large box and was smiling down on her, hands on his hips. "Your fan club."

"I have to go," she said to him, her voice soft.

"Okay, kids, let Peyton out of your mighty little grips. She has to go. Peyton, you have a date or something?"

"No...no, I just...well, I'm a little tired, and I left the car running." But as she said that she had an arm around each child's little waist, holding them closer.

"Are you worn out from your weekend away?" Scott asked.

She shook her head forlornly. She was sunk, and she knew it. She kissed a couple of hot little cheeks.

"Why don't you give me your keys, and I'll turn off your car?"

She made a small sound, a kind of weak whimper, as she handed over the keys.

"Don't let them take complete advantage of you. I was just about to make them some popcorn," Scott said. He went out the door. That's when she noticed he was wearing worn leather slippers. And she found them incredibly sexy. That wasn't a good sign. Her sister Ginny called her Fancy Pantsy; designer clothing was supposed to be sexy to her.

By the time Scott came back in the house, perhaps only thirty seconds later, Will had the Candy Land board opened on the living room floor. The kids were literally bouncing on the floor in excitement. Given they were only four and five, Peyton expected it would be a long game, but they'd played it so often they'd become fast. After two games, Will wanted to play War using three decks of cards. On their third game, Scott was hovering again. "I'm making popcorn. You have to let Peyton have a break. Glass of wine, Peyton?"

She had gathered her composure by now. "I wouldn't mind."

"Have you eaten?"

"No, actually. I was planning on heating up one of those low-cal frozen dinners. I ate enough over the weekend to keep me for days."

"I happen to have a box of some of the best Basque takeout there is, and I bet you never get sick of it. I think I'll start warming it up. White or red?"

"That Rioja is from my uncle's vineyard, but if you have any cold white I'd love some. If you wait till we're done here, I can help get everything ready...."

"I got it. I'm an expert at warming. By the time you finish your next game, their popcorn will be ready."

A few minutes later Scott was back holding a

big bowl of popcorn. "All right, you two. I'll put a movie on for you. Peyton's going to have a little dinner with me."

"Can we play some more?" Will asked.

"Maybe after our dinner and your movie. Come on, up on the couch." He reached out a hand to Peyton to pull her to her feet, then he settled the kids with their treat and started the movie. They settled in just that fast. Scott pulled her into the kitchen where her wine sat on the table. "Sit down, Peyton. Tell me about your weekend while I warm some of this."

"Can I help?"

"Relax. Talk to me."

"Where's the sitter?"

"Date night with Charles, the love of her life. How's your family?"

While Scott busied himself around the stove and microwave, she talked to him and enjoyed her wine. She couldn't remember the last time she'd been served so efficiently, as if she were an honored guest. Plates and utensils appeared, he added a little wine to her glass, and they were serving up plates and bowls. Conversation turned to the food as Peyton explained what they were eating. He had a hundred questions about the farm and the extended family who were involved in vineyards, restaurants, more farming and ranching.

He glanced into the living room and smiled at her. "You're off the hook for more Candy Land or War."

"They're out cold," she said.

"I knew that would happen. We were busy today.

I love the way they sleep—Will sprawls just like I do, Jenny curls into a little ball."

He went to fetch the popcorn bowl before it landed on the floor, then whisked away the dishes. She started to get up to help, and he said, "Sit tight, we're not doing dishes. I just want to save the leftovers. We're going to finish our wine and enjoy the quiet."

"You're awfully good at this," she said.

"Practice." He came back to the table.

"You've been on your own for a while now," she said.

"I've had help. I've had the grandmas, sitters, day care, nannies. And Gabriella for the past two years. I don't know what we'll do without her. I'm on the hunt—there has to be someone out there."

"You must miss your wife so much."

"It's a process," he said. "At first I was in so much pain and shock I couldn't move. Then I was angry. Angry that she'd leave me with such impossible responsibility. For a couple of years, I just pedaled as fast as I could, afraid to lift my head or I'd miss something important. And then I realized that I wasn't the only person in the world who had this kind of life. Mostly women had been in my shoes. I saw a lot of single mothers and their children in the ER, young women struggling to make ends meet, some of them working two jobs just to squeak by. In fact, my mother had that life—my father died when I was ten and my sister was fourteen, leaving my mom on her own with a couple of kids. I decided I'd better live the life I had or I was going to be sorry. I had to let go of that anger at being abandoned and show a little gratitude for what I had. That's when I broke my mother's heart by looking for Thunder Point and a small clinic where I could work and raise my kids."

"I don't think that's the way most widowers or divorced fathers do it," she said, thinking of Ted. "Most men who find themselves single fathers just install a new mother or at least a babysitter."

"Well, so did I," he said. "Gabby's parents were friends of mine, and when the kids were babies, she was a babysitter. She wanted to be a full-time sitter and go to school, so we struck a deal. If she'd work for me full-time, I'd pay her well and cover her tuition. The bonus for me was that she loves the kids. She came with me to Oregon and met Charles here, so I think she'd tell you it was worth it. Any day now she's going to tell me that Charles is going back to Washington with her."

Hiring a devoted sitter wasn't what Peyton had been getting at. Handsome young doctors like Scott shouldn't have much trouble finding a woman who would live for the chance to be his partner, help raise his kids…. "So, no pretty young nurses lobbying to be the next Mrs. Grant?"

He laughed uncomfortably. "I haven't dated much. I've been out with a few women but not with that in mind. At some point I realized if I didn't have a social life of some kind, I was going to remain that miserable, unhappy character who moped around resenting two perfect children who wanted only to make me happy. I was turning mean."

"I can't imagine you mean," she said, most sincerely.

He shrugged. "People are all mean in their own way, Peyton. Some will lose their temper and lash out, others just let themselves be negative and moody. I became inattentive and self-absorbed. I had to get out of that cycle. I've done my best. Once I got to Oregon, I made it a point to socialize more."

She impulsively reached for his hand. "It must be impossible to forget your wife."

"Forget? Forget the mother of my children? The best friend of my youth? Is that required? Because if it's required that I forget or pretend she wasn't one of the most important parts of my life, I guess I'll be alone forever. Of course I won't forget her. She was amazing, and she'd want me to have a full, happy life. She'd want me to laugh and live fully and find love again." Peyton pulled her hand away, and Scott reached for it, pulled it back and held it again. "Let me tell you what I think is happening here. We like each other. We're attracted to each other. You're probably more nervous about that than I am because you just came out of a painful breakup, but pretty soon you'll decide it's going to be all right because you know I don't treat people the way he treated you."

"I haven't told you that much about—"

"You didn't have to, you said enough. Look at the time, Peyton," he said.

She glanced at her watch and was startled.

"You got here three hours ago. You played with

the kids, ate a big meal with me, had a glass and a half of wine, talked to me for hours. It's going to be okay, Peyton. I'm not going to use you or take advantage of you. And if this conversation were happening at a nice restaurant I'd be asking you if we could go someplace where we could be alone. But because I have two little kids who wander into my bed in the night and a babysitter who will be walking in the door anytime now, I can't seduce you. I want to, but I can't."

"Look," she said, trying to pull back her hand, but not trying too hard. "Was I clear? I fell for my boss. He used the workplace where he had all the power to—"

"I'm not going to do that, either. That might be my clinic, but it belongs to the town. And it belongs to Devon. I'm not going to use that venue to try to fumble together a love life for myself. I know the situation isn't ideal, but I am going to figure out when I can take you out. Besides, I have no power."

Is he kidding? she wondered. But of course, he didn't realize it! He thought brute strength or big bucks or notoriety made power. And so did Ted; those were his priorities. What Scott didn't know was that honesty and integrity held the greater power, far greater than the awards and citations and certifications that could be framed and hung on the wall. Love for your children was a powerful force; kindness and sincerity held more power than money. And how about loyalty and fidelity? She was very fond of those things. It didn't hurt that he put a kick-ass physique and eyes that seemed to listen and an electrifying smile with it all....

"I would like to kiss you good night," he said.

And love, she thought. Love for others, that would make life whole. Had Ted ever truly loved her? He'd wanted her, she knew that. To a great extent, he'd needed her. But had he really loved her? Maybe in his own pathetic way, but he had always loved Ted best. Did he love Lindsey as much as he loved himself? Because Ted being Ted might have followers and even worshippers, but until he knew how to share love, Ted would end up being alone with the love of his life—himself.

"I can do that," she said to the idea of a kiss.

He pulled her over onto his lap, and she put her arms around his neck. He tested her lips softly. Carefully. Then he pressed a little harder, a little longer. He was coming in for the kill, she could tell. She stopped him and said, "What about the kids?"

"They watch TV, Peyton. Kissing isn't against the law. It won't cause them to have immoral thoughts...."

With that, he pulled her closer, holding her against him, and went after her mouth like a starving man. He devoured her, using his lips to open hers. One hand rose to her jaw, holding her tight, working her lips with his tongue. His hand slid under her hair at the back of her head, pressing her firmly against his mouth while his tongue deftly played with hers. He groaned into her mouth, and she welcomed him with a little moan of her own.

He was the best thing she'd tasted in a very long time. While he held her tighter, she held him as closely as she could. When he plunged his hand into her hair, she ran her fingers through his. His stubble was rough on her lips and chin, and she didn't mind. In fact, she liked it. His breathing grew a little more rapid and coarse, panting. She pulled back, her lips still touching his.

"I'm getting immoral thoughts," he whispered against her mouth.

"I should go before things get out of control."

"I'm not going to lose control," he said. "I won't hold it against you if you do."

She laughed lightly. "You seem to be…ah…" She wiggled a little on his lap. "Responding."

"Oh, yeah. A lot of ideas are running through my mind right now. All inappropriate."

"Like?"

"The bathroom. The dining-room-table fort. Right here, right now."

She laughed. "I better go."

He pushed against her a little bit. "Can I take you out to dinner this week?"

She lifted one brow. "Will I actually get dinner?" she asked suspiciously.

"Yes, Peyton. You will get dinner—your choice of restaurant. And dessert is up to you. Completely up to you. You're the one in charge."

"Check your schedule," she said. "I'm free every night."

Just that promise of an evening together caused

him to kiss her again, long and hard, deep and wet. His arousal was all too obvious, and she was well aware of the erotic feelings he had stirred up in her. His kiss left her gasping.

He buried his face in her neck, breathing hard. "Gimme a minute, okay? And then we can get up...."

She held him there, comforting, soothing, murmuring. She inhaled the smell of his hair. Oh, God, she had so missed the comfort and affection of this— warm bodies close, the promise of excitement and fulfillment.

"I haven't done this in a while," she whispered.

"I haven't done it in even longer. I say we get right back on that horse and ride like wind. What do you think?"

She sighed. "Like the wind..."

Ten

Scott stuck to his word. He did not make any romantic overtures toward Peyton at the clinic. He could
tell by the sly looks she slanted his way that this surprised her. It was difficult; she would never know
how difficult. Every time he saw her he wanted to
grab her in his arms and just kiss the daylights out
of her. He had a hard time pulling his eyes away
from her. But he didn't touch her. He wouldn't. It
was very important that she not get the impression
she was dealing with another Ted Ramsdale. He was
not going to be that guy, a boss with a lot of bag-
gage on the make.

Fortunately he worked at the clinic on Monday
and Tuesday mornings, went to the Bandon ER for
the afternoons and then was scheduled on call both
evenings. Monday night he was called out, but so far
on Tuesday evening his cell phone remained bless-
edly quiet. On the way back to Thunder Point he
called Gabriella and asked how everyone was doing

at home. Dinner and baths were already done, she reported. He let her know he wanted to run a few errands, and could be called back to Bandon so might not be home before bedtime.

He stopped at an Italian bakery. He drove to Peyton's little duplex and rang the bell. When she opened the door, he held up the bag. "Cannoli," he said with a grin. And then he noted the look on her face. "I should've called."

"No, it's okay," she said. "Come in."

"I have the feeling I'm interrupting something," he said. There was music playing; it was a mellow, moody old tune. "At Last" by Etta James. He put the bag on the small kitchen table. "I think something's wrong. And we're too new for anything to be wrong."

"Just an unexpected development," she said. "There's a pediatric heart surgeon in Seattle. I met her at a conference, and we made the occasional, though rare, referral to her. Christine Sullivan. She's one of the best in the country, very impressive credentials, quite well known. She heard I left Ted's practice, and she hunted me down. I got an email from her this afternoon. She made me a job offer."

"That's wonderful, Peyton! That says a lot about your reputation."

"I'm pretty experienced in cardiology now...."

"Why does this upset you?" he asked, perplexed.

"I don't know how to respond."

"Oh, I get it," he said. "You want the job."

"That wouldn't bother you?"

"Oh, Peyton, I'd hate it if you left. I don't want

you to leave, not ever. I'll make every argument I can think of, but I'll never hold you back. I think we could have a successful practice here. Not a wealthy practice, but very successful and very satisfying."

"Her PA is leaving on maternity leave in October. She'd like to take six months and then come back part-time...."

He pulled her against him. "That gives me a little time," he said. "If you're not leaving tomorrow, maybe there are things I can tempt you with." He began to sway with the music. "I bet she offered you a big pile of money."

"She did."

"Well, that's one thing I don't have. But I have other things. Great things."

She pulled back and looked into his eyes. "Like what?"

"The ocean," he said. "Football games. Cute kids. A little clinic everyone loves and needs. Quiet. You don't have to lock your door. You should, but really, it's so unusual for anything bad to happen here. Storms over the bay—they're amazing. People bring things to the office—cookies, cakes, all kinds of stuff, and you have a relentless sweet tooth."

"Let me ask you something," she said. "You don't have a lot of experience with women, right?"

He shook his head. "I married my high school girlfriend." His hands rested on her hips and pulled her closer. "That was a miracle in itself, that I had a girlfriend in high school. Especially one like Serena, she was beautiful. But I was a nerd, not a jock.

I got very good grades," he said, resting his lips on her forehead. "I bet Ted got good grades and is athletic, too."

She nodded. "Golf, tennis, polo…"

"Polo? Jesus, he is so easy to hate."

"You met a girl, you loved her, you married her, you were committed," she said.

"Try not to hold that against me," he replied.

"I think it might be best if we just reel this back in, refuse to take it any further and keep our relationship strictly professional."

"That's very wise," he said, holding her. "I'm afraid that's no longer an option for me. If it's what you want, I completely understand. But I hope you'll at least think about it a while longer."

"I'm afraid if I let myself get any more involved, you'll eventually hate me."

He shook his head. "That's not possible. Listen," he said, lifting her chin with a finger. "I was interested in you the second I met you. I just got more interested every day. Then I crossed over into seriously wanting you. If it turns out you're not mine to have, I'll be really disappointed. But if you think I'm going to walk away without trying, you're crazy. I'm not that big a fool."

"I should at least take another day or two to figure out if I can deal with this," she said. "Even though you brought cannoli."

"Much to my disappointment, you're going to get a couple of days…."

"Ah, you do see the wisdom to that!"

"No, Peyton. My phone is in my pocket, set to vibrate. I'm on call tonight till midnight. It would be so embarrassing if someone bled to death because I was getting laid." He made a face and shrugged. "It might be worth it, but it would be embarrassing."

A huff of laughter escaped her. "What makes you think you're getting laid?"

"I'm a dedicated optimist." He heard a sound and looked over her shoulder to see the old turntable release another record. "Wow. I haven't seen one of those in twenty years."

"I collect old vinyls. Very old."

"Aw, see, you're just way too classy for me...." He swayed with her in his arms, wishing that he'd learned to really dance. As he was feeling her against him, he was listening to the lyrics while Ronnie Milsap sang that any day now his wild and beautiful bird will have flown away. The words were just plain too telling, enough to depress him. He felt her arms tighten around him, and he kissed her. Damn, he liked kissing her. They had such a nice fit, such a good rhythm and movement. He couldn't remember ever tasting anything so right for his mouth. He kissed her through an entire song—probably three minutes.

As the next record was being released, she said, "What am I going to do about that job offer?"

"Honey, that's the easy part. Answer it. Tell this world-class surgeon that you're flattered, intrigued and you're thinking about it. That's the truth. Just out of curiosity, would you tell me what she offered you?"

"One-twenty," she said.

"One hundred and twenty thousand? *Dollars?*"

She nodded.

He whistled. He ran a hand over his head and down his neck. "I guess I'm going to have to win you with charm."

She smiled at him, "You are very charming. And cute."

"*Cute*. You really know how to gut a guy."

She ran her hands over his shoulders and down his arms. "Just in case you were worried, you completely outgrew that nerd thing."

"I did?"

"Oh, mama," she said, kissing him once more. She finally broke away with a little laugh. "You're cute in a very manly way."

He shook his head. "That wasn't exactly a save. I'm going to go. Otherwise I'll undress you and show you a few things. And my phone will ring. That's how my day has been going."

"I'm sorry, Scott. About the news, about the dilemma."

He ignored that. "Dinner tomorrow night?"

She nodded.

"I'll see you in the morning." He gave her another kiss and left. He hoped they were the best cannoli she'd ever had.

There was a nice restaurant in Coos Bay that was extremely small and very quiet, just the perfect place

for good food and talking. It was an American menu,
everything from steak, chicken and fish to pasta. The
drive was rather long just for dinner, but for a couple
who liked to talk about things, it worked. Once they
were settled at a corner table and each had a glass of
wine, Scott started the conversation. "Tell me about
the job offer. How did you handle it?"

Peyton thought she was going to get that question
before she even got in the car. In fact, she had wondered if he would ask her while they were both at the
clinic, but he had restrained himself. She gave him
a smile. "I did exactly as you suggested, which was
what I was going to do, anyway. I emailed her and
said it was a very tempting offer, and I'd like a little
time to think it over. I heard from her immediately.
It happens she has a family vacation scheduled as
well as a conference in Europe, and to accommodate
those trips, she's pulling a very crazy schedule. She
said if I wanted the job it was definitely mine, but
asked one thing of me—if I'm considering turning it
down, would I please visit her practice, meet the staff
and let her show me around the hospitals where she
has privileges before making a final decision. One
of her hospitals, she boasts, has a pediatric coronary
care unit. She'll be back and available in Seattle in
September. I told her I'd see her then."

"So you didn't accept the offer?" Scott asked.

"No. I think visiting her office is a good idea before making a final decision."

"So, you're staying in Thunder Point your full
three months?" he asked.

"Unless you'd rather I just leave now."

"Not a chance. I have a proposition...."

"Indecent?" she asked with one raised brow.

"Incredibly decent," he said. "We've got a month and change. Let's have some fun."

"Sex?" she asked.

"God, I hope so. But I was going to suggest a few other things. Let's go into the mountains to see the sights, let's check out the redwoods south of here and look at the beaches up and down the coast. Let's learn to paddleboard. We should date and play and hang out. And there's one thing I'd really love to cash in— You said if we were friends, you'd take me to the farm. We're friends, right? Can the kids come? They've never seen a working farm, and they love animals. I've discovered I love Basque food as much as I love Basque women."

"We also have a clinic to run," she reminded him.

He smiled. "Yes, we do. And you have the baby coming."

She nodded. "Adele. The middle of September."

"There's a lot to do in the next several weeks."

On the drive home from dinner they talked about all the things they could do, and she realized what a brilliant strategist he was, distracting her from the negative side of this deadline on both her job decision and their relationship and focusing instead on the positive, the fun they could have for the next several weeks. It was like a free pass. She'd never known a man so well in such a short period of time. It felt as though she'd known him for years, not weeks. She didn't have the slightest sensation of doubt until they stood together at her front door. That's when she was suddenly hit with misgivings. *Can I do this? Really?*

He pulled her into his arms, gently. He kissed her soundly. He was a great kisser—sensual, thorough, delicious and tempting. Against her slightly parted lips he said, "Let me come in, Peyton."

"Are you sure you want to?" she asked. "When all is said and done, this could turn out to be complicated for us. Please, be sure."

"I'm sure. I want to be alone with you. Unless you're hiding a couple of little kids in there…."

She shook her head. "We'd be very alone."

"I want that. I want you," he said, running a hand along the hair on her shoulder, caressing it, stroking it. He lifted a sheath of her hair to his face and kissed it, breathed in the scent.

She was waiting for one of the better-known, clever lines. *Let's not fight this any longer. I know you want this as much as I do.* But instead he said, "I'll never hurt you. I promise." And she pulled on his hand, drawing him inside. Turning and leaning against the wall, she pulled him against her for more kissing. He threaded his fingers through hers, held her hands against the wall on either side of her and pressed himself against her. "Feeling you against me…it's the best feeling I know," he whispered. He began to unbutton her silk blouse, very slowly, stopping every few seconds to kiss her again. And then he pushed the blouse off her shoulders, and it slid to the floor. She wore only a silk camisole under it, and he drew in his breath at the sight. "Whoa," he said softly. "Come with me. Let's get rid of some clothes…."

She just laughed and let him take her hand and lead her to the bedroom. It was such a small place, he didn't need directions and he didn't take very many steps. He got rid of his own shirt and shoes in a split second and advanced on her again, burying his lips in her neck, inhaling, licking, nuzzling. His hungry hands found the button on her slacks, and he slid them over her hips. She was wearing white silk panties that were loose and flared and matched the camisole. All silky, flowing fabric… He could make them disappear with hardly a touch, and she wished he would, but he just put a hand to his heart instead. He took slow, even breaths.

"Come on, Scott," she said, reaching for his belt. "Let's level the playing field here."

"Right," he said, helping her. "I like that idea so much."

He got rid of his pants, leaving him in boxers. She slid back on to the bed and waited for him to join her. He crawled on the bed and reclined next to her, taking her in his arms. "This is good," he said, his hands running all over her silk underwear, pausing for a moment under the curves of her breasts. He slid one hand under the loose leg of the flared boy-cut panties, grazing her belly and sliding to the inside of her thigh. "This is a very fine fashion idea," he muttered against her lips. His fingers roamed.

"I had no idea," she whispered. "I'll have to get some more...."

"I just want to touch every single part of you."

"All right," she said. Then her hands began to move, and she slid them down inside his boxer briefs. "Maybe you should just take these off."

"Anything you want. And these should go, too," he said, clutching a fistful of silk. "But, damn, don't let them get too far away. Just looking at you in these is enough to bring me to my knees. You're so beautiful." Then, almost reluctantly, he lifted the camisole over her head and gently pulled down the briefs. He gazed down at her. "I take it back. There's nothing more beautiful than you, just you."

His hands on her were so gentle, his caresses so slow and measured from her breasts to her knees. He kissed each breast, the inside of her arms and her belly. His fingers slid lower, and he smiled, murmuring, "Oh, baby."

"Condom," she whispered. "Top drawer."

"I've got it." And he reached inside, finding a brand-new, unopened box. "Thank you for this," he said. When he was ready, he didn't enter her. Instead he kissed his way down her body, spread her legs and used a strong tongue on her.

She grabbed his hair and arched against him, moaning in such beautiful pleasure she wasn't sure how long she could wait for him. Then he lifted her legs behind the knees, put his hands under her bottom and entered her slowly. Filling her.

"God," she said. She looked at his face, and it had

turned to stone. His eyes were shut, and he clenched his jaw, and she knew trying to wait was going to be a problem for him, as well. She put a hand on his cheek. "Look at me," she whispered. "Just look at me."

He opened his eyes and slowly he smiled, but he didn't move his hips. He threaded his hand down between their bodies, two fingers slipping down, rubbing her until she began to push back at him, panting wildly, and then he began to move. He thrust deeply, rhythmically, powerfully. He kept his eyes open, watching her face, his expression so intense. The second he felt her internal muscles clench around him, he moved a little harder, faster, deeper. Her orgasm held her a long time, and she gripped his shoulders fiercely, her nails digging in, riding it out. Just as the power of it was starting to ease, he thrust and held, and she could feel him pulsing into her. And it was magnificent. He was magnificent.

A moment later he carefully lowered his lips to hers. He kissed her softly, then more deeply. She held him close, the small patch of hair on his chest brushing against her breasts, his pelvis flush against hers as he stayed inside her. She reached up and ran her fingers through the hair above his ear. "Scott...."

He smiled. "Thank you."

She laughed softly. "The pleasure was all mine."

"Am I too heavy?" he asked.

She shook her head. "Stay with me like this," she said. "You feel good."

"Next time will be better," he said. "Now that we know each other's bodies a little bit."

"You're kidding, right? Scott, my toes curled. My eyes watered. I haven't felt this good in too long to even…" She put a finger on his lips. "It was wonderful for me. And I think it was good for you, if I'm any judge."

"Oh, baby." He laughed. "Thanks for thinking of condoms. I wasn't sure you'd have any…."

"We probably don't need them. I'm on the pill, but Ted was a cheater so…. We should talk about it, but for now…"

"I have a couple in the pocket of my pants, but yours were closer. Were you expecting this to happen?"

"Uh-huh. Since that kiss at your house while the kids slept on the couch."

"Only since then?" He laughed. "Honey, I've been having a party in my pants since the day I interviewed you."

"Even though you thought I was playing for the other team?"

"Somehow, that made it worse…or better."

"Men…" she said, but she laughed.

"I just had a few harmless fantasies, that's all."

"I hope you're over it."

His eyes were so dark and hot. "Honey, being with you tonight was a lot better than anything I could dream up."

She looped her arms around his neck. "For me, too, Scott."

* * *

He held her for a long time, whispering to her. He wanted to be totally honest with her. "As much as I wanted to make love to you, I really didn't think it was in the cards. First, I thought I wasn't your type. Then, I thought your bad heartbreak would keep you from me until you could get past it, and since I only had you for a little while, I didn't like my chances. And then I thought you would see what a flawed decision you made working in this little clinic, in this little town for that little paycheck, and you would leave."

"I told you I'd keep my word," she said.

He turned so he was spooning her from behind. "I admire that," he said. "I admire it in anyone, but that was a hard promise for you to make, and you made it, anyway."

"I thought maybe this was a good place to take a break, to remember what my priorities really are. All the people I've met here seem to know something about that."

"Most of the people you've met have done exactly the same thing. Cooper came here because his good friend died suddenly, and he wanted to know what happened. Sarah came here to recover from a nasty divorce. Eric—who owns the service station—he came here because he needed a fresh start, and he has a daughter here. I'll let Devon tell you her story herself, and it's remarkable."

"And there's you," she said.

"There's me," he said, pulling her a little closer. "I was looking for something, but I didn't know what. There were the practical reasons. I always think about the kids and what would be good for them. But I wanted my work to be more than a job. I wanted to be a part of something. When you're the only doctor in a small town, believe me, you're in it and it's in you." He moved her hair out of the way and kissed her neck.

"A lot of doctors follow the money," she said.

"Good for them," he said. "A lot of doctors are only good at doctoring and get in financial trouble and file bankruptcy. If a big wind comes and blows away all our material wealth, I want to be worth something."

"Character," she said.

"Okay," he said, kissing her neck again. "You're intoxicating. You're delicious. What if you're addictive?"

"No," she said. "I'm not."

"You turn me on like crazy. And really, I can't get enough. If you could read my mind, you'd hear the most embarrassing things...."

"Tell me," she begged.

"I wanted to be here, like this, next to you, inside you, closer to you than possible, closer than this. Part of you, you part of me, driving each other to the most pleasure there is for a man and woman. I already want you again. And again. You're electrifying. Hmm, I don't think this is human, what you make me feel."

She wiggled her butt against him. "I can tell…."

He slipped a hand over her hip, across her flat stomach and down. He separated her legs, lifting the top one, and deftly pressed against her soft center. "What do you think of this idea?"

"I think… Ohhh… I think, yes…."

He entered her from behind, slick and easy. With his lips on her neck and his hand making her so happy, he moved against her, within her. The angle seemed to stimulate her in a different place, and it was heavenly.

"Good?" he asked.

"Good," she said.

"I love it when you come," he whispered. "It's powerful." And he stroked harder, pumped his hips, driving deeper. "You're ready," he whispered.

"Oh, God," she whispered back, pushing against him, loving his thrusts, loving his fingers. He rocked into her for a long time, murmuring to her that she was amazing, that he'd never have enough of her.

And he brought her all the way, leaving her trembling with satisfaction.

He wrapped his arms around her, holding her against him, neither of them speaking for a long time, just melting into each other.

"I think this is my favorite part," Peyton finally said, her voice soft. "Post-coital bliss, no rolling away for sleep."

"I can sleep like this. I could every night of my life," he said.

Another long moment of silence passed. "What's going to happen to us, Scott?"

He kissed her neck. "All the best things, I think."

Eleven

August changed things all over Thunder Point, and most definitely in the clinic. Scott spent a little more time than usual in town, cutting back his on-call schedule somewhat because of the flood of school and sports physicals that were required. Peyton handled as many of the physicals as she could manage because Scott had to keep his clinic hours in Bandon where they had a busier month than usual for the same reason.

And yet, the month was more fun. It began with a big party on the beach as Cooper and Sarah prepared to send Landon off to the University of Oregon where the Ducks football training camp was starting. Of course, Peyton was invited. After a little more than a month as a resident of this little town, people treated her like an old friend. But she was a bit unnerved when Cooper dropped an arm around her shoulders and said, "So. You and Scott? That's awesome. He's a good guy." And not long after that,

Mac gave her a little shoulder-squeeze and said, "The doc's a great guy, Peyton. You're in good hands."

When Scott brought her a beer, she challenged him. "Have you been bragging around town that you finally got in my pants?"

"Of course not," he said, taken aback.

"Then it must be the way you look at me! So, stop it!"

He just grinned and said, "Maybe it's the way you look at me, Peyton. Every time I get a free pass and show up at your house, you're all over me like a starving animal." He touched her nose with a finger. "I am not complaining about that, by the way. I'm just as hungry for you. Every minute." And then he went off to bond with the men over beer, sports stories and off-color jokes.

And Peyton thought, *I probably do look at him that way.* She found him wonderful in every way, and he was an adventure in bed. Not only was he handsome, when he touched her it made her wild for more, made her wanton and eager. He was lusty and powerful, yet he could also handle her as if she might be as fragile as a newborn. She wanted him all the time. She couldn't remember ever wanting a man this way. She realized it had to be written all over her face.

She also loved to watch him with people. He had a great sense of humor and had compassion for absolutely everyone he came into contact with in the clinic and around the town. He was the most skilled listener, whether it was a complaining old lady or feisty sixth grader. He somehow conveyed with his eyes and by his touch, *You can always trust me. I'll always tell you the truth.*

But she was nervous about these feelings, and for good reason. She'd been in a very similar position before, thinking herself to be in love with the doctor she'd worked with. She'd thought he was everything she'd ever wanted, then she came awake one day and realized she'd been kidding herself. Ted hadn't been the man she thought he was at all.

What could Scott need her for? Love, for one thing—that was obvious. He'd love her every day if she didn't hold him off a little. Did he need a dirt-cheap PA to help him get his clinic functional and successful? He did need a babysitter—desperately! Gabriella would be leaving soon. It didn't help that she wanted to be needed for these things. But what if it wasn't as good as it seemed? What if it fell apart? It would break her heart to pieces because her instincts said she'd found the man she'd been waiting for all her life.

"You're thinking too hard," a voice said, jolting her out of her contemplation. She snapped out of it and saw Devon standing next to her.

"What makes you say that?" she asked.

"You've almost gone cross-eyed you're staring so hard at Scott. I've known him a year now, Peyton. He's exactly what he appears to be. Believe me, I'm in a position to be very suspicious of men who seem perfect and are hiding something. Scott is the real deal. You don't have to be nervous about liking him."

"What makes you think I like him in any particular way?" she asked.

Devon laughed. "You look at him like you're trying to look into him. Relax. He's okay. Want a hot dog or hamburger? People are eating."

"Great, I'm starving!" she said, happy for the distraction.

She wanted to spend a little time in the hayloft. She wanted to fall into this man and stay in his arms for life, and it scared the hell out of her. She was not at all afraid of holding him and loving him tonight.... She was afraid of finding herself trying to hold it together in two or three years.

Peyton got a plate and visited with Carrie for a while. Carrie sat with Gina and Mac at one of the new picnic tables Cooper had brought to the beach, and for the first time in a long time her leg wasn't elevated. "How's the knee these days?" Peyton asked.

"Excellent. I've been careful the last few weeks, not standing for such long hours. All thanks to my daughter, granddaughter and Rawley. They helped me with the cooking and baking. I only lost one catering job and the dinner meals for only a week or so. I think I'm going to be fine."

"I think the next time, you're going to have surgery," Peyton said. "Have you been thinking about that?"

"Thinking and researching. I'm determined to come to some kind of conclusion before the next time my knee gives out. I'm going to be ready before that happens!"

"Good for you," Peyton said. And right then, Rawley delivered Carrie a plate holding a hamburger, deviled eggs and an ear of corn. Buttered. "It seems Rawley takes very good care of you," Peyton observed.

"He's an old friend," Carrie said. "I never asked him for his help, but he's been wonderful lately."

"Mom made sure he had food at his house after his father died, and he's been indebted ever since," Gina said. "Rawley doesn't have much to say, but he's a good old guy. Good to have him watching over us all."

"That's nothing to complain about," Peyton said, giving Carrie's hand a pat.

She moved on to where Cooper and Sarah were sitting with the baby in the stroller beside them. And right next to the stroller, Ham towered, watching closely. When Peyton approached with her plate of food, Cooper jumped up and flipped open an extra canvas beach chair for her. "Thanks," she said, taking the seat. "How's the baby doing?"

"She's very loud," Sarah said with a laugh. "I'm afraid Ham is going to wig out any day now."

"He looks so calm," Peyton said.

"When she's quiet, he's quiet. When she starts screeching, he runs in circles and moans until she's quiet again. Then he lays his big muzzle as close to her as he can get, usually on my lap. He's adorable. I don't think even I love Summer as much as Ham does."

"Maybe when she wakes up, he'll let me hold her," Peyton said, taking a bite of her hot dog.

"He's very generous," Sarah said. "He doesn't care who holds her as long as she's being comforted and stops crying."

"And, are you ready to give Landon over to the Ducks?" she asked.

"Not really, but he's ready to go. Everything is going to change around here," Sarah said. "See those kids over on that blanket? Landon's leaving, and Eve will be looking for ways to earn gas money so she can visit him and go to the games. I doubt Landon will be around much during football season, and when he is around, I bet he's with Eve. Frank, the tall dark-haired kid? He's going to Princeton—but every college wanted him. I hear he's brilliant. I bet anything Ashley follows him eventually. She's wild about him. We're going to have to hire some help for the bar. Cooper and I can't run it without Landon and also go to his games. Plus, Summer needs parents who don't work twelve hours a day, seven days a week, and Rawley can't do everything. Cooper wants to pour two more foundations along the hillside. He likes the building more than anything."

"Spec houses," Cooper said around a mouthful of hot dog. "I want to build and sell a couple of spec houses. Need to get that foundation poured and the houses framed before the wet and cold settles in." Then he grinned and added, "You should see what me in a tool belt does to Sarah!"

"He's dreaming," Sarah said.

"And it's a great dream," he said with a laugh. "You should join me, honey!"

"So, Peyton, rumor is you're seeing Scott these days," Sarah said.

"I see him all the time," she said. "We work together."

Sarah tilted her head and gave Peyton a sly smile.

"Okay, we've gone out a few times. It's not serious," she was quick to inform them. "I have a job offer in Seattle that I'm considering."

"Oh, I hope it turns out to be a lousy offer! Not that I don't wish you the best, but we'd love to keep you here. You fit in, you know?"

"This is a nice place to fit in to," she agreed.

Cooper lifted his empty plate and said, "I'm getting seconds. Want anything, babe?"

"Deviled eggs!" Sarah said.

When he was out of earshot, Peyton said, "You used to fly for the Coast Guard. What made you decide to give it all up for this little town?"

"Besides this little town?" she returned with a laugh. Sarah nodded toward Cooper. "Look at him. I held him off as long as I could, but Cooper is the best man in the world. He loves my little brother as much as I do. He'd go anywhere for me, even if it meant leaving what he loves. And besides, he's right about the tool belt. Don't tell him I said that—he's a little arrogant."

The baby started to stir, and sure enough, Ham was upright, watching. "My turn," Peyton said, putting her empty plate on the sand and scooping up the baby. She jiggled the fussiness out of her, and little Summer snuggled in, quieting at once, mollified. Ham sat again, at peace.

"But would you have stayed here? If not for Cooper?"

"I wanted to stay at least another year. That was mostly for Landon, so he could finish high school without moving for his senior year, but the thought of leaving really bothered me. I had made friends. I had a wonderful man in my life. The Coast Guard definitely pushed my decision, but I'm completely happy with it. Everyone is family."

"I grew up in a small town," Peyton said. "Sometimes too much family is too much."

Sarah laughed. "That's true anywhere, I think. This town is no exception. People get very nosy. That takes getting used to. But if you're ever in trouble, in need of help, this is a good place to be."

"I remember that, as well," Peyton said. Indeed, so often it seemed like too much family. But then when the sheep needed to be sheared, the potatoes and fruit harvested, butchering to be done, not only did the Lacoumette family gather en masse, there were folks from neighboring farms, townsfolk the Lacoumette family had aided, present to lend a hand. They helped on each other's farms, put out fires, gave shelter to friends in need, congregated to build and assembled to party.

The baby squirmed a little. "Is she hungry yet?" Peyton asked.

"Well, she's hungry most of the time, but she had a bottle a couple of hours ago."

Peyton gazed at the baby. She had held every single niece and nephew and a multitude of other infants. They always felt secure in her arms; she had always felt confident holding them. She'd started holding babies when she was a baby herself—her younger brother and sister, George and Ginny, twins, had come along when she was two. She had never longed for one of her own until the past few years. She was over thirty before it occurred to her that a child of her own might feel slightly different, somewhat more precious. And now she supposed she'd never have one. She had known better than to add one more to Ted's tumultuous horde. And not only did Scott have his children already, childbirth might have cost him his wife.

When Cooper returned, she passed over the baby and went to sit with Scott and his children.

"I thought you were avoiding me," he said, putting his arm around her.

"Not at all. I was visiting people."

"Having a good time?"

"How could anyone not have a good time?"

Before long, Gabby and Charles said their good-byes and ambled across the beach, headed for home. Soon after they left, Spencer was at their table. "I've got a dilemma," he said to Scott. "I've got a few football players who are uninsured, and their families find the cost of a sports physical pretty steep. There might be as many as five or six, a couple of whom might not go out for the team because of the requirements. They can get their school physicals at a free clinic, but, as you know, we need something a little more thorough than just a student physical, and we need it done before practice starts."

"No problem, Spence. Send 'em by the clinic."

"I don't know if everything will be covered by state aid, but before these boys play for me, I have to be sure their health is sound. I have a few issues with the team because of the income of some of the families in the area."

"Issues like what?" Peyton asked.

"Well, some of them won't get enough balance in their diet during the season. I've gotten in the habit of bringing some high-octane fiber and heavy duty vitamins as well as a lot of beef jerky that I get wholesale. They not only have to have the stamina for football, they have to build muscle if they're going to go up against those inland farm boys. Some of 'em are already big and muscled from working with their families on the fishing boats and eating a ton of solid fish. These boys get a lot of pasta—white pasta. The carbs keep 'em going, but they need muscle and brain food. I have a protein drink I give them during training. You'd be amazed how big and healthy I can get these kids if I concentrate." Then he smiled with satisfaction.

"And does the school pay for that?" Peyton asked, though she was pretty sure she knew the answer.

"Nah. But teachers have been known to bring supplies to schools for years. This is just as important as pencils, believe me. Some of our families live close to the poverty line. Like the Russell boys, before Al took over as their foster father. You know what I'm talking about. And these guys need things like sports and academics for scholarships or they won't get to go to college. Everything we do now changes the face of this town for the future."

"I have an idea," Scott said. "Pick a practice day early in the schedule. Tell the boys we're doing physicals at the gym. Tell them if they have insurance information to bring it, and if they don't, don't worry about it."

"That'd be great, Scott. I'll help shoulder the cost of that," Spencer said.

"Nah, don't worry about it," Scott said. "I'll do blood draws and urine tests, and if we find anything hinky, FHIAP will step up to the plate for low-income families."

"FHIAP?" he asked.

"Family Health Insurance Assistance Program," Peyton explained. "If they're sick, that is. They don't provide football physicals, but it's one of the best ways to find out if they're sick. I'll come with Scott. How many boys on the team?" she asked.

"Thirty," Spencer said. "Sometimes we get thirty-five."

"We'll clear appointments for a morning," she said. "What time of day do you start practice?"

"Early. Six-thirty."

"Awww…" she whined. "You're as bad as a farm!

My dad wasn't happy unless everyone was out of bed at five!"

Scott laughed. "I'll be there and Miss Slug-abed can catch up."

"I'll be there," she groaned. "I can help. And since Scott is pretty incompetent at paperwork, I'll help keep that straight so Devon doesn't eat him alive. Too bad hunting season is so late in the fall—we get some amazing venison jerky off the farm."

Scott covered her hand. "Every time I'm at the store, I'll throw some jerky in the cart for Spencer."

"Daddy, I have to go to the bathroom," Jenny said, tugging at Scott's sleeve.

"The house is unlocked," Spencer said. "I better find Mercy and make sure she's under control. Thanks, you guys! On behalf of the team, I owe you one."

Scott talked Will into making a bathroom run at the same time, Spencer left in search of his family, and suddenly Peyton was there alone. *What just happened here?* she wondered. *We're not just a clinic. We're propping up our neighbors. We're feeding the hungry kids, making sacrifices to be sure they're educated, all for one, one for all. Everything was a community project.*

It was a lot like being at home.

Ted had given to charitable causes. He'd usually done so in a tux, writing a check. But checks were important, too. Very important. And he'd taken on the occasional patient who couldn't meet the cost of the best cardiologist in the state, but it just didn't feel the same as this. He didn't ever get his hands dirty.

She looked around the beach. The volleyball net had gone up. Al, the foster father, was having a beer and laughing with his lady friend, Ray Anne the Realtor, while his boys were playing in the game. One of the boys was helping young Austin watch for the ball and position his hands so he could bump the ball. Over at Cooper's area, Landon was holding his baby niece, rocking her against his shoulder while Ham repeatedly nudged him in the waist. Rawley was having some dessert with Carrie. Mac and Gina were surrounded by family—a bunch of kids, Mac's aunt Lou and her husband, Joe. All her new friends were here.

Peyton tried to remember what it felt like to be completely dazzled by Ted, by his polished good looks, his brilliance, his mystique. He had the classiest practice she'd ever worked in, a six-thousand-square-foot decorated beauty to live in, expensive late-model cars to drive. And she believed he had loved her. Until he'd stopped. When had he stopped? She wasn't entirely sure. Maybe when they began to argue about his kids. Every time she thought about them, it made her sad. She had wanted them to find in her a kindred spirit, a woman who shared a bond in loving Ted.

That hadn't happened.

Ted had given her beautiful clothes and jewelry. Items she made sure to pack when she left his home, most of which would look painfully out of place here.

Scott brought her cannoli. It made her smile. She had almost never tasted better cannoli in her life. They were almost as good as her mother's.

Carrie packed up her beach-mobile with coolers, thermoses, tablecloths and other picnic things. She was ready to head for home when Rawley approached her and said, "I'll drive over in a few minutes and just help you unload that."

"I can do it if you have other things to do."

"I'll be there directly," he said.

So, off she went across the beach. She arrived at her house and right behind her came that cranberry-red restored truck that Rawley drove. Without a word, he started carrying things into her house. When all was inside, they met in the kitchen. "I hope you know, I appreciate your help. I'm much better now, Rawley. My knee hardly bothers me at all. I don't want you worrying."

"I ain't worried," he said, but he didn't look at her.

"Good. Don't feel you have to keep up with me."

"I don't," he said.

"You're here a lot," she pointed out.

"You'd rather I be scarce?" he asked.

"No. I like you."

"Good. We have ourselves a deal then."

"Do we? What kind of deal do we have?" she asked.

"I help out. I don't have to keep up. I like it. You like it."

"True," she said. "Cup of coffee?" she asked.

"I reckon."

"Have a seat. I'll put on the pot."

Before sitting, Rawley put away a few of the things they'd brought in the house. He was so comfortable there, he knew where everything went. Then he sat at the table. "You serve up a good cup of coffee," he told her.

"I'd better. It's my business."

"There's a thing or two you know about me already. I'm not good around a mess of people. I like being on my own more or less. When your knee went all gimpy, I found out I liked cooking. I'd rather be cooking than serving. On the other hand, you're awful good with people."

"Caterers have to be," she reminded him. "But you like being with me."

"I don't mind them other women much, either. You're all kind of alike."

"What other women? You mean Lou and Ray Anne? We're *nothing* alike!"

"You think not?" he asked. "Well, maybe I can take you in groups of three, then."

"Maybe," she said, sitting at the table with him. "What is it you're trying to say, Rawley? That you like to cook?"

"I always liked to, I just wasn't sure of that before. And you make passable company."

"Thank you. I think," she said. "I'm not exactly looking for a man in my life. But there's a thing or two you probably don't know about me. I've been alone a very long time. My husband walked out when

Gina was five years old and never bothered to drop a check in the mail. Not once. The next time he turned up, he turned up dead. Gina was around thirteen, I think. He never divorced us, but he did get himself a new family—a new wife and child. I've been in a bad mood about that ever since. Consequently, I don't much trust men."

"I don't much, either," he said. "But I do find I like to cook. I couldn't leave Cooper. He's perfectly useless on his own, and he does need me around. He's talked a bit about hiring on some new help, but there's no evidence he's done anything about that. I wish he'd get on with it because I'm game to help him around the bar, but I'm not crazy about serving. And there ain't nothing to cook there. Bear in mind, I have to be around those kids. I don't know that anyone would see to it they get to go fishing if not for me."

"That's pretty obvious. But how many hours a day can one man work? Living in Elmore and all?"

"Well, that has come up as a problem," Rawley said. "Cooper did offer up that apartment over the bar, but that wouldn't be right. I think that place is the guesthouse now. But I'm looking for a change or two. I been in that bar five years now, and I don't know if you noticed, it just keeps getting busier."

"I noticed," she said with a smile.

"I like it quiet."

"And you'd like to cook."

"I guess that's right. I don't mind stocking, cleaning, opening early, closing up. I like to get in a little fishing, work a little on the truck. I particularly like to cook with you. I hope that doesn't put you off."

She leaned back in her chair and smiled. "If I didn't know better, I'd think you were making me a proposal of some kind."

"Some kind, but what kind I can't say." He cleared his throat. "I wonder if we should keep cooking together. I can do the heavy lifting and make sure what cooking you need gets done."

"And that's all?" she asked.

"Ain't that enough?" he asked.

She just chuckled and shook her head. "For the time being," she said. "What am I paying you for that?"

"Can't I just have all the good food I can handle?"

"You could stand a few pounds, I guess. And I can use the help."

"The way I see it, Miss Carrie, you need the help, I need a little company, and who knows? Maybe I won't live in Elmore forever."

"Don't get any ideas, Rawley Goode. I like living alone!"

And he flashed her a very handsome smile, showing off his false teeth. "I haven't had a passable good idea in a hundred years, Miss Carrie."

And so they left it at that. He wanted to work less at the bar, more in her catering kitchen and he liked her company.

A match made in heaven.

Twelve

Peyton quickly learned that the people of Thunder Point had their own ideas about what was and was not their business. Scott remained thoroughly professional on the job and completely respectable about demonstrations of affection in public when they weren't on the job, but people still regarded them with twinkling eyes and sly smiles. When they went to the high school to provide athletic physical exams, she overheard one of the high school boys make a cute comment about "the doc's new girl." It made Peyton blush and Scott laugh.

"Come over to dinner tonight," Scott said. "Let's grab something from Carrie's. I'm on call, but it will probably be quiet."

"Famous last words," she said.

"It's okay. Gabby and Charles are on duty if I get called. They're staying in tonight. We won't see them unless I text her and tell her to come upstairs for the kids."

"Does she have a whole apartment down there?"

"Close. No kitchen, but a little refrigerator, a microwave and lots of space. It's a nice suite with a big bathroom. They'll fix something to eat upstairs and then hide away, watch TV, whatever. If I'm on call, they have date night at home so Gabby can take care of the kids if I'm called out. She's going to be irreplaceable."

"How *are* you going to replace her?"

"For call-outs, with Devon and Spencer. Right now, Eve is willing to do a lot of babysitting during clinic hours. She'll be in school full-time so I'll have to get a backup sitter, but Devon has some ideas. She found a preschool-slash-day care for Mercy and Jenny, Will will be in school, and they have an after-school program for working parents. We're ironing out the details. Devon was educated in early childhood development, and she's the perfect person to find our next solution. Come over for dinner. When the kids go to bed, we can curl up on the couch and...talk."

"You don't want to talk!"

"I love to talk to you," he said. "And do other things."

Of course, she went. The four of them had spaghetti and meatballs from Carrie's deli while Gabby and Charles had a pizza downstairs. When the kids were bathed and in bed, they curled up on the couch and made out like a couple of teenagers while Gabby and Charles were probably doing the same thing downstairs. "This is crazy," she said. "Don't you feel strange, making out up here while your baby-sitter is making out downstairs?"

"I feel young," he said with a smile. "This is all I have to offer tonight. It's Gabby's night off, unless I'm called for an emergency. Tomorrow night she's on, and I can come to your house. If you feel like company."

Peyton toyed with the idea of saying no, that she needed a night off, but she couldn't. She didn't want a night off. And she was aware that their time together was running out. She might take that job in Seattle if it was just too good to pass up. But she knew that if he came to her house without the kids, they would do much more than talk. She might climb him like a tree. And she trembled at the thought.

She couldn't resist him. It was enough to make her think about whether she needed that greater income offered by the surgeon. There was something about making love with Scott that rang all her bells and whistles. He was just a small-town clinic doctor. He had no power in the medical community, in any community. His picture would never be on the cover of *Medicine Today*. He didn't even have a website. He needed a website! He was not a mover and shaker…. Okay, he moved and shook a little in Thunder Point, but you'd never know it; he was treated like a friend, a pal, a buddy. He didn't influence people, make things happen anywhere but in his small bubble. He helped people where he could and sure, people noticed, but they weren't important people.

They were just regular people. And that was exactly who he wanted to be.

But when they made love…

That was it, she thought. They made *love*. Love was what they were doing. With Ted it had been sex. But even though Ted had said the words, she hadn't really felt loved.

Scott hadn't said the words, and yet he was completely convincing. She felt them. With each passing day, the thought of saying goodbye to him became more impossible to imagine.

One Saturday they took the kids south to California to see the largest stand of redwoods in the area—they were magnificent. They picnicked, hiked through the woods, hugged trees. The following weekend they drove north of Coos Bay to Echo Beach and Canon Beach where the haystack rocks offshore were the most stunning. It was so chilly on the water, they had to dress warmly and snuggle close. The four of them had many dinners together, and twice Scott was called to the hospital, and once a Thunder Point resident called his cell phone in the evening with concern over an injury on his foot. It was a deep cut that he'd closed and been treating himself, and now it was worse with a mysterious red line running up his leg from the site of the wound. Gabby was called upstairs to be on duty for the kids, and Peyton went with Scott to the clinic where Scott cleaned the wound, stitched it and loaded the guy up with antibiotics.

If the whole town didn't have his cell phone number or if Scott had been on ER duty at another hospital, it could have meant a trip to another town's emergency room for the man. Or she would be the only other option. She could have met a patient at the Thunder Point clinic. If she was still in town.

But a person had to be out of town sometimes and, while Peyton could treat and prescribe for patients, an MD usually had to sign off on her work. So Scott made arrangements. Scott's clinic hours were Monday through Friday, nine to five, and he always answered his cell phone, but a man needed days here and there when he could be completely unavailable. To that end, a doctor from an urgent care in Bandon agreed to trade off practices with him from time to time. Dr. Stewart was a young, ER-certified physician, looking for more income, and was willing to be the doctor on call to Thunder Point if Scott could return the favor now and then. Scott's patients could call Dr. Stewart when Scott was away, and Dr. Stewart's patients could call Scott in emergencies.

The first time for this new partnership was coming up in another week. Scott and the kids were following Gabriella back to Vancouver; he was pulling a trailer with her belongings. The kids couldn't be left behind—the coming separation was going to be difficult enough.

"I can keep the clinic open if Dr. Stewart will work with me," Peyton said. "He can sign off on any procedures that come up while you're away, but we'll stall most of the appointments until you're back in town."

A few days before the scheduled departure to Washington, Peyton had dinner with Scott and the kids. He was on call and his phone rang. There was a family with a bad flu in the ER, and the youngest was two years old. They were all sick, dehydrated and feverish.

"I'll text Gabriella to come upstairs, and then I'll take off," he said.

"Don't bother her," Peyton said. "I know the bedtime drill. I'll get the kids settled. Gabby doesn't have much time with her beloved Charles before she has to leave Thunder Point."

"Are you sure? I know how you feel about being taken advantage of in off hours."

"I'm good," she said. "Just go. Maybe you won't be too long."

There was one thing about being the ER doctor on call, it was very rare that Scott felt his time had been wasted. This night there was much more to the story than a family with the flu. It was carbon monoxide poisoning from a dysfunctional water heater. A mom, dad, four-year-old and two-year-old had come to the ER The kids had low-grade fevers while mom and dad were just sick as dogs. Scott had to decide what the devil it could be if he ruled out fever. Then he asked if they were the sole inhabitants of the house and learned that Grandma and Grandpa lived there, as well. The fire department was dispatched, two more patients were admitted, the water heater was turned off and the house aired out.

All this took quite a while.

Scott texted Peyton as he was leaving the hospital, but she didn't respond. He wondered if she had fallen asleep in the fort again. That thought made him smile.

If Peyton knew how much he fantasized about her joining their family, about a life with her, he feared she'd run screaming into the night. He had no idea how to pursue her, but he was moving as cautiously as he could. He knew a little about what she'd been through with Ted and gathered it had more to do with being stuck with his bratty kids than with him. Scott couldn't guarantee his kids would always behave; he often wondered if he didn't just find them way more precious and sweet than other people might. One thing for sure—they were his responsibility. Not hers.

And if his kids weren't enough of a wild card, how about the grandmothers? Holy Jesus, they made *him* want to run away! They were each high maintenance in their own way—his mother could be domineering and controlling, Serena's mother could be wheedling and manipulative. When they weren't bickering, they were forming an alliance, with him as the common enemy. While he and Serena lived in Vancouver, the grandmothers, both widows, competed for time. "She got Thanksgiving, so I get Christmas." Even though they invited each other to all family events. They disagreed on how to take care of the children, fought over what discipline was appropriate and what was not and who was the better cook or more nurturing grandma or whatever. They'd been like that even when Serena was alive. When Will was born, Serena's mother took up residence in her daughter's house, staking a claim as the mother's mother. Scott's mother had snidely asked, "If I drive past the house slowly, will you please hold the baby up in the window so I can see him?"

When Serena passed away, it was even worse. They were both determined to take care of him. It had been torture.

Not only was he reluctant to tell Peyton how much he cared for her, he had no real experience in this. He'd grown up with Serena; they'd been together since they were kids. She'd passed away when she was only thirty-three. He remembered moments of passion, of sexual hunger, but more common in a relationship over a decade old, there were feelings of security, enduring love, safety, partnership. As a medical student and resident, he could not have managed without a wife like Serena, so supportive and patient. God, the number of times he'd worked sixteen-hour days and left her abandoned, barely talking to her, too tired to have a meal with her unless she came to the hospital, too exhausted for sex, broke and struggling. And yet she'd held so strong, knowing they were headed for a better day. He had adored her. He thanked God for her every day.

That was the love of his youth, a love they created over time, through hardships and triumphs. It was a love they'd grown into since he was a boy and she was a girl.

This thing with Peyton was somehow different. Now he was a man who had endured the rigors of loss, a man with a family. He looked at this new love differently. This was a woman, a love he might never have found. The love of his youth, the love that grew between a boy and girl, felt sweet and tempting and hopeful. What he was feeling for Peyton felt explosive. Powerful, complex and consuming.

He really didn't want to screw it up.

Scott wasn't sure what he should be doing with this romance. He hadn't truly wooed a woman since he'd convinced Serena to marry him—and that hadn't been difficult. He was going to have to think very hard, strategize with great cunning, to capture Peyton. She wasn't a young innocent who had fairy-tale ideas about relationships; she was a grown woman who had been through her own heartaches and disappointments.

But when he walked into his house, into his bedroom, the woman he found didn't seem to be the same one he was worried about convincing. She was on his bed, stocking feet, yoga pants and T-shirt, one of his kids tucked under each arm, all of them asleep.

He couldn't remember ever loving anyone as much as he loved her. It felt brand-new.

He quietly changed into his pajama bottoms and slid into bed with them.

"Um…oh," she said, stirring. "You're here. I should go—"

"Shh," he said. "Go back to sleep." He raised up on an elbow, leaned toward her and kissed her lightly on the lips. "Wouldn't they go to bed?"

"They were fine. We found a bed big enough for all of us."

He smiled. "Happens that way a lot around here."

"I figured." Then, in what almost seemed a choreographed movement, she rolled over, spooning Jenny while Will turned into Scott's arm, resting his little head on his father's shoulder.

She took my children under her wing and rocked them safely to sleep.

For him, there was no turning back.

Peyton was not surprised by the way the town responded to Gabriella's departure. Even though, as a college student, her closest friendships were among the coeds and young couples she and her boyfriend socialized with, she was also well acquainted with many in town. The Saturday Scott was helping her load the small trailer to take her and all her belongings back to Vancouver turned into a party. Peyton went over to Scott's house with a big plate of cookies and found a number of her friends already there with food, music, drinks and good wishes. Someone made a big sign that was hung on the trailer that said, *Happy Trails, Gabriella.* Devon, Spencer and the kids were there; Cooper, Sarah, the baby—and Ham—came. Al and Ray Anne were there with two of the three boys, Eric Gentry was working at his gas station, but his significant other, Laine, arrived with a platter of submarine sandwiches. Mac and Gina stopped by; Ashley and Eve, the new part-time baby-sitters, came by to give hugs and wish her well. Even though some of her young friends from the community college she had attended threw her a farewell party the night before, some of them dropped by for a final goodbye. There was a constant flow of people throughout the afternoon.

This was the kind of place that honored good people, even if they were just passing through. Gabriella had been Scott's nanny for the past year, and her reputation was solid—she would be missed. This filled Peyton with nostalgia. Even though she'd not been able to wait to take her job abroad after college, couldn't get on the plane fast enough, her entire huge extended family had shown up at the farm for a spectacular send-off. They'd been armed with messages to Basque family members they'd barely heard about in forty years…and they'd been so proud of her.

Scott and the kids and Gabriella and Charles left for Vancouver on Sunday in two cars. Peyton and Dr. Stewart would cover Scott's duties until Wednesday.

But early Monday evening there was a knock at her door, and Peyton opened it to find Scott standing there holding a bouquet of flowers and a bottle of wine. He was smiling, and his eyes had grown dark and smoky. She had talked to him by cell phone several times Sunday and Monday and had had no idea he was coming home so quickly. There were grandmothers to visit in Vancouver!

"Scott?"

"I left the kids with their grandmothers," he said, smiling. "Got a corkscrew?"

"Why didn't you tell me you were coming right home? I would've showered and changed! Planned dinner or something."

"First, a glass of wine," he said, coming inside and closing the door. "Then a shower for both of us. Then maybe we'll take our time getting dressed. And if you show the proper amount of gratitude, I'll take you to Cliff's for crab cakes and fries."

"*Gratitude?* Shouldn't you be the one to show gratitude?"

"That's right, that's my job. I'll get it right. Then we'll come back here, and if you want me to, I can spend the night. And show even more gratitude. Up against the wall and sweaty!"

He always made her laugh. She slid up against him, holding him close. "I want that," she said. "All of that."

"Good. All I could think about all day was a long, hot intense night with you. I don't like being away from you."

She didn't like being away from him, either. And he had rushed back to her. The thought made her smile down to her toes. Nothing, she thought, could possibly go wrong.

Deep in the night, Scott reached for her and pulled her close against him. "Are you awake?" he whispered.

"Hmm-mmm," she answered sleepily, snuggling closer.

"I want to tell you something." He stroked her cheek. "I didn't think it would feel like this. I thought I would have a woman in my life again someday. I was open to the idea. Hoping. I didn't want to stay alone. I wanted what everyone wants—someone they just can't live without. And I thought when I finally found it—her—it would feel nice. I didn't think it would feel like this—overwhelming. I wake up thinking about you. I fall asleep wanting you. I'm in love with you, Peyton. Not in an ordinary, comfortable, easy, compatible way, but in a desperate, passionate, powerful way. Completely gone. I want to be with you forever."

"Forever is a lot longer than three months," she said, her voice sleepy.

"Lots longer. I understand you're at a crossroads. I know you aren't sure where you should be next. Maybe you're not completely sure who you should be with. But, Peyton, I want you to know how I feel, while you're figuring things out. I love you. I love you completely. I want to be with you. I want us to be together if we can. I think I can make you happy, I really do. I promise you I'll do everything in my power, and when I give everything I've got, it doesn't fall short—it's really *everything*. I want you, you make me feel like there's nothing else in the universe I need. It's just you. I want you to know that."

"Is that a proposal?" she asked weakly.

"It can be whatever you want it to be. I love you.

I want you. You're the one for me. I dated a little bit, it wasn't even interesting to me. It's you, honey. It's you I fell for. Just know that. It's not just lust… okay, there's a lot of lust. You really do something to me. But there's more to it—it's deep in me. It's solid in me. I know how to treat those feelings, too. I can be steady for you; you can count on me and lean on me, and I'll always give everything. I promise. Whatever you decide is right for you—at least you have the facts."

"I have things to figure out," she said. "To understand, get over."

"I know."

"I'm not ready to say all that. Not yet."

"I know. And I want you to be sure because I'm not interested in being the consolation prize. I'm here when you're sure."

"Maybe while I'm figuring things out, someone else will come along and distract you, make you see there are other fish in the sea."

"I'm not him, Peyton," he said. "There won't be anyone else."

Peyton was pretty much walking on air when she got out of bed the next morning. She didn't doubt Scott's sincerity for a second. He had treated her to a lot of snuggling, hugging, deep kissing and three very lovely, earth-shattering orgasms. For a man who showed love with every sexual move he made, it was clear he never held back the power of it. He could love gentle; he could love hard. They hadn't been a couple long, yet he already knew her body so well, evidence that he paid attention.

And she knew his body. Oh, God, did she know it! She knew how to touch him, tease him, blow his mind. She could bring him to his knees, leave him gasping. And then his reciprocation caused her to cry out, he was so tuned to her desires.

They'd parted ways in the early morning so Scott could go home for a shower and change of clothes. When Peyton walked into the clinic, she asked Devon if she had talked to Scott.

"He's here!" Devon said. "Did you know?"

"I talked to him last night," she said, smiling. "He's a freewheeling bachelor for a few days. I take it saying goodbye to Gabby was hard for the kids, so he left them with the grandmothers for a few days."

At that, Scott walked into the reception area. "The grandmothers drive me bat-shit crazy," he said. "But they can take on the task of buying new clothes. School starts for Will pretty soon, preschool for Jenny."

"I hope to meet these grandmothers someday to better understand," Devon said.

"Their next visit, they'll stay with you," he said. "How's our schedule today?"

"Light," Devon said. "I didn't expect you back, and I went easy on Peyton. Dr. Stewart came by yesterday afternoon, looked over the charts, approved Peyton's exams and procedures for the day. He's nice, by the way. Good choice."

"Thank you," Scott said with a smile.

"We had walk-ins yesterday, of course," Devon added.

"Nothing earthshaking," Peyton said. "Some allergies, a strained muscle, and I taped up a broken toe—the baby toe."

"I thought you talked to Scott last night," Devon said to her, clearly a little confused that she was left out of the loop.

"We didn't talk about work," Scott said.

"Oh. I see," Devon said, looking between them. "I hope you two didn't think you were fooling anyone, because you're very obvious."

"I wasn't fooling," Scott said.

"Me, either," Peyton said. "I really had no idea Scott was coming back right away."

"The grandmothers are thrilled," he said.

"I'm going to pull up the schedule and see how I'm spending the morning," Peyton said.

Once she was sitting at her desk, laptop open, her cell phone buzzed. She answered it briskly. "This is Peyton," she said.

"Hi," Ted said. "I need to talk to you."

"No, you don't," she said. "We have nothing to talk about. We had a clean break, remember?"

"It's serious," he said. "We have issues. Unfinished business."

"Take it up with Lindsey," she said, clicking off. The phone immediately buzzed again. *"What?"*

"Listen, Peyton, what would it take to get you to come up here and have a meeting with me?"

"Am I being investigated for malpractice? Non-feasance? Embezzlement?"

"Don't be ridiculous...."

"I'm not coming to Portland, Ted. Not now, not ever. You made your choices, some of them irrevocable, and I'm no longer a part of your life."

"Think of the patients! Think of the kids!"

"I'll think of them as much as you do. How's that? The answer is no." And she clicked off again.

Again the phone buzzed immediately. "This is the last time, then I stop answering."

"Things are not okay here," he said. "The practice is a mess, the office is falling apart, Lindsey can't do the job, can't do any job, the kids are in a state of mutiny, everything is chaos."

That gave her great satisfaction. She tried not to smile.

"Please," he said.

"I'm working, Ted. I'm very busy. And you made it clear you didn't need me. You didn't even need my help in the practice. Obviously you needed someone else. Good luck with that."

"Just tell me what it would take. Name a price."

"There is no amount of money in the world that would get me to Portland! You used me and then cut me loose. You cheated on me, and you didn't even have the decency to apologize for it!"

"What did you expect, Peyton? Really? I wasn't being taken care of at home, for God's sake. All we did was fight, and when I crawled into bed, I got your cold back! What did you really think that would do for our relationship?"

Scott walked into the office and put a cup of coffee on her desk.

"You ungrateful son of a bitch!" she hissed into the phone. "Don't call me again. You made your bed. Good luck."

She clicked off and looked up at Scott. "Ted."

"Glad to hear that was Ted," he said. "Otherwise we were going to have to start working on our patient communication skills."

The phone buzzed again, and she declined the call. "How do you block calls?"

"I don't know, Peyton. I've never blocked a call," he said.

"Devon!" she called. The young woman showed up in the office doorway, a stunned look on her face. She had never been summoned so rudely. Peyton held up her phone. "Do you know how to block calls on one of these?" Devon shook her head. "My ex is calling. He's going to keep calling. He's used to getting whatever he wants. I don't want to change my number—I have a hundred relatives. I want to keep him out. Can you find out how to block calls?"

Devon's features relaxed. "I think I know someone who will know. I'll get right on it. Want me to answer your phone in the meantime?"

"Oh, that would be nice," she said, holding it toward Devon.

"Or I could," Scott offered.

"No, not you. I don't want him to think I need a

man to stand up to him. I can stand up to him just fine. I just want to block him. I want to block his office numbers and his cell number."

"What kind of trouble is he in?" Scott asked.

"I don't know. I don't care. But I got the impression the new woman can't handle the work at the office and can't deal with the kids at home. I'd put money on it." She shook her head. "I thought, of all things, he was smart. But he couldn't figure out what the rest of us could see coming ten miles away."

An hour later, after thirty missed calls, the numbers were blocked. It turned out that Devon's best friend, Laine, had been an FBI Agent—she knew exactly what to do.

In that hour, Peyton did a little thinking. It was nearly lunchtime when she pulled Scott aside. "Listen, is there any chance you can get some time away? If Devon can clear the schedule, maybe we could drive up to Vancouver, pick up the kids and take them to the farm for the weekend."

"You sure? Because if you feel you should go to Portland—"

"I'm not going to Portland," she said vehemently.

"Think of closure, Peyton. Think of closing doors before you try to open new ones."

She ignored him. "It's crazy busy at the farm. We'd be crowded together. It might mean sleeping bags or someone's camper shell. They're picking pears—it's that time of year. Pears don't ripen on the tree like apples, they have to be picked before a freeze. There will be Lacoumettes all over the place. The kitchen will be full of dark-haired women cooking for an army, speaking strange languages, everything from French to Spanish to Basque to Ameri-Basque. And all over the farm—trucks, people, equipment everywhere. End of day, the wine is busted out, sometimes there's a big fire and dancing. It can be a lot of fun. The new lambs aren't too big, there's a Shetland pony, barn dogs and cats, chickens to chase. It's a circus. But it's my circus, and I think the kids might like it. It might take their minds off saying goodbye to Gabby."

He smiled. "Sounds like fun."

"We could drive up to Vancouver on Thursday. Back south to the farm on Friday. We could spend a couple of days and be back to work on Monday morning. If you can close the clinic and get coverage."

"Did Ted ever go to the farm? Ted and his kids?"

She nodded. "They were appalled. They thought we lived like dust-bowl peasants because our clothes got dirty and there was manure used as fertilizer all over. And everyone didn't have their own bathroom with whirlpool tub. There's not one walk-in closet on the property. There's only one TV. And it's Paco's, my father's. They were shocked."

He looked at her for a long moment. "The kids will be in heaven."

"Sometimes my mother serves squid," she said by way of warning.

"I tell Will and Jenny that everything is chicken. Let me make a couple of calls. We can move our appointments and direct our emergencies to Dr. Stewart's urgent care. So, Thursday?"

"Yes. Let's spend a little time with the grandmothers. Dinner Thursday night and breakfast in the morning? Then we can hit the farm Friday afternoon. And really, if it's too much, we can pack up and head back here. I know this is a little spontaneous," she said.

"Are you running away from Ted?"

"No, Ted is blocked! But I want to show you my world. *You* might want to rethink everything."

He took a step toward her and gave her a little kiss on her lips. His first demonstration of affection in the office. "I want to know your life. I want to be part of it. I want to call Ted and thank him for being such an impossible asshole."

There was a sound in the office doorway, and they both turned. Devon was leaning in the frame, arms crossed over her chest, smiling. "Now that's what I'm talking about."

"Were you spying? Eavesdropping?" Scott asked.

She nodded, still smiling. "I'll start working on the schedule."

"Devon, you were eavesdropping!"

"I know. Very few perks in this job. I'll get right on that schedule." And she turned and left them.

Thirteen

There was something so intimate and protected about a road trip. Peyton and Scott started out at seven in the morning, stopped for a leisurely breakfast in North Bend, then shot up the freeway to the Washington border. Within the privacy of the car, it was time for some details she hadn't previously shared. "It's not as though I didn't see the warning signs. I did. I thought they were warnings we could deal with. It felt like minutes after I moved into his house, he spent less time there. I confronted it immediately. I didn't mind the unofficial role as stepmother, but I knew his children needed his parenting. The kids competed with me and defied me, signs that they needed their father. He seemed to try, but too soon we were back to the routine of Ted being too busy. When I found myself sitting in parent-teacher conferences, I knew we were in serious trouble. And yet, I kept trying to turn it around."

"But didn't you work, too?" Scott asked.

"At least forty hours a week while they were in school or summer programs or occasionally at home under the housekeeper's supervision. Ted listened to the housekeeper. She would regularly threaten to quit if they made her life miserable. He would threaten the kids. 'If Mrs. Hardcastle quits, you will all go to boarding schools.' They would stay pretty invisible on her watch. But Mrs. Hardcastle didn't carpool or take them to doctor or orthodontist appointments. For that, someone would have to leave work, and it wasn't the cardiologist." She cringed. "Red flag."

"How did you plan to get around all these red flags?"

"By reasoning with him," she said. "By reasoning with *them*. I even tried to make friends with the ex-wife, to enlist her help with her kids. That was a futile exercise."

"How long did you try reasoning?"

She sighed. "Scott, those kids are in trouble. Literally. Conflicts at school, dropping grades, tantrums at home, ignoring rules. Pam was caught shoplifting once, Krissy had marijuana in her backpack, curfews were disregarded. Ted and I fought over discipline—he was inclined to just let things go while I wanted to bring the hammer down. Then there were two or three days a week when they'd be with their mother, and I could breathe deeply. I honestly don't know if they were well-behaved for her, or if she, like her ex-husband, ignored their antics. I'm inclined to think she ignored. Those kids would be better off raised by wolves."

"Yet you kept trying."

"I've been called stubborn. But I made a commitment," she said. "When I agreed to move in with Ted I thought I had a fighting chance of turning those kids around. I did everything I could."

"Sounds like it was a nightmare," Scott said. "It also sounds like you were stalwart. You gave a lot."

"In the beginning I think I had something to prove. That I hadn't made a mistake, that I wasn't delusional. I think I wanted to prove it wasn't that hard to be a good parent.... Shows what I know. That was closely followed by feeling like a fool. I'd complain to my mother or one of my sisters, and they'd say, 'Peyton, he just wants one more qualified person to work for him,' or 'Don't you see that he's taking much more than he's giving?' and it put me on the defensive. The last people you want to criticize you are family! Couldn't they see we were doing the best we could with three kids bruised by divorce? I realized I was still there because I was embarrassed to be a failure, to be an idiot. Almost nothing in my life was working. Well, those hours I spent with cardiac patients worked—that was the one thing I got from Ted and his practice—excellent training and experience in cardiology."

"So he was smart in that," Scott said.

"He's brilliant. I hate him like crazy right now, but if my mother had a heart problem, I'd probably take her to Ted. He's too arrogant to fail at that, even if he despises the patient."

"Listen, about that commitment thing," Scott

said. "It's admirable, but—sometimes you have to know when to walk away. At least you didn't quit too soon."

"My parents are very serious about commitment. It's the last bastion. The last barrier to fall. Your word is your life. I have one divorced brother. He was in agony with a crazy wife, and the entire Lacoumette family rallied to offer suggestion after suggestion, solution after possible solution. My brother George, the oldest son, finally said, 'Enough! Cut your losses!' And Matt bailed."

"And did everyone treat him like he failed?" Scott asked.

"In a subtle way. Sometimes among extended family someone would say, 'That's Matt, the divorced one.' Or it was implied he should have saved that commitment for someone he could partner with, which makes it his failure, doesn't it? I wonder what they'll say about me."

"Listen," he said, holding her hand across the front seat. "Commitment is great. Being sure is great, too. But sometimes we find ourselves up against things we can't control and couldn't have predicted. Then, letting go becomes a virtue. A tough one, though."

"Has that happened with you?"

He gave a nod. "The one that comes to mind was when I was eleven. It'll sound silly…."

"No, tell me," she said.

"I played softball. There was a rule to keep things fair—everyone gets to play. I was small. I wasn't that bad, but I was smaller than some of the ten-year-olds. I could hit a ball a mile even if I couldn't catch much. The coach left me on the bench week after week, giving me the requisite two innings to keep things fair. The coach's son was eleven, like me. He pitched every inning and was up to bat all the time. I wanted to quit, but my mother said no. She said I had made a commitment to the team, and they might need me at some point. She talked to the coach and said, 'You never let Scott play, this team isn't worth his energy or mine if he never gets a chance.' And the coach said, 'I'm playing him. Not a lot but the eleven-year-olds—this is their last year in this league and then they have to move on, so I'm giving them more opportunities.' And my mom informed him that I was also eleven, and he said, 'He is? I didn't realize that.' So the next week he benched me again—and I was the only kid on the bench. Nine- and ten-year-olds played while I warmed the bench. So my mom talked to him again, and the exchange was exactly the same. 'Oh? I didn't realize that.' By the fourth game of identical conversation, she told the coach she was pulling me off the team and writing a letter to the head of the league. A harsh letter." He chuckled. "You'll meet my mother tonight, and you'll probably have no trouble understanding the kind of letter she can write. But the moral to the story—I was getting screwed on that team. I needed to walk away. I needed some family support to do that."

"I was raised in a pretty black-and-white world order...."

"But did they urge you to try harder with Ted and his family?" Scott asked.

"Ironically, not at all. They asked me what I was doing. They pointed out that he was not like 'our people.' Which of course, made me try harder to prove I knew what I was doing."

He chuckled. "I'm not surprised. So, can we talk about you and me? When it comes to things like commitment—I appreciate it. Respect it. But I don't want you to stay one day longer than you feel is right for you. Just because you said three months, I won't hold you to it. I like commitment, but I like intelligent, adult choices even more. I don't want a reluctant PA. I *really* don't want a reluctant lover filled with doubts, struggling to find some happiness in the ruins."

"Scott, you don't have a reluctant lover. Have I done one thing to give you the impression I doubt my choices so far?"

He pulled her hand to his lips and kissed it. "Not one. Which is why I'm such a happy man. But promise, you don't stay if it's not working."

"You think just because we get along so well and have such great sex, it'll stay perfect? Forever?"

He laughed at her. "You think I didn't ever fight with Serena?" He whistled. "We had some beauts. I even slept at the hospital a couple of nights. That really pissed her off. I was probably tired and grouchy, but...underneath it all, we knew we could work things out. Deep down, we knew at the core of things, we were good together. I never doubted that." He glanced at her. "You doubted with Ted, yet you stayed."

Doubted? She *knew!* She just had a hard time facing it.

"You don't have to do that with me," he said.

"One thing I feel sure about is it won't be your kids who drive me away...."

"Oh-ho, we have our issues, Peyton. You haven't been present for one of Will's legendary meltdowns."

"And then what happens? What do you do?"

"It varies, because I'm never quite sure what to do. Sometimes he gets a time-out, sometimes he gets punished, sometimes I just put him in the shower. It's really hard to be taken seriously if you're naked, screaming your brains out under water."

She couldn't help but laugh. "But won't it break your heart if I leave you?" she asked. "Even a little bit?"

"It would break my heart to pieces. But it will heal. What would kill me is you staying with me by sheer dint of will when you know you should move on. Let's not do that to each other."

She threw him a gentle smile. In a whisper she said, "Let's not."

"You've probably come across a few red flags with me," he said.

"Just to save time, why don't you lay them out for me?" she suggested.

He laughed at her. "They're so obvious, Peyton. I'm poor for one thing—I still have some med school debt. I have a complicated family life. I have a ter-

rible schedule. I have a difficult mother and an annoying mother-in-law. I'm an incurable idealist—I
always think things will work out eventually—that
can be draining. My kids are pretty cute right now,
but one of them might have pot in a backpack someday. I don't know. I'm messy—I use my car as an office. Devon will tell you, paperwork makes my eyes
roll back in my head. I don't dance… Oh, that's right,
you experienced that for yourself. I can't cook, but
I'm good at laundry."

He wasn't messy, she thought. And he wouldn't
ignore pot in the backpack.

"That's a pretty scary list," she said. "I'll have to
give this some more thought."

"You do that."

When they arrived at Scott's mother's house, the
kids came flying out the front door. "Peyton's here!
Peyton, Peyton!" They completely ignored Scott and
wrapped their little arms around Peyton's legs. She
tried to ignore the way their arms felt, the way their
smiles and shining eyes filled her up inside. She
could not afford to fall in love with them.

Scott's mother, Patricia, was a small woman of
angular lines, but she had a very tall personality.
Her hair was colored a soft brown with blond high-
lights, teased for height, her nails were manicured
and shiny red, she wore plenty of makeup and she
was businesslike. "You look tired, Scott. You're not
getting enough rest."

Indeed, he had not, Peyton thought with a slight blush. And it had been glorious.

"You saw me a few days ago, Mother. I've gotten plenty of rest since then."

"I wonder if you take care of yourself," she said. "Do you eat right?"

"Yes," he said. "Enough," he added. "Stop it."

Patricia was a paralegal who managed a law office, and Peyton had no trouble imagining all the partners taking orders from her. And she could also see where Scott got at least some of his good looks; Patricia was a fetching woman. She had never remarried after her husband's premature death, and Peyton found that surprising.

Suzanne, his mother-in-law, was softer, rounder, seemed more nurturing and kind of cuddly. She had a quick smile, a high-pitched laugh, plump hands with clipped nails, had let her hair go gray in a very attractive short cut. At first glance she seemed far less threatening than Patricia, but Peyton knew looks could be misleading. "Scott, the kids are so well behaved, Serena would be so pleased with how well you manage with them. Nice to meet you, Peyton. Are you and Scott dating?" she said.

"That's really not our business, Suzanne," Patricia said. "Are you?"

"We've been out to dinner a couple of times," Scott said.

"So, are you single? Widowed? Divorced?" Suzanne asked.

My God, these women are as bad as my mother! "Single," she said after a moment of hesitation.

Scott had been so right. Within ten minutes Peyton could see that these women might be polar opposites, but were bent on a single mission—to have control over their grandchildren. Suzanne was Grammy and Patricia was GiGi—they were even named appropriately.

Scott's older sister, Nancy, showed up for dinner with a twelve-year-old son and a fourteen-year-old daughter. Aside from being thrilled to see their uncle Scott, they were self-contained—iPad, texting, TV—entertaining themselves while listening should Patricia ask them to do something or inquire as to what occupied them.

If Peyton had been a little intimidated by the grandmothers, Nancy put her quickly at ease. "I didn't think I'd get a chance to meet you unless I went to Thunder Point to see Scott. He talks about you, you know. I know he got you in the clinic by sheer accident. He claims you are a much sought-after PA who happened to be in the area right when he was looking for help."

"That pretty much sums it up, though I don't know about the much sought-after part," Peyton said.

"She has a great deal of experience," Scott said. "She suggested we show the kids her family's farm— a quick weekend before school starts."

"Tell me about the farm," Nancy begged. "What kind of farm?"

Peyton happily explained about the pears, potatoes and sheep, about the huge extended family that included Uncle Sal and Aunt Sophie's vineyard, Lucas's Basque restaurant in San Francisco, Adele having a baby soon, the side of the family that fished off the coast near Tillamook. There were other family farms and restaurants and fishing fleets between Portland and Reno. "There will be a lot of people around the farm this weekend, picking pears, getting ready to dig up potatoes. Then my family will end up at the vineyard for a few days between the pears and potatoes to help harvest the grapes. In the spring it's lambing and shearing. They have to get the wool off early so the sheep can get good sweaters before the cold comes. All the kids love the lambing season. They're not that crazy about picking pears."

"And where do the pears go?"

"Mostly to Harry & David and surrounding food retailers. Potatoes go to a lot of restaurant suppliers, grocery chains and Frito-Lay. It's a pretty large farm."

"What a wonderful way to grow up," Nancy said.

"It's a demanding way to grow up. My father brags that he takes them off the breast and into the grove or fields."

"What kind of talk is that?" Patricia asked tartly.

Peyton laughed. "That's a proud Basque farmer talking. He swears he took it right out of the Old Testament, but I suspect that's pure legend, not fact. He also claims we descended from royalty and my mother whispers that that's bull. Basque businessmen, fishermen and landholders like a lot of family

to help them get the job done. I have three sisters
and four brothers and too many aunts, uncles and
cousins to count."

When Suzanne took the kids outside to wear off
a little energy before dinner, Peyton casually remarked, "She seems like a sweet lady."

And Patricia, busy over by the sink said, "You
don't want to get on her bad side."

Peyton covered her laugh with a hand. She sat
with Nancy at the kitchen table while Patricia put-
tered with food, yet obviously hadn't missed a word
of their conversation.

"The pot speaketh of the kettle," Nancy said with
a laugh.

Peyton was put to bed in Patricia's craft room
while Scott and the kids shared the guest room. She
actually had a very nice time, but it wasn't hard to
understand his decision to get out of Dodge.

In the morning, they were up early. Scott took
over the kitchen and made a big breakfast for everyone. Of course, Suzanne was there, but Nancy
and her kids declined. Once he had filled his kids
with food and run them around the block a couple
of times, they were off in the direction of Portland
as the farm was southeast of that city. The kids, in
their safety seats, had their little movies to occupy
them, and within a half hour, they were out cold.

It seemed that was just the moment Scott had been
waiting for. At the very next rest stop, he pulled over
and parked under some big, leafy trees, unsnapped
his seat belt and turned to Peyton. He grabbed her

chin in a hand and kissed her. "I don't like not sleeping with you," he said softly. "I'm sorry about the craft room. I don't think my mother even does crafts!"

"It was just fine," she said with a laugh. "I can't wait to see where my parents put you for the night. Do you like chickens?"

"Was it unbearable? The visit?"

"Not at all," she said. "The grandmothers are a little intense in their own individual ways, but their hearts are in the right place—they love their grandchildren. Are they always like that?"

"Always. They don't spend any time together that doesn't include Jenny and Will. Before Will came along, it was the same with Serena and me—everything had to be perfectly divided or there was hell to pay in the form of guilt and badgering. We only spent a few years in Vancouver, always looking for an opportunity elsewhere."

"Didn't your mothers realize they were driving you away?"

"Of course not," he said. "Not even when we said so. But with the kids, they have this interesting division of duties. Suzanne spoils and plays, Patricia teaches and disciplines. Suzanne excuses, Patricia praises. Suzanne fusses, Patricia rewards. They need all of it. They're in heaven. As long as they're not a pressure on the kids, I can deal with them. At least they're getting old enough to spend time in Vancouver without me. I can take them up there, spend a day or two, leave them for a couple of weeks, go back for them." He grinned at her. "Thunder Point was pure genius. For a lot of reasons." And then he kissed her again.

"You'd better get it all out of your system, Dr. Grant. My family is completely different but no less challenging. Don't be too surprised if my mother or father takes you aside and questions our relationship and your intentions."

"I have the best intentions in the world. It's your intentions that need a little work."

"My parents are actually more progressive than a lot of the family. They knew I lived with Ted. They still put us in separate bedrooms, but they knew. They're good, except when they're plotting to arrange marriages."

"Seriously?" he asked.

"A time-honored custom. Their kids were not very excited by the notion and didn't want the assistance. I suspect meddling, just the same. I don't think Lucas and Adele are purely an accident, even if she did do some PR work for his restaurant."

"Just make out with me a little before we take on the next family challenge."

She giggled and put her arms around his neck, kissing him intensely.

"Dad?" Will said from the backseat. "We there?"

Scott let go of her reluctantly. "Almost," he said. "Not much longer. Watch your movie."

Even with all of Peyton's description, nothing could have prepared Scott for the farm. When they pulled into the yard the dogs were set to barking and that brought a woman of around sixty to the porch. She was tall and slim like Peyton, wore jeans and laced boots, a gingham blouse over a tank top, and her long hair was pulled up into a clip. Her hair was dark like Peyton's, with the slightest bit of gray threaded through it. Her face was rosy with health, and her smile was bright, her lips red. She was drying her hands on a towel, and she began waving at the car.

Scott parked and helped Will out of his seat while Peyton helped Jenny. Their feet had barely touched the ground when Mrs. Lacoumette was swinging her dish towel over her head, yelling, "Hurry, hurry, hurry! We have so much to do!" Then she crouched down to better receive the kids. "Well, now, you must be Will! And you would be Jenny! Are you hungry? Need the bathroom? We can have a snack, take care of business, then it's time to collect the eggs. Do you know how to collect eggs?"

They just shook their heads in wonder, making Scott laugh.

She extended her hand. "Dr. Grant, we're so pleased to have you join us."

"Please, it's Scott."

"And I'm Corinne, Peyton's mother. Come in, everyone."

Parked between the house and barn was a very large semitrailer surrounded by trucks and cars. The sound of engines of all types could be heard, but they seemed to be far off. Then a pickup truck pulled up next to the trailer, and two men leaped out, grabbing bags of what he assumed to be pears and loading them in the trailer. He watched for a moment, and they were quickly done and off they went.

Scott was the last one inside. He found his children had been swept up in kitchen activity. He counted five women including Corinne, all busy with chores. One was white-haired and at least eighty years old, one was around Peyton's age and embraced her, three were Corinne's approximate age, all dark-haired, all working at meal preparations. Pots were steaming, vegetables were being peeled, sliced and diced, meat was searing, bread dough was rising.

Garlic and drying herbs hung from the shelf over a triple wide sink, scoured pans hung over the work island, and extra-large cooking spoons occupied big ceramic pots. The stove was commercial size—three ovens and six burners. There were several wooden knife caddies on the countertops. Jars of all shapes and sizes lined the counters and held ground spices, flour, sugar, grains, pastes and liquids he couldn't possibly identify. Linens were folded and stacked on several open shelves, dishes and glassware were neatly stored in glass-front cupboards and there were drawers full of eating implements. This wasn't a kitchen. It was a cooking and eating factory. The pots and pans in use on the stove were very large, large enough to imply an army would be eating here.

Corinne swung the kids up on to stools at the long breakfast bar. She opened the refrigerator and pulled out two already-prepared sandwiches, then she ladled a little soup into two soup cups. She poured milk, shook out napkins, brought out spoons—all done like a woman who knew how to feed eight children in just minutes. Then she smiled at him. "Can I get you something to eat, Dr. Grant?"

"He can always eat, Mama," Peyton said. "He has an unbelievable appetite. Scott, this is grand-mamma Josephina, Aunt Sophia, Aunt Maria, my cousin Maida. Maida only cooks for momentous occasions, like harvest and holidays."

"Tell him, I'm very good," Maida insisted with a smile.

"She's very good," Peyton agreed with a laugh.

"Do not eat that," the woman introduced as Sophia said to the kids, pointing at the soup. She reached into the freezer and pulled out two chips of ice. "First, stir this around the bowl, test with your upper lip, this part here," she said, pointing. "If you need, I'll give you another ice. Not to burn your tongue. We have much eating to do today!"

Food was being scooped from all kinds of places on to a large plate. Vegetables, salad, meat, more meat, sauce, a bowl of soup, beans and creamy pota-toes. It was placed before Scott, a napkin appeared—all the napkins were cloth—utensils came out. A basket, almost big enough to be a laundry basket, was full of bread in many different shapes. Corinne tore off a large chunk of a French loaf and put it on the edge of his plate. "Just a little sampling for you, Dr. Grant."

"Are you ever going to call me Scott?" he asked.

"Perhaps on your next visit," she said, but her smile was very mischievous.

"All right, Mrs. Lacoumette," he said. He picked up his fork and tried some beans. He chewed. His eyes closed. He took a deep breath and said, "Ahhhh."

All eyes turned to him. Corinne frowned. "It's not good?"

"It's amazing!" he said. "Amazing!"

There was a collective sigh and smiles all around. He suspected he'd passed the first test, but it wasn't much of a challenge as everything he put in his mouth just sent him to heaven. The meat was tenderized with spices he didn't recognize. The greens were unlike anything he'd ever tasted. He dipped into the soup and grunted, and once again, all the eyes turned to him. "Good," he said, relaxing their sharp stares. "Very, very good."

He hadn't even noticed that Peyton had disappeared, but she was back, her clothing changed. She wore rough, worn jeans, work boots and a sweatshirt with cut-off sleeves. She helped herself to a small bowl of beans and a large chunk of bread and sat down beside him.

"When we've eaten, get the suitcases. Jenny's sandals will have to be replaced with tennis shoes. Will's good, but it might get chilly in the orchard. They'll need their sweatshirts. Can you dig out your old jeans?"

He nodded, his mouth full. Was she putting him to work straightaway?

He took a forkful of a tender fish or something. "What is this?" he asked.

She leaned close and said, *"Txipirones en su tinta.* Calamari. Squid. Cooked with Mama's tomatoes, onions and garlic."

"So tender," he said. "I'm used to calamari being chewy."

"Pah! Not in this house!" Corinne said. "It is *el punto.* Cooked the right way, the Basque way."

He was going to like her. He tasted the soup and murmured his approval. Delicious.

"Potato and chorizo with Mama's tomatoes," Peyton said. She pointed to his plate and identified lamb, tenderized beef, the pinto and kidney beans and greens. "There will be lamb stew later—you'll faint it's so good. And some things you can try if you like. Oxtail soup, beef tongue, tuna belly." She grinned. "No obligation."

Scott ate everything and even had seconds of the squid, lamb, beans and soup. A little extra bread to dip into the beans and soup. This made Peyton's mother smile broadly and brag a little about the food coming for dinner. It was time for Scott to bring in the luggage, to find his jeans and Jenny's tennis shoes. He groaned when he stood.

"I knew you went overboard," Peyton said. "Get going, move around a little bit. We have to get Mama's eggs, then we can visit the animals. Tomorrow I'll take you over to my brother's, and the kids can see the lambs. Come on, Scott."

"Maybe we should lay down in the hayloft for a while...."

"Oh, you're going to make a bad impression."

"Your mother loves me—I cleaned my plate. Twice."

"And had to be stopped before you did it a third time. Come on!"

The kids scampered along with Peyton to the chicken coop; Scott followed more slowly. "We should hurry to get the eggs. Mama saved them for you, I think. She's usually out here early. We need a lot, so I hope the hens haven't been lazy." They had to shoo the dogs away, and Peyton stomped at a couple of roosters, sending them skittering off. The kids were a little hesitant until she told them the chickens were gentle and rarely pecked, being used to having their eggs collected every day. Then she showed them how to slip a gentle hand under a hen and pull out an egg. She put her hand over Will's and guided him, whispering, "Please, don't squeeze the egg. It's very fragile. Hold it light as a feather." When he got the first one, he lit up.

"Me," Jenny said. "Now me!"

"Shh, no jumping up and down. We have to stay very calm around the hens or they'll get upset, and hens who are upset can't lay eggs."

"How do they lay the eggs?" Will asked.

"Well, I've never actually seen it happen, but the eggs are carried inside them, and they settle on the nest, and when the eggs are ready, the hens push them out."

"Like babies?"

"Like babies," Peyton said. "Jenny, let's get the next egg together. Put your hand under mine. When you feel the egg, tell me."

"I feel it!" she whispered. "I feel two!"

"Jackpot," Peyton said. "Bring them out one at a time."

By the time they'd collected a half dozen, the kids could do it without Peyton's hand. They pulled out another half dozen, a very good crop. Corinne was impressed and praised Will and Jenny.

Scott was looking as if he might need a nap. But she dragged him along to the barn. The kids met the few cows and goats, but the popular winner was the miniature pony. Peyton put a lead on him and brought him into the corral so the kids could take turns on his back. Jenny was chased by a rooster, Will was nipped by a goat, but even so, it was a completely positive barnyard tour.

Chasing dogs, cuddling kittens, racing through the barn—it all served to wear them down. And then, as the sun was lowering, a parade of people started returning to the house. Men, a few women, teenage boys and girls, all looking weary and dirty. They washed up in the barn and in the outdoor vegetable sink on the back porch.

"Time for dinner," Peyton said. "Can you take the kids inside and get them cleaned up for dinner?"

"Change their clothes?" he asked.

"Just brush them off outside and take them to the upstairs bathroom to wash hands and faces. That should do. These guys aren't going to get dressed up to eat. They'll probably fall into bed right after dinner."

When Scott got inside, he saw the table was set for many—at least twenty. He was introduced to Uncle Sal who was putting open bottles of wine on the table. Aunt Sophia was adding pitchers of tea and lemonade. Platters and tureens and bowls were being readied in the kitchen, and a great hodgepodge of people migrated to the table. Aside from being introduced to Peyton's father, commonly known in the family as Paco, there was very little talking. Everyone, it appeared, was tired to the bone. But then wine was poured, tapas came out, a couple of baskets of bread were put on the table along with olive oil and some kind of fish paste. And with the wine, conversation loosened up. By the time the first tureen of soup arrived, there was laughter. Scott was asked who his people were, where he came from, what his town was like, how his clinic was getting along. Paco soon shifted his attention to Will and Jenny, made a place for each of them beside him, sharing his bread, making them laugh.

"What meat do you like?" he asked Will. "Sausage? Lamb? Chicken?"

Will shrugged. "Are they the same chickens? Because I got their eggs today, and I liked them."

"You'll get around that. Corinne, bring the boy pears and cheese!" Paco yelled. And then to Jenny, he said, "Do you like potatoes and beans? Corinne, soup for my guest!"

The platters of meat came out, and Paco showed the kids how to gnaw the lamb off the bone, and they tried it, both of them liking it. They ate tapas, not realizing there was fish lying atop the pimento and cheese slice. Paco was large and robust, with the broad shoulders of a man who had been physically challenged by hard work every day of his life.

Dinner was a social event that went on for some time, but immediately following the meal, everyone who had worked in the orchard drifted off, headed straight for bed. The women gathered in the kitchen both to clean up and store food and to eat, gossip and laugh around the work island. Peyton's brother George took some of his relatives across the property to his house, Corinne and Paco put up several in their house, there was one RV and one fifth wheel that housed more aunts, uncles and cousins. Scott was given a room with two bunk beds in it.

On Saturday, Peyton drove them around the property in a Rhino, a vehicle perfect for getting around the farm. They saw the orchard, the potato fields and George's sheep. It was a long and busy day.

Dinner that night started out the same, but it didn't end with exhausted workers headed for bed. A fire was built behind the house, and there were chairs surrounding it. Everyone gathered, and a few instruments came out—a clarinet, a drum, an accordion, a horn. Music began to serve as a backdrop to conversation. Some men lit thin cigars or pipes, and wine bottles were passed around.

And then Uncle Sal got up and began to dance.

Paco followed his brother. George joined them, and within a few minutes there were a couple of teenage boys joining in the traditional dance. If they'd been wearing their cultural garb of white with red vests and caps it would have felt like a Basque festival, but these were tired yet energized men who had worked hard all day and wore the dress of farmers. And they danced like young men, whooping, slapping the air, grinning, twirling, kicking.

Paco pulled Will into the group, and he looked completely confused, then one of the teenagers showed him a couple of steps and kicks, and he was immediately into it.

Peyton grabbed little Jenny's hand and took her behind all the chairs and danced around with her. Some of the girls and women clapped for the dancing men.

And Scott thought, *I'm on another planet.* It was like a fairy tale filled with excellent food, great wine, good cheer, celebration. Then the thing that brought it all home for him happened. Paco grabbed his wife of over thirty-five years and planted a big kiss on her mouth, holding her tight for a moment, laughing lustfully as she tried to get away from his coltish playfulness.

They were still hot for each other after all the hard years and eight kids. That was perfect.

Scott and the kids headed for bed before the older men gave up their wine, cigars, dance and laughter. Peyton went into the house with him, helping to get the kids bathed. "We can leave in the morning. The harvest is done until next Friday. Tomorrow they'll all go to church and then home. Papa will send pears, slaughtered and frozen lamb and extra food with them all. When they help Uncle Sal at the vineyard, they bring home many bottles of wine—that's the best. Are you exhausted?"

"I'm exhausted," Scott said. "The kids have had the time of their lives. I think this was better than Disneyland!"

"They'll be asleep in seconds. Let's go out to the front porch swing and snuggle up for a little while. In the morning we'll head back to Thunder Point. I'll talk Mama out of some of your favorite dishes," she said.

"Ohhh." He sighed. "You are a dream come true."

"And you, Dr. Grant, are a glutton!"

Fourteen

It was the first week of September, school had started for Will. Jenny and Mercy were attending a preschool in Bandon three days a week, with Eve McCain babysitting the other two days. And Scott Grant felt truly alive for the first time in four years.

He tried to play his cards close to his vest, not behave too demonstratively, but when he touched Peyton, his feelings were as raw and honest as they could possibly be. And naturally, since Scott had no guile, his words followed suit, especially when they made love. Nuzzling her neck, he asked. "Do you know what your skin smells like?"

"Yes. Right now it smells like you," she said with laughter in her voice.

"Before it smells like me, it smells like rain. And faintly of flowers. And freshly washed linens. I can't get enough. It's intoxicating. Do you know what you taste like?"

"You?"

"Before that, you're candy floss and champagne. Sweet and delicious and so soft on my tongue."

They had been changed by their few days away and talked endlessly about their families and the differences in where they'd come from, even though they'd actually grown up just a hundred miles apart. It hadn't exactly been planned, yet it did a lot to cement their relationship. Now all he could do was hope that Peyton was beginning to feel the same way. She was everything he had wanted in a woman for such a long time.

They fell into a nice routine in the clinic the week after their trips to Vancouver and the farm. Peyton had some ideas and suggestions for improvements— for one thing, she felt strongly that the clinic needed an X-ray machine. When Scott told her he had considered that when money loosened up a little bit, she began drafting grant proposals. The clinic assisted so many patients on federal and state entitlement medical programs, and there was grant money available. Not only did she begin researching qualifications and drafting copy, she brought Devon up to speed on the process, increasing her already impressive office skills.

It was Friday, and the clinic was empty of patients at the lunch hour. Devon had gone across the street to the diner for a bite to eat, Peyton was busy at the computer in Scott's office and Scott was sitting at Devon's desk in reception looking through patient notes. A man walked in. Scott knew who he was immediately. He was either Superman or Ted

Ramsdale. He was exactly as Peyton had described him. Six-two, thick dark hair, broad shoulders, a face handsome enough for feature films, chiseled enough to cut glass. And above all, poised and confident.

"Hello," Scott said, standing from the desk. "Can I help you?"

"Dr. Ramsdale, here to see Peyton Lacoumette."

Scott was a healthy six feet tall, yet this man with his square jaw and piercing blue eyes somehow made him feel puny. "Let me tell her you're here," he said. But when he turned toward the back of the clinic, Peyton was already standing in the hallway.

"What can I do for you, Ted?" she asked smoothly.

Ted looked around briefly. "Is there a place we can have a private conversation?"

"Scott, is your office available for a few minutes?"

"Of course," he said.

He watched as Ted let himself through the break in the counter and followed Peyton down the hallway. He noticed that Ted reached out to grab her elbow as if to escort her, and she shook him loose, throwing a grimace over her shoulder at him. Scott wished he hadn't even seen that. He was afraid it would fill him with false hope. He stood at the counter. He let out his breath. *Wow. He came after her.*

And then Scott overheard them speaking.

"Peyton, what the hell are you doing here?"

"Well, I'm practicing in a clinic. And it's going to be a very busy afternoon, so, please, get right to the point," she said.

"Peyton, with your ability you deserve far better than this little dump."

"This is a very respectable clinic, Ted. We have an outstanding staff. We do good work here. If you're just going to be insulting, please, leave. At once."

"Stop, stop, I didn't come here to discuss your current place of employment. We have to talk about us. We had our problems, but I think we can work them out. We were a very good team, and I'm not managing very well without you. I didn't realize how much you meant to me until you were gone, and now…I really need you back."

"I'm sorry to hear that," she said. "I'm sure you'll find a way to manage."

"I'll do whatever it takes, Peyton. I need you back in Portland. The kids need you."

"I'm sure Lindsey will be more than happy to lend a hand," she said.

"Look, I know you're very upset about Lindsey, and I admit, it was a terrible mistake on my part and I'm sorry. She's out of the picture. She's gone, and I have to straighten out this mess with you."

"Out of the picture," Peyton said slowly. "Aren't you expecting a baby with her? A baby you created while we were a couple? While we were still living and sleeping together!"

"We've been over that. You were freezing me out, ending it with me. It's no excuse, but that's how it was at the time. I might not have made the best decision, but there certainly was provocation. It's reasonable I'd turn somewhere. But that's over, so—"

"No, Ted, it's not over. What about the baby?"

"I'll support her and the baby, but she'll have to work elsewhere. I should have known better than to fall into that trap. Now, what's it going to take, Peyton? I have more problems than I can count since you left, and I'm sorry. I regret damn near everything, especially her."

Scott was shaking his head in absolute awe. *He did that to her? And he expects her to accept his apology and come back?*

"You're too late," she said. "I have no intention of going back to Portland."

"You have to listen to reason," he said. "I want you to—"

Scott took quick steps back to his office. He swung the door open without knocking, and Ted whirled around with a scowl on his face. "As fascinating as I'm finding this conversation, I've already heard too much," Scott said. "I need you to take it out of here. Now."

"I have appointments soon, Scott. Ted and I are finished talking. I have a busy afternoon ahead," Peyton said.

"I'll cover for you. It sounds like you have things to settle. Go, settle them."

"Apparently there's no privacy in this clinic," Ted said. "Let's go somewhere we can talk. How about your place? You do have a place around here somewhere?"

"We'll walk down to the dock at the marina. You're not coming to my house," she said. She grabbed her sweater and headed past both men, down the hall and out the clinic's front door.

Ted followed her, and Scott watched them leave together. From the clinic's window he saw them cross the street and head down the hill toward the marina. Devon was on her way back from the diner, carrying a couple of take-out cartons—one for him, one for Peyton. He had completely lost his appetite.

Devon came into the clinic, still looking over her shoulder. "Who's the good-looking guy with Peyton?"

"The ex," Scott said.

"Does that Lamborghini belong to him?"

Scott leaned over the counter to look out the window. "Probably," he said.

"Where are they going?" she asked.

He watched as Ted dropped an arm around Peyton's shoulders, and she stepped away, escaping his touch. "Down to the bay so he can demonstrate walking on water," he said. Then he turned and went into his office, closing the door.

Peyton was stunned to see Ted at first, then realized she shouldn't have been surprised. She knew the man. He believed he could turn any situation to his advantage.

"Let's just get something straight," she said. "I had plenty of legitimate complaints about our relationship, but I always trusted you to be honest and faithful. You might be over this infidelity, but I'm not. For all I know, there might've been others.

There's no way I'll ever trust you again, no way I'm willing to take that kind of chance. Tampering with Lindsey was a fool's move, but the next time, you might find a woman of more maturity and substance, a woman you can actually move on to, leaving me devastated and broken all over again. No, Ted. I'm not going there. No way."

"You were devastated?" he asked a little too hopefully.

"I'm over it," she snapped. "I'm over you! I can't believe you. Lindsey didn't quite measure up, and you ousted her. For God's sake, can't you at least take responsibility? Or is this just one more child for you to throw money at and ignore? How many more will there be?"

"No more, and that's a guarantee. I've done what I should've done years ago and had a vasectomy. But that's not the point. The point is—"

She laughed outright. "Oh, but it's a very good point, let's stay on it. Now you're completely safe, except for disease, of course. Now you can screw around without the possibility of pregnancy. How very clever!"

There was a painful clench in her chest. Before Ted's home became too much to bear, she had wondered if she would perhaps have a child of her own. It was a decision that had to be made sooner rather than later. It wasn't very long after getting to know his children that she'd decided she'd never bring a baby into that household. She stomped off ahead of him, and he grabbed her arm, spinning her around.

"Are you listening to me? I made a terrible mistake! I have regrets. I'm sorry, more sorry than you can imagine, and I believe I can make it up to you. And I'm not going to ignore the child. I'm having documents drawn for support and visitation— everything necessary to be responsible and meet my obligations. No matter what you think of me, I have never ignored my responsibilities!"

She shook free of his grip and said, "Don't you ever lay hands on me again or I'll have you arrested, you son of a bitch!"

"Sorry," he said. "Sorry. You make me desperate. For God's sake, am I not getting through to you? I need you. The kids need you!"

"How many need me, Ted? The three that probably threw a party when I left? Or three plus a baby who will be *visiting?*"

He lifted his hands again, as if he might grab her upper arms, but then he dropped them to his sides. His face was a little twisted, and he glanced away as if looking for some courage or inspiration. "You were right about them. The kids. You were right about *me*. I should've listened to you. They needed a firm hand. They needed discipline, and I fought you. I don't even know why, but I just didn't want to think they were that much trouble. When I was around, there weren't many problems. I was confused. You were so angry with them, but when I was around, they were mostly fine."

"You weren't ever around!"

"I see that now. I realize now, I should have listened to you."

"Fine. There's still time," she said. "Take a firmer hand now."

"That won't be enough," he said dismally.

"Ted! Get into counseling. With them. Learn to be a better parent. Learn to show your children you love them enough to be sure they're safe, and help them learn to respect themselves and their family. For God's sake, I can't do it for you!"

He looked at his feet. "Krissy's pregnant," he said.

That silenced her. *Krissy? Fifteen-year-old Krissy?* "Oh, God," she said. She backed away from him and sat on one of the pilings holding up the dock. "How pregnant?" she asked weakly.

"Not very. Six or eight weeks. She got scared and told her mother. Her mother called me."

"She must be terrified," Peyton said.

"She's a wreck. Her mother didn't prepare her for this."

"Did *you?*" she asked.

"Me? I'm her father!"

"My point," she said, shaking her head. She stood, surprised to find her legs were trembling. "Ted, I can't fix this for you. You have to get some family counseling, maybe get her mother involved. Krissy needs some family support right now. You all have decisions to make, and it's very important that everyone is on board, going forward with this family event."

"The decision is made," he said. "She'll terminate."

"That's what she wants?" Peyton asked.

"It doesn't matter what she wants! She's fifteen!"

"Oh, God," Peyton said. "Is Krissy okay with that decision?"

"She'd better get okay with it because she's fifteen, and that's what's going to happen!"

Peyton swallowed. She hated herself for even asking the next question. She didn't particularly like Krissy. Krissy had always been mean and selfish around her. She was a horrible fifteen-year-old. She had lied, defied and treated Peyton not just disrespectfully but cruelly. But she was fifteen and pregnant. "Ted, has Krissy told you what she wants?"

"Irrelevant," he said with a wave of his hand.

"What did she say?" Peyton asked.

"She thinks she wants to keep it, but that's absurd. She can't be a mother, she's too young, she's in high school. She'll terminate."

"Oh, man," Peyton said, shaking her head. "You can't force her to terminate the pregnancy. You guys need an intervention in the worst way."

"What do you care? You're pro-choice!"

She sighed and shook her head in frustration. How had she managed to ignore this side of him until she was giving up, until she was leaving him? Was it because in the beginning he hadn't acted that way toward her? She took a deep breath. "Actually, you don't know anything about my politics, but it appears you think *you're* pro-choice, though I'd have to wonder if you even know what it means. *Choice,* Ted. Not pro-abortion. As far as I know, there is no pro-abortion network. I'd never condone forcing a woman to terminate a pregnancy. What the hell do you think a choice is?"

"Bullshit! I've seen you at work in my practice with women who jeopardize their lives with pregnancy because of their cardiac condition! I've seen you!"

"No, you haven't," she said coolly. It was true, they'd had the rare patient who couldn't survive a full-term pregnancy, and neither could the fetus. It was an awful situation, one rife with heartbreak. "My patients get the facts, the best information I have, but I would never force anyone to make a decision that they'd always regret. Not even if it threatened their life—that's not my decision. It's the patient's decision. Krissy could be irreparably damaged by being forced to do something she's violently opposed to. It could be harder for her to recover from that than from early motherhood. Besides, there are other options. There's adoption. There's even open adoption. Oh, Ted, talk to your daughter."

"That's her mother's job!"

"It's also yours!" she shouted. Suddenly she realized her forehead had broken out in a sweat, and she wiped it with her palm. "Listen, Ted, I can't help you. Even if I wanted to, I couldn't help you. Krissy has never listened to a thing I've said. She hates me. If she doesn't actually hate me, she definitely resents me. I would be of no use to you. You're on your own."

She walked past him, heading for the clinic.

"Peyton, please," he said. "Please. There isn't anyone else to ask."

She slowly turned back. "Yes, Ted. There are lots of people to ask. Call an OB. Maybe a women's health NP. Tell them what you're up against and ask for some real high-end counseling. Explain you're divorced, a single father, you're up a creek and you don't know how to help your fifteen-year-old daughter, but you need to hear all the options. If you can't think of anyone, ask the triage nurse in your practice—she's very savvy. She can point you in the right direction. But don't come back here and ask me. When all I wanted in the world was to love you and your kids, none of you cared. You didn't help. You didn't support me, and then you betrayed my trust." She started walking again, then she turned back toward him. "My God, did you really think I'd go back to your practice and your house?"

"I hoped," he said.

"Ted, why did you fight for joint custody when you and Olivia divorced?"

"Don't make this about my divorce! I've always loved my kids!"

"I think you really believe that, but you've never spent time with them. You never gave up a golf game to be with them."

"I worked like a bloody slave to make sure they had everything they needed, that they'd have a decent school, a good house, a college savings…."

"That's all money. Most of my college was paid

for by scholarship. I also worked and saved. Did you think I'd take care of your office, your three kids, your new baby *and* a grandchild? Did you?"

He didn't answer right away. "You have no idea how much I need you."

"And here I thought you loved me," she said softly.

"I do love you! I've always loved you! I tried to show it."

"Why didn't I know this about you?" she asked in a soft voice. "I thought you at least loved your kids in your own clumsy, inadequate way. I thought you were just too permissive, but you just couldn't be bothered." She shook her head. "Those poor kids. They're going to be such a mess, and they have nowhere to turn."

"You could help," he said. "I'll do anything you say."

She shook her head. "I can't help you. Ted, I don't love you."

"You did once," he argued. "You could love me again."

"No. I can't manufacture that just because it's what you want."

"We could try one more time."

"No," she said firmly. "What you have to do is admit your mistakes, live with them and take responsibility."

"What is it you think I'm doing?"

"Trying to get someone else to take up your responsibility, that's what you seem to be doing. As usual."

She put her hands in the pockets of her sweater and, head down, she went back to the clinic. The whole situation made her heart hurt. They were doomed unless someone helped them, and it certainly couldn't be her—no one in that entire family cared for her or respected her enough to even take her seriously. But left in her wake was a man she had deluded herself into thinking had really loved her, and a teenage girl facing the biggest crisis of her young life. It was crushing.

The fact that there was nothing she could have done didn't make it any less painful. Or maybe the worst was that she'd thought herself so smart, so perceptive and intuitive that a man like Ted couldn't get anything by her. Yet he had. She'd never seen it coming.

When she got to the clinic, she found Mac McCain and Eric Gentry standing in front, ogling the midnight-blue Lamborghini parked there. Eric had a reputation as one of the best classic car restorers in the Pacific Northwest. And Mac's office was the clinic's next-door neighbor.

"Hey, Peyton," Mac said.

"Hey, Mac. Hey, Eric."

"Peyton, this here's a Lamborghini," Mac said.

"It is," she affirmed.

"Belong to a friend of yours?"

"No," she answered. "Belongs to my former boss. Dare I hope you have a reason to lock him up?"

"Not for having a car worth about a billion dollars," Mac said with a chuckle. "You unhappy with your old boss?"

"No," she said, shaking her head. "I hate him a little, that's all. He's a shit."

"Oh, well, that'll do it," Eric said, laughing.

"He hasn't broken any laws that I'm aware of," she said. "Maybe if you hang around the car, he'll let you take it out for a spin. But then, no, he won't. In fact, if he sees you touching it, he'll want to press charges."

"Well, now, I'm craving a cup of coffee," Eric said, heading for the diner and out of harm's way.

"I believe I'm due a cup, too," Mac said, following.

There were no patients waiting yet, but Devon stood behind the counter, wide-eyed and looking a little anxious. "I brought you back a grilled cheese, like you asked," she said a little nervously. "Here's your change."

"Thanks. Is it in the fridge?"

"I left it out so it wouldn't get lardy."

"Thanks. Where's Scott?"

"In the back somewhere. You okay? That guy upset you?"

Peyton shrugged. "He brings back some sad memories, that's all." She went to the office. Even though Scott was not there, she occupied her small table, not his desk. *It's all so sad,* she thought.

Scott walked in, a clipboard in his hand. "Well?" he said.

"He's in a mess," she said. "He's in over his head. He can't manage his office, his children, anything.

His girlfriend is pregnant and he's not going to marry her, but his daughter is pregnant and she's fifteen and he decided he needs me. He said he just can't do it without me."

"So?" Scott asked.

She shook her head. "I can't help him and wouldn't if I could. But I wish things hadn't gone the way they have."

"Do you feel sorry for him or something?"

"I do. I tried to warn him. But I don't get any pleasure from the way he thinks he needs me."

Scott leaned a hip on the edge of his desk. "I might be having a little trouble understanding this…."

"I knew I did a good job in the practice. I didn't think I was managing his kids very well, but apparently I was better at it than he is."

"I'm not surprised," Scott said. "Why would it surprise anyone to hear you're good at everything? Most women would like hearing that, I think."

She stood. "My conversation with Ted sounded like a quarterly review—he didn't know how much he loved me until he had to take care of his own practice and his own kids."

"He said that?" Scott asked. "He didn't say that."

"It sounded like it to me. Can I ask you something personal?"

"I think you'd better," he said.

"If your wife had lived, do you think you'd still be crazy about her when you were in your sixties?"

He didn't hesitate. "Yes," he said.

"And what did you love so much?"

"How much time have you got?" he asked. "She was funny. She could make me laugh even when I was mad. It pissed me off, have a good mad going and she acts like a simpleton, undercutting my bad mood when I was really getting into it. She was way too generous. It drove me crazy—she couldn't pass a bum on the street without giving him a couple of bucks, even though we didn't have a couple of bucks to spare. I'd say, 'Serena, he's just going to go to the bar with that,' and she'd say, fine, maybe it's the last cold beer he enjoys. She wouldn't pick up her clothes for anything, she was a draper—over the chair, the exercycle, the dresser, even the toilet. Half the time she got dressed right out of the clothes dryer. She was disorganized and forgetful, except where long columns of numbers were concerned. With numbers, she wouldn't even misplace a decimal point, but hell if she could remember what day it was. She sang off-key, she was gentle-natured unless she was ovulating, and then she was a bear. She fell asleep reading every single night. She left lights on all the time, hours after she left the room, like we had money to throw away on utility bills. She burned half of what she cooked, but she was amazing in the garden—the flowers worshipped her. She was clumsy, her feet were huge—size tens. She battled her weight, she was eventually going to be round and soft like her mother—she gained sixty pounds with Will. And when she smiled, people went into a trance. She cried at movies, and she couldn't stand scary movies. I love scary movies and fall asleep during chick flicks.

She could do the taxes, but she'd forget to file or pay them. Want anything else?"

"So…you didn't adore her because she was a great physician's assistant or excellent nanny?"

He frowned darkly. "She was a terrific CPA and was going to manage my private practice—we looked forward to being partners. And she didn't live long enough to be a great mother."

"I'm sorry," she said softly. "I meant no disrespect."

"You better get some things straight, Peyton. It sounds like you think Ted used you when he said he loved you. It's not a crime to praise someone with amazing talent—you're not only a better PA than I can afford, you're the best PA I've ever worked with. It's an absolute crime to say you love someone when all you love is what they can give you. Or do for you."

"I want what my parents have."

"I spent only two days with Paco and Corinne. He is very proud of her. He brags about her cooking, her mothering, her gardening and her figure, but I don't think he lusts after her for any of those reasons. And that Paco." He whistled. "He's filled with lust—for your mother, his farm, for life. You can have what your parents have. If you think you can have that with Ted, you can probably catch up with him. Or maybe not," he said with a shrug. "I'm sure that Lamborghini really moves."

"You're angry," she said.

He shook his head. "I want you to know something. I want you to think about this. There is nothing you have that I can't live without, except *you*."

"Scott…"

Her cell phone rang.

"Go ahead and take it," he said. "Ted showing up rattled me, too. I'm going to walk around outside for a few minutes. We need to get a grip before we say things we can't take back."

And with that, he turned and left the office.

She stared after him for a second, then looked at her phone, saw that it was Adele calling, and she picked up. "Hey, girl."

"Peyton, I know this isn't on your schedule. I'm sorry. But my water broke."

"You're early!"

"But not too early. It's okay. I know you might not be able to come."

"No! I'll come! Are you in labor?"

"Nothing yet. But I'm going to be spending the night at the hospital."

"Okay, darling, okay. I'm going to throw some things in a suitcase and start driving. We don't exactly have hourly flights out of North Bend. I'll be there in eight hours or so and will call you for updates when I'm on the road."

"I'll try to hold her back," Adele said with a laugh. "Are you sure your doctor can spare you on such short notice?"

He'll probably be glad to see me go, she thought. "It'll work out fine. Love you, kiddo."

Although there was a part of her that wanted to

break into a run, to rush to Adele, another part hated to leave Scott like this. She went to find him. As she walked out of the office, she noticed the back door to the alley behind the small strip mall stood open. He was out there. He probably didn't go out the front door for fear he'd run into Ted. And if he needed some time alone, he wouldn't want to bump into his friends and neighbors.

She peeked out. He was pacing, head down. It made her smile. He didn't have an easy time with being angry. And no matter what he said, she knew he was mad. "Scott?"

He stopped pacing and looked up. She wanted to smooth out those lines across his forehead.

"I'm sorry about what I said, what I asked, about your wife."

"Forget it. I know you didn't mean anything. Listen, I'm not trying to replace Serena. In fact, I didn't think I could fall in love again. And I hoped if I did I wouldn't fall for another woman who tripped over her own damn feet."

Peyton smiled in spite of herself. She hoped Serena heard all that, knew that she had been loved even for her flaws. "I've been called a perfectionist, which I never took as an insult until my mother told me that perfectionists are very hard on the people around them."

"And did she mention that perfectionists are rarely perfect?" he asked.

"Something else came up, Scott. It's Adele. Her water broke. She's going to be having that baby within twenty-four hours. She's a little early, but not too early. If she doesn't go into labor, they'll induce, and if that doesn't prove productive, they'll do a C-section."

"When do you have to leave?"

"I'm afraid I have to leave right away. Babies don't watch our schedules. I promised I'd be with her. If it was anyone else…"

"Don't worry. We'll manage."

"Devon made several appointments for me today."

"The clinic has been operating on a best case schedule for the past year. I can't be everywhere, every day. There have been times we've had to close up the shop and send our people to an urgent care or ER in the nearest town, just like before I got here. That's how it is when you're the only doctor in town. Go." He reached out and touched her cheek. "Do you want me to come with you?"

"You can't, Scott," she said, shaking her head. "You have patients and kids and lots going on. You took four days last week and—"

"If you need me, I'll find a way."

She tilted her head and smiled. "You're a dear, sweet man."

He looked away from her, and she could see he was grinding his teeth. If he wasn't angry, this was a very good imitation. "Scott?"

"I don't want to be a goddamn *dear man!* I want to be the one you can't break away from, the one you can't resist, can't leave behind. I want to be so far under your skin you can't escape. I want to drive you crazy with want, with lust. I want you for a lot more than your PA training, and I want you to be completely unable to say no to me." He pulled her up in his arms and held her tight, kissing her hard, invading her mouth, groaning against her lips. Her arms wrapped around him, her mouth yielding and even deepening the kiss. He bruised her lips with the fury in his kiss. They stood like that for at least a minute. His hand rose slowly until he captured a fistful of that soft black hair and held on. Then he eased his grip. He let go reluctantly. "I'm sorry. I shouldn't lash out at you."

"I think I understand," she said.

"Tell me something, and tell me the truth—were you tempted, for even a second, to follow him home and get him back on his feet?"

She looked at him pleadingly. "I invested a lot in him, in his family. All I wanted was to be appreciated. And now he does appreciate me. Too late, but…"

"Ouch," Scott said.

"But I wouldn't," she said. "I wouldn't."

"Listen. Take some time," he whispered. "Hold the baby, help your sister, think about what you really want. Make your next move the right one. For both our sakes."

"I will. I'll call you," she said. "I'm not running away. This is pure coincidence."

"I just want you to be safe. And happy. Take as much time as you need. Come back if you're…." He swallowed. "Take your time. Be sure," he said.

Fifteen

Gina watched her husband walk across the street toward the diner from his office. She admired the fine figure he cut in his deputy's uniform. The young girls in town called him Deputy Yummy Pants.

Ever since he'd moved to town over four years ago, he had occupied that office, and from the beginning, before they'd become a couple, he'd been having his morning coffee break with Gina unless there was other pressing police business. Mac had four deputies working for him, and between them, the town was always covered. Mac had taken good care of the town.

And now this was going to change. He was moving on. Moving up.

He walked in, took his usual seat at the counter and collected his kiss. It was the public kiss—just a little matrimonial smack.

"I got the call," he said. "Would you like to sleep with Lieutenant McCain tonight?"

"Is he as lovely as Sergeant McCain? Or should I just put a call in to Mac, who always steps up? When is it happening?"

"Soon. A couple of weeks. My replacement is coming in about a week. He's held a satellite office like this before, though in a smaller town, so it shouldn't be a big transition for him. And then I start working in Coquille."

Gina and Mac had been talking about the possibility for months. This promotion gave Mac more responsibility, worse hours and a small raise. "It feels like the end of an era to me," Gina said. "We did our whole courtship right here at this lunch counter."

"Except for the really good parts," he said with a distinct twinkle in his eye.

Mac and Gina had been good friends, both single parents whose teenage daughters were best friends. They were in love for years, neither of them daring enough to cross the line from friends to lovers. Gina took all the credit for finally making him see they had much more potential. Once she pushed him, Mac was ready to marry her right away. The funniest part was that the whole town had known they were in love before they did.

"I bet you know the new guy pretty well—Seth Sileski," Mac said.

Her mouth dropped open. She was speechless. She knew Seth worked for the county sheriff's department, but she'd seen him very rarely over the years. It wasn't as though they'd ever been friends. They hadn't been in the same class in high school, and he ran with an entirely different crowd.

"He's been trying to get back this way for years," Mac said. "I can't wait to talk to his dad."

"Ah, you might want to brace yourself," Gina said. "There's some bad blood between father and son."

"Really? He seems anxious to get over here. He's even talking about moving. What's up with that?"

She shook her head. "I'm not sure of the details. I mean, I'm aware of the gossip, but I wasn't part of the *in crowd* when Seth was the town football hero— I was a high school dropout with a baby. But gossip is an equal opportunity sport—of course I heard it. He's the youngest of three Sileski boys, and he went to the University of Oregon on a scholarship, quit school to take a nice pro contract, then something went wrong. He was in some kind of accident, he couldn't play ball anymore and lost the contract. I gather it was his fault or something. Norm's been pissed off ever since."

"Is that so?" Mac asked. "Well, Norm's a little on the cantankerous side even when he's happy. I don't know Seth that well, but he's a good enough guy. He's respected in the department. I know he hasn't had an easy time—took him a long time to get hired on, but he was determined. I wonder if that's what's wrong with his leg—the accident."

"What about his leg?"

"He has a limp," Mac said. "Haven't you noticed?"

"I can count on one hand the number of times

I've seen him in the last fifteen years. I don't recall noticing a limp."

"He must be okay—he made it through all his physicals and the academy. And he said he was looking forward to this transfer because he has family here."

"His mother. I think he's close to his mother and brothers. It's just Norm who can't get over Seth failing at his big break. And the two older boys aren't in Thunder Point, but they're still around. Jeez, it's been a good fifteen years since he went to college. Norm might be holding on to his disappointment a little over-long. Besides, I can't imagine holding a grudge because a kid lost a football contract—no matter how stupid my kid had been, I'd be so damn grateful he wasn't killed!"

"I'll say. Maybe I won't raise the subject with old Norm."

"Brilliant idea," Gina said. Then she smiled, leaned over the counter and whispered, "Congratulations, Lieutenant McCain. I'm very proud of you."

Scott walked into the diner just after the lunch hour. When Gina saw him coming, she smiled and gave a little shake of her head. This was the second time he'd come in today. Gina had worked on Saturday, and he'd been in then, too. She sure hadn't seen this much of him before Peyton left town.

"And what can I get for you, kind doctor?" she asked.

"Is the tuna fresh?"

"Yes." She laughed. "Stu may not be the best fry cook, but we're very conscientious about the quality and freshness of the food. Have you ever been sick after eating here?"

"Sick? No. But I had to struggle to get through his meat loaf."

She laughed. "I don't recommend the meat loaf. Or the meat loaf sandwich. I don't know what's in that recipe, but isn't it awful? We've talked about it, but obviously Stu is in denial." She slapped a ticket on the cook's counter and then got back to Scott. "Drink?"

"Coke."

She poured it, put it in front of him and asked, "How's Peyton?"

"Good," he said. "She called a little while ago. The baby is perfect, the Bay Area relatives are visiting in droves, and she's managing them. Her sister is doing very well."

"When will she be back?" Gina asked.

His gaze dropped.

"We can either keep tiptoeing around this, or you can spit out what's bothering you," Gina said. "You know I only love listening to gossip, but I never repeat it. Especially when it concerns a dear friend."

"Be careful with that word...."

"Friend?"

"Dear," he corrected. She frowned in total confusion. He took a deep breath. "You saw the Lamborghini on Friday, right?"

"Scott, people took pictures of the Lamborghini.

This is a little fishing village. Devon said the car belonged to the ex, who I didn't see, but she described him as an older version of Brandon Routh. You know, Superman. And she said he wasn't nice."

"Devon talked to him?" Scott asked.

Gina took a breath. "I believe she talked to Peyton."

"Oh. Sure."

"Scott! Why shouldn't I say *dear*?"

"After Adonis left, Peyton was a little upset. Understandably. She told me I was a dear, sweet man, and that was not what I what I wanted to hear. So I was an ass and jumped all over her for calling me that."

"Really," she said with a cynical tone. "Lost your mind a little, huh?" She turned and picked up the sandwich from Stu's counter and delivered it. "I guess a handsome guy driving a Lamborghini is a little in-your-face, huh?"

He picked up his sandwich. "I could pay off the clinic and stock it with state-of-the-art equipment we need with what that car cost." He took a bite, chewed and swallowed. "I bet it's the only one in the state."

"Well, I've never seen one before," Gina said. "I had a similar thing happen. Not quite a Lamborghini, but still... Before the clinic was open, before Mac asked me to marry him, this woman came into the diner. I thought some movie star had missed a turn, gotten lost and ended up here. She was dressed to kill in designer clothes, jewelry, gorgeous thick dark hair, perfect makeup and a dazzling smile. I thought

I'd seen her in toothpaste commercials. Great figure, too. I know this is hard to envision, but she was even more beautiful than Peyton."

"I'd have to see that to believe it," he said.

"I know. But I thought any second George Clooney might walk in to join his girlfriend. She even drove up in a Lexus convertible, one of those sporty things. And the second I saw her I felt like I should probably have a little work done."

"Come on," Scott said. "You're one of the prettiest women in town. Maybe *the* prettiest."

"Aw, that's very kind of you to say. But, no, this woman made me feel frumpy, dumpy and pathetic. And then it got worse. She asked me if I knew the deputy because she wanted to see him and the office was closed. I told her I thought he'd be stopping by for coffee. He usually did. I asked her if she'd like me to give him a call to be sure he was headed this way, and she lit up. She'd appreciate that so much, she said. And in the meantime, she'd have a cup of coffee and piece of pie. So I served her and asked her if I could tell Mac who was waiting to see him. And she said, 'His wife.'"

"Mac was married?" Scott said. "I thought he was divorced."

"He's been divorced for years, but the beautiful woman still thought of herself as his wife. I'm surprised I didn't faint. She had walked out on Mac and the kids ten years before, and I knew that. That doesn't exactly recommend her, right? But I still had visions of her moving that fabulous wardrobe into his closet. I was panicked for a while, until I remembered who Mac was. And until he had a chance to catch his breath and figure out how to deal with her. It was very hard to be patient, to trust him."

"I know there's a lesson in here somewhere," Scott said.

"Well, you keep coming back here, and I know it's not for the tuna!" Gina said.

"Lay it on me," he said.

"You should trust Peyton," she said. "You should believe in her if you love her. She's a smart woman. She knows—some people are what they drive and some people are what drives them. She knows that."

"Have you seen what *she* drives?" he asked, referring to the hundred-thousand-dollar car.

"Yup. We've had some laughs about it. She said it drives like a dream, but now that she's had time to think things over, she probably wouldn't have done it. Her father calls her moneybags, and she thinks she bought it to be less lonely. My money's on Peyton's good sense. I know she likes nice things, but she's not motivated by them. At least, that's my impression. She's not superficial."

"It's not easy," he said. He looked at her and smiled. "When you love someone you want to give them everything. You don't want them to have to settle for less."

"I guess you have to know what's more and what's less to them."

"And I guess we'll find out," Scott said. He put

down the sandwich and wiped his mouth with his napkin.

"You finished?" she asked. "Or can I get you dessert? Maybe a little self-pity to go with that?"

"Go easy on me, Gina. I love her. I never thought I'd find her, and now I have and I love her."

"I understand completely. Just don't be a fool. Don't judge Peyton by the short measure you're using on yourself right now. She knows what's really valuable. If you resembled the guy in the fancy car, she would have been out of here weeks ago. I believe that."

"Well, we both know I don't resemble him." He stood and threw a few bills on the counter. "Thanks for the tuna. And the advice."

It was about nine Monday evening when Scott heard his cell phone singing. He opened his eyes, sat up and whacked his head on the dining-room table, then crawled out of the blanket fort. He was on all fours in search of his phone. He found it in the living room and answered before looking at the ID.

"Were you in the shower?" Peyton asked. "It took you so long to answer."

"I was in the fort," he said. "I fell asleep."

She laughed. "Did you hit your head?"

"I did," he said, rubbing it. "I think I'm going to get rid of the table and pitch the tent in the dining room. It's probably safer."

She laughed some more. "Why don't you do something with the basement, now that Gabby's gone?

Turn it into a playroom and pitch the tent down there? Where they're safe and out of your hair sometimes."

"I've thought about that. Will wants to know if he can move down there."

"Are you going to let him?"

"Eventually, I guess. I think it might lose some of its charm once he's allowed down there all the time. How are you? How's everyone?"

She sighed. "I'm exhausted, but not from Adele and the baby—they're easy. My brother-in-law Lucas is around so much these days. He runs between home and the restaurant. He accepts his family's offerings, but only he cooks for his wife and for me. And his family—typical big Basque family—are here every day. Some of them drive for hours to stay a little while because Lucas and Adele have a pretty small flat in the city, and I have the baby's room right now. They're looking for a house, but they want to stay near the restaurant because his hours are crazy. When they find a bigger place and his entire family can come and stay over, I will be sure not to be here. They're lovely people, but seriously—how much extended family can one person take?"

"Will your parents come?" he asked.

"Ah, they can't. The pears have been harvested, and the potatoes are coming in. It's such a busy farm during the harvest. And this year they're going to cut Christmas trees."

"Christmas trees?" he asked.

"Part of the farm is a tree farm. Papa started them a long time ago, and they're finally reaching the height needed to bring the best price. And get this—rather than selling them to a distributor or retailer, he's going to hire flatbeds and send my brother Matt and some crew to sell them where they'll have the best chance of succeeding, like Las Vegas or Phoenix." She laughed. "I'm dying to see if Papa goes with them to manage them. He can't keep his nose out of anything."

"Christmas trees," Scott said. "That farm does it all."

"They try. Adele will take the baby to the farm before it gets too cold up there, but I don't know if Lucas can stay sane through much more time off. He's starting to twitch. How's the clinic doing?"

"It's limping along. The doctor misses you, but I miss you most when the clinic is closed."

"Ah, you are so brave, going it alone," she said.

"I wasn't going to ask this," he said. "Have you heard from Ted?"

"Not a word. But then, his number is blocked, remember? And he doesn't know I'm in San Francisco unless you told him."

"Me? Believe me, Ted isn't going to check in with me!"

"I talk to you at least twice a day, and you never ask me when I'm coming back."

"I have no backbone," he said. "I'm afraid of the answer."

"*You* have no backbone?" she asked with a laugh. "You, who took two preschoolers on a hunt for a perfect small town in which to be the only doctor? You, who hired a young woman who had just escaped from a cult to manage your office? You, who will go out to a bus accident when they're not your patients and you're not on call just to see if you can help?"

"Me, who wants you to be sure this is what you want before you come back," he said.

"I owe you a month," she said. "I made a commitment."

"That's off the table. I'd rather have you in the best possible place than here for another month out of obligation. It's so important you have no regrets, Peyton. But I do miss you and want you, enough to crawl through the phone. Seriously, I'd give up my life savings for one hour with you."

"Oh, Scott, that's so lovely...."

"My life savings will probably buy you a slice of Stu's pie. You should stay away from the meat loaf. No one is sure what's in it."

She laughed at him. "I miss you so much. And there's no one I'd rather have a slice of pie with than you. Do you have a lot of patients tomorrow?"

"A few in the morning, then I'm in Bandon in the afternoon, on call tomorrow night. The week looks busy. I'm glad of that—I want the time to pass quickly right now. When are you going to Seattle? To see that clinic?"

"I don't know. I'm not sure I will."

"You shouldn't wonder if it was the right thing," he said.

"Right now all I can handle is a sister and newborn. But you're right—I should make a decision if

I'm going to visit, talk to the surgeon there.… You know what, Scott? When I hold the baby, she curves right to me, and I have a hard time thinking about more practical things. I just pick up a book, and I can read for hours with her warm against me, and I don't give her up until she wants food. I feel so guilty—I shouldn't leave a spoiled baby when I go. I'll never hear the end of it if I do. But Mama always said you can't hold a new baby too much. She used to tie each new baby to her in a sling. So, it's been hard to think about things like practices in Seattle—that's so far away."

"Don't leave doubts about whether you've done the right thing, Peyton. Be sure. Maybe you want to check around San Francisco, close to Adele."

"Yes, we agreed, didn't we?" she said somewhat sadly. "My next move should be the right one for both our sakes.…"

"I don't know about you, but I don't want to be in limbo forever."

"Of course you don't. I bet you need to get the kids in bed."

"I don't know," he said. "I might just crawl back under the table again."

"Those are the things they're going to remember," she said. "Camping on the beach, sleeping under the table…"

Gina had an evening completely to herself and decided to drop in on her mother. She laughed to herself as she pulled up to the little house where she'd lived her entire life and saw that Rawley's cherry-red restored pickup truck was parked in front. And here she'd been so worried that Carrie would be lonely when she'd married and moved out six months ago.

Ordinarily she would have walked right in but no more. It was a surprise enough that Carrie was keeping company with Rawley. Who knew what else might be going on behind closed doors? She knocked.

"Well, Ulna," Carrie said, opening the front door. "You're knocking?"

"I didn't want to interrupt anything. I think in the future, I'll call to make sure you're receiving."

"You're such a goose. But what are you doing here? Alone? You seem to have more and more people trailing you every time I see you!"

"I know. I married a large family. They all went to Eugene to watch the Ducks play, just in case the coach puts Landon in. The van was full, Cooper and Sarah were following, and I'm more than happy to just hear about it later."

"Tea? Coffee? Glass of wine?"

Rawley was sitting on Carrie's sofa, apparently watching football, his cup of coffee beside him on the sofa table.

"Hi, Rawley," Gina said. He lifted a hand in her direction and mumbled something back. "I'd love a beer if you have one. For old time's sake. Remember all those times Mac used to come over with two beers, one for me and one for him, and we'd sit on the front porch in the dark?"

"I'm afraid it'll have to be Merlot," Carrie said. "Have you eaten?"

"I have, thank you. I nuked some leftovers, ate them by myself in an empty house, fed the dogs and took a long, leisurely bath. Then I thought, I hardly ever have an evening to myself, and decided to drop in on my lonely old mother."

Carrie handed her a glass of wine and said, "I'm certainly not that old," she said, ignoring the comment about being lonely.

"What are you doing here, Rawley?" Gina asked.

He looked over at her and said, "Helping your mother."

"Oh? What are you helping with?"

He lifted a bowl. "This here popcorn."

"We were just watching football. Come in the living room, sweetheart."

"But, Rawley, who's minding the bar?"

He turned the volume down and gave her his attention, looking a little animated. "Ain't you heard? We got us a part-timer. Kid by name of Troy. School teacher by day, bartender and sweeper-upper by night four nights a week. Cooper can manage those three nights Troy isn't around. Troy Headly is the kid's name."

"I hadn't heard that. When did that happen?"

"About the time that baby kept Cooper and Sarah up half the night a couple weeks running, he got serious and hired himself some help. He can't do without help around there. Besides, if Cooper's honest with himself, he likes putting up those houses. It's not like he does a lot of the physical labor, but he can't be accused of letting the builder do it without plenty of advice." He had some popcorn and said, "I prefer the mornings. I ain't never been interested in taking care of all those people, but I'll serve a little in the mornings, do the supply runs and keep it cleaned up, now that Landon's quit."

"It turns out Rawley enjoys cooking. And since he's promised not to **share** my best recipes, I'll accept his participation," Carrie said.

"Had me sign a document," Rawley said. "Confidential agreement."

Carrie laughed. "I didn't."

"In blood," Rawley said.

My God, Gina thought. *They're made for each other!* And no two people could be any more different. Her domestic, all-business, independent mother who dealt with people all day and this old soldier who didn't like people. Did they talk about things? Snuggle? *Kiss?* She coughed suddenly. "So, you two have been dating a couple of months or so now…."

They looked at each other with nonplussed expressions. "Dating?" Carrie said. She shook her head. "This sure isn't the way I remember dating!"

"I can't remember it at all," Rawley said.

"We cook, watch TV, eat. Rawley helps around here or the deli if there's something that needs to be done. If I ever go out to eat, I'm normally with Ray Anne and Lou—Rawley has very little interest in public places."

"I go to the stores," he said. "I get all the supplies

for Cooper and Carrie. I ain't called upon to be real friendly at the stores."

Gina shook her head. "And I bet they just love to see you coming."

"I reckon they do love it. I bring 'em plenty of money, buying up supplies for two businesses now."

"Gina, Ashley said Mac got his promotion," Carrie said.

"He did. He'll be supervising a couple of units or squads of deputies, and his office will now be in Coquille—not a bad commute. And since he lives here, I suppose they'll take advantage of him when they need help around here. But his schedule will change, and he'll be working nights. Two to midnight."

"Should we throw him a party?" Carrie asked. "It's such an achievement."

"I never thought about it, but maybe we should. We can have a backyard thing on a Sunday afternoon right before he leaves his Thunder Point office."

"Oh, let's," Carrie said. She reached for her handy notebook. "Picnic-style barbecue or something else?"

"Barbecue chicken, crab and pasta salad, spinach and cheese stuffed French loaves..." Gina said.

"Stuffed mushrooms, braised red potatoes, vegetables cooked on the grill. Broccoli, cauliflower, peppers, carrots?" Carrie asked, writing down the possibilities.

"Oh, this sounds wonderful! I wish I'd thought of it. Maybe we should ask Mac what he'd like, since it's his party."

"Don't be silly—I know what Mac likes as well as you do," Carrie said.

"If we do it in a couple of weeks, it'll still be warm enough. And the new guy will be here. The new guy is Seth Sileski, by the way."

"That'll make his mother so happy," Carrie said. "We'll invite the Sileski family! And while we're turning the chicken, we can upend Norm and pull that bug out of his ass."

Gina burst into laughter. "Perfect!"

Sixteen

Peyton folded her freshly laundered clothes on the bed while Adele sat in the rocker, nursing the baby. "I have to admit, I'm going to miss the city," she said.

"You'll have to come back on a weekend," Adele said. "Bring Scott and his kids. Except…"

"Don't worry," she said with a laugh. "We'll get a hotel room. We should show the kids the pier, cable cars, the sea lions…. Wait till you meet them. The kids were so excited at the farm, they were speechless. Papa was feeding them from his plate, talking the whole time, telling his lies and spinning his tales. Then he had little Will dancing with the men."

"A little different from the time Ted and his kids visited?"

"Oh, just a little! That didn't work out the way I thought it might, but I have to let go of it. It's time to move on."

"You're sure this time?"

"It's everything I ever wanted. Scott is everything I've ever wanted, though I have to figure out what's bothering him so much right now. He's so glum, so unlike him. It's probably just the fact that he misses me, and no matter what I say, he worries that I'll leave Thunder Point and we'll never see each other again."

"Did you talk to that doctor in Seattle?"

"I called her this morning. It's kind of too bad I'm not going to get to know her better, she's a remarkable woman. We talked for almost an hour, and I learned things about her that I didn't know, that had I known before I met Scott I would have run to her practice. She spends six weeks a year on a hospital ship doing surgery on infants and children for a nonprofit. When I told her what I was going to be doing, she didn't even argue her case. She thinks it's wonderful. Her specialty doesn't lend itself to a small-town clinic—she has to make herself more widely available. But they take on a number of needy patients every year, and they're very proud of their work."

"Ted did that, too, didn't he?"

"Of course, though not a lot. But that's how I fell in love with Ted—the way he works with patients. I might have noticed his good looks first, but I actually fell in love with his brilliance and his bedside manner. He could charm the doorknob off a door." She laughed at herself. "Or charm the most stubborn patient into the right medical protocol to change their lives and make them better. It just took me a bit too long to realize all that ended when he left the office. If he cared half as much about his kids…"

"Or his girlfriend!" Adele said.

"He doesn't get it, Adele."

"Does Scott?" Adele asked.

"Yes, I think so. I hope so. There are a few things for us to sort through when I get back. The day you called about the baby was the same day Ted came to Thunder Point and begged me to come back to him and help him get out of his messes. Without thinking, I asked Scott about his wife in a careless way that made it sound like I was afraid he'd use me as a PA and nanny. I apologized, but I think he might be having a hard time getting past it."

"Oh, Peyton…"

"It was an honest mistake, Adele. Even though Scott has never treated me the way Ted did, I was emotionally distraught after Ted's visit, and I popped off. I think once I get back and we start to live normal lives again, it'll fall into place. I can tell he's a little unsure of me, even now. Afraid I can be talked into giving Ted another chance just because he's got a real strong presentation—rich, handsome guy with a lot of nice stuff. Ted's intimidating, you know…."

"Oh, I know," she said. "We all know!"

"Poor Ted. He's so clueless."

"I don't think I can go the poor Ted route," Adele said. "He could be a real man if he knew what a real man was." She stood. "I'm going to change the baby," she said, and she left the bedroom.

Peyton folded the rest of her clean clothes, ready

to start packing to leave early in the morning. Her cell phone rang, and she frowned as she saw it was a cell phone with a Portland area code. Had Ted gotten himself a new number just so he could get through to her? If so, she'd have to call Devon and ask her how to block another number. "Hello?"

"Please," came a small, tearful voice. "Please, help me."

"Hello? Who is this?"

"Peyton, please," the voice said. "They're going to make me get an abortion!"

Peyton sank on to the bed. "Krissy?"

"It's me. No one will help me. Please," she said in a whisper and a sob. "Please, help me."

"How do you think I'm going to help you, Krissy?"

"I don't know. Please, come and get me!"

"You don't even like me, Krissy. You didn't like my rules. You didn't like having me in your house."

"I know. I was a bitch, I know. But I don't have anyone, and this is very bad. They made an appointment!"

"Who did?"

"My mom and my dad."

"Krissy, I know of no doctor who will give you an abortion without your consent."

"Are you sure? Because my parents think they can get this done. And if they do this to me, I don't even want to live!"

Peyton gasped. Krissy could be melodramatic and demanding and threatening, but she hadn't ever played the suicide card that Peyton could remember. "What about the baby's father? Can he help you? Can his parents help?"

"There is no father. It's just me."

"Of course there is, Krissy. Just tell him what's going on and—"

"I don't know who the father is, okay? There's no one. I don't have *anyone!*"

Did this girl's parents even begin to realize how much help she needed? "Krissy, I'm not in Portland...."

"I know. You're in some little town somewhere down the coast, but that's okay. I have money. I can take a bus or something. I just need somewhere to go."

"No, honey, I'm in San Francisco with my sister. I drove here. I'm a good twelve hours away from you by car."

She started sobbing. "Oh, no! Can I come there? I have to go somewhere! I have to do something!"

"Krissy," she said, but the girl kept crying. "Krissy, you have to stop crying and listen to me. Can you do that?"

"Okay...okay..."

"All right, calm down. I can't talk to you unless you can stay calm."

"Please...please, I'm sorry for everything, but, please..."

"Krissy, be calm. Can you listen to me?"

"Okay," she said tremulously.

"I'll come to you. It's going to take me a long

time—I won't be there before tomorrow. I can talk to you from the car, but it will be a long drive for me. And I'm going to have to tell your father that I'm coming."

"Why do you have to?"

"Because I'm not your mother or even your step-mother. I'm nothing more than an ex-girlfriend involving myself in his family business."

"But you took care of us for three years!"

Well, not quite that long, she thought. As for the caretaking, since she'd been totally unsuccessful, how would that give her any leverage in this situation? "He's your father. I take it you're at his house right now, not your mother's?"

"I'm here. If you tell him, he might just make me go to that doctor right away."

"Well, he can't. If you think that's about to happen, if you think you're going to be forced to have a medical procedure against your will, you can call the police. I don't know exactly what will happen, but you won't have a procedure before I get there. But you have to stay calm, and you can't lie to your father, do you understand?"

"But..."

"No, Krissy. If your father asks you, and I believe he will, you have to tell him the truth, that you called me and that I'm coming. Are we on the same page?"

"Yes, ma'am."

Ma'am? Well that was a switch. She must be truly desperate. "I'll call you as I'm driving, just to check in with you."

"Are you going to drive all night?" Krissy asked, her voice so small, so scared.

Adele wandered into the room, the baby snuggled against her shoulder. She frowned as she listened.

"Probably. I might have to stop somewhere for a little rest, but I'll be there as soon as I can. Now, I'm going to call your father. I'm going to tell him I'm coming to see if I can help you. I don't know how I'm going to help, but I will come. I'm sure you'll hear from him."

"He's going to be so mad at me...."

"Well, that would be a first, now, wouldn't it? Just stay calm and tell him you called me because you were scared, and I'm coming. Can you do that?"

"Yes. Yes, I'll do that."

"All right. I'm going to hang up so I can pack and make a couple of phone calls. Will you be all right now?"

"Yes. And...thank you, Peyton. I'm sorry, but thank you."

"I want you to be calm because this is going to work out. I'm not sure how yet, but it will."

"Okay," she said.

Peyton disconnected and looked up at Adele, who was swaying in the bedroom doorway with the baby in her arms. "Did I hear what I think I heard?"

Peyton nodded. "Ted's daughter. Begging me to come to Portland to help her because her parents are planning to force her to get an abortion."

"And you're going?"

"I'm going. She said a couple of things that could be melodrama or...or could be suicidal."

"What can you do?"

"I have no idea. I think I can buy her twenty-four hours. Maybe forty-eight. Forcing a minor to have a surgical procedure is abuse. How the police handle that isn't up to me. And her parents—Ted and Olivia—they're pretty forceful people. But my biggest concern right now is that the girl definitely needs some kind of intervention before she does something crazy—like run away or kill herself or God knows...."

Peyton started putting her folded clothes into a suitcase.

"When are you going to be free of that loony bin?" Adele asked.

Peyton stopped what she was doing and went to Adele, taking the baby from her to hold her close for a moment, kissing that little head, inhaling the fresh powdery scent of her. Then she looked at her sister, her best friend. "It's pretty sad that I'm the only one they have to reach out to, isn't it? I mean, Ted's a doctor and Olivia is a geologist with a post-graduate degree, they're very successful, and apparently not a lick of sense between the two of them. And Krissy calls me? I swear, she hated me the whole time I was there. No matter how hard I tried, I couldn't reach them. And yet when their parents should be getting them help, who do they call?" She shook her head sadly. "I could turn my back right now. No one would blame me. But I don't think I could sleep at night if I didn't at least try."

"She's fifteen, Peyton. Maybe it would be best if her parents won this struggle."

"That's just the point, Adele. There will be no winner."

"But what's your stake in it? Proving to Ted you're right?"

"Ted?" she asked with a laugh. "Ted is so yesterday's news! My stake in it might just be in my head. I was there for over two years, trying my damned hardest to make a difference in the lives of three spoiled rich kids who had no attention from their parents. They never once asked for my help. I prayed they'd ask me for help, for advice, for anything that would make it seem they wanted to be decent, civilized people, and it never happened. And I finally gave up. Now one of them asked me for help. I resent the hell out of it, to tell you the truth. But she's fifteen, and I'm thirty-five. I can afford to give it a couple more days. It'll help me sleep at night."

Adele just smiled. "Oh, you are your father's daughter."

"How so?"

"Stubborn. Committed. Proud."

"Foolish," Peyton added, handing the baby back to Adele. "Papa has been foolish a time or two. But with grand flourish."

"What do you want now?" Adele said, mimicking their father. "My pockets are empty! My wealth is under the dirt, my pears are hanging from the trees waiting to be picked before a freeze, my sheep are skinny, my chickens are too nervous to lay. You want something—you know where to find it!"

"Remember how we used to call him Paco Poor Mouth?" Peyton laughed. "He wouldn't make it easy, would he?"

"But if anyone was really in trouble, he was there. You got nothing for wanting things easy, you got nothing for being lazy, but if the world turned on you and you had no one, just blink and Paco Lacoumette would bring an entire clan to your feet. Listen, Peyton, just remember one thing, okay?"

"What's that, honey?"

"You're only one person. And there's only so much you can do."

"Thank you, baby. I'll remember. I'll give it a shot. And then I'll pass the baton and walk away. I promise."

Peyton left right away. She spent the first hour of her drive thinking about what she was going to say to Ted, then once she was out of the Bay Area, she pulled off the road and called his cell. As she thought he might, he picked up right away. "Peyton," he said. "I'm so glad to hear from you."

"You might not be when you hear what I have to say. I'm headed to Portland from San Francisco. I'm driving. I'm coming because Krissy called me. She was close to hysterical and asked for my help."

"And you're coming. Thank God," he said.

"Ted, whatever it is you think you're going to do

to that girl, just don't. She's unstable. She needs help. At least let me get there and talk with her, maybe find her a counselor or some professional therapy."

"Everything will be all right if you're coming," he said, sounding greatly relieved. "You can talk some sense into her."

"That's not why I'm coming, Ted. I'm not coming to convince her she has to take any action she can't live with. What she ultimately decides to do should be up to her. But she begged me to come, to help her, and I'm going to try. I have a long drive ahead, and I'll reach out to a couple of people while I'm en route, see if I can get some leads on resources for her, for all of you."

"You'll stay at the house, of course."

"Ted, I'm not coming back to you. I'll stay with Krissy for a night or two. She's very needy right now."

"She'll be fine once you're here. And you and I can work on a few of our issues."

"Here's what I need from you, Ted. Are you paying attention?"

"Anything, Peyton. I told you, I'll do anything."

"Okay, that's a great start. I won't get there until tomorrow. When you go home tonight I want you to tell Krissy that everything is going to be all right, that I'm on my way and you're not angry. Do not confront any of your problems—leave it alone until I get there. Can you do that for me?"

"And then you'll take care of it?"

Jesus, she thought. *He is so dense.* "I'm going

to try to find her some professional help, but, no, I won't be taking care of it."

"But you're coming back to me. You'll stay. Once you're here, I know you'll stay."

"I'm afraid that's not in the cards. Now, will you promise to reassure your daughter? Will you?"

"If that's what you want. Peyton, I'm very grateful, you must know that. And I think once we talk, we'll be able to straighten some things out. I know I have a long way to go to get your trust back, but I'm willing to do anything."

"Will you please just make sure Krissy doesn't feel any more threatened? That's all I want from you right now."

"I will, if that's what you want."

"It's what I want. Think of Krissy as a patient. A nervous, frightened, confused patient who needs the best, most charming bedside care and support you can give. It's what you're known for. Don't argue with her, don't try to convince her of anything, just be kind to her."

"When will you be here?" he asked.

"I'm not completely sure. I think I'll have to stop and get some rest. There's no point in me arriving at midnight when everyone's asleep. I'd rather have Krissy rest. And maybe it will be best if you're not there when I arrive. I can talk to her alone."

"But you'll call me when you're here?"

"Sure. I have to go now. I have driving to do."

After they signed off, she thought, for the hundredth time, *we have got to get that man a good hearing aid.* He was a bad dream, that's what he was. Just when she thought the nightmare was over, he was looming there, ready to invade her peace once more.

She got back on the road. She wanted to spend the night in Thunder Point. Ideally, she'd go to Scott, but if that wasn't practical because of children or if he was working, she did have her duplex. At least she could see him before heading the rest of the way.

Since she knew there was no risk of a panic attack or argument during her next couple of conversations, she drove and made hands-free calls. Her first call was to Amy, her friend from Ted's practice. She told her what she was struggling with.

"I know who it is, Peyton. Even though Lindsey isn't working here anymore, she hasn't been at all discreet. She couldn't wait to spread the word that Ted's home life is a disaster and that his daughter is pregnant. My sister works for a really great OB in the area, but don't you have a sister-in-law who has volunteered on a crisis hotline or something like that?"

"Yes! How did I not think of that?" Peyton said. "George's wife, Lori. She's perfect. She knows everyone. She can get me a referral of some kind. She'd know exactly who to call."

Peyton waited until she'd reached the halfway mark and was still six hours from Portland before stopping for gas and a bite to eat in the car. She bought herself a pretty sad-looking half sandwich, some jerky, some chocolate and some hot coffee and sat in her car behind the gas station's mini-mart. It was six in the evening. She had no idea where Scott might be. He could be home, getting the kids dinner. Or he could be at the hospital. This was the call she'd been looking forward to, the one she thought would soothe and comfort her.

"Scott," she said. "Where are you?"

"Just wrapping it up at the clinic," he said. "I stayed to finish my charting and clean up a little, but I'm done now. Devon picked up the kids, and I'm headed to her house to scoop up mine. If I drag my feet a little, she might feed them."

Peyton laughed, missing him. Missing the whole group. "Don't be mean."

"I'm on call tonight, so she might get stuck, anyway. And then there's always payback. How's it going?"

"Ah, yes, how's it going. Well, there's good news and bad news."

"Lay it on me," he said.

"Well, the good news is, I've left San Francisco a little early. The bad news is, I'm headed for Portland."

"Portland? That wasn't in your plans, was it?"

"Nope, I had a very abrupt change of plans. There's a crisis—one of Ted's kids called me—she's in some trouble and I'm needed. I don't know how much I can help, but I'm going to try. It's serious or I wouldn't bother. But I was wondering—"

"You're going to Ted's house?" he asked, sounding a little brittle.

"Well, that's where his kids are."

"I thought you had decided you'd done all you could for that family," Scott said.

"And as it turns out, there might be one or two more things I can do. You have to believe me—I'm not doing this for Ted. It's his daughter—she needs me right now."

There was a long moment of silence. "Of course," he said. "How long do you suppose she'll need you?"

"Hey, you're upset!" she said.

"I'm surprised," he said. "You were very convincing when you said you were all done there. The kids hated you, you said. How much can you do for kids who hate you?"

"Don't do this, Scott. I wouldn't be going if I thought I was just being exploited by Ted or his kids. It turns out to be quite important. His pregnant daughter reached out to me."

"And I suppose you'll have quite a lot of discourse with Dr. Ramsdale while you're there, helping his daughter."

"I don't give a crap about Ted, though I pity him! But at this moment I'm beginning to feel pretty sorry for you, too."

"I'm sorry, Peyton," he said. She could picture him rubbing his eyes with his thumb and forefinger. "I'm reacting. I guess I'm disappointed."

"Apology accepted," she said, but it really stung.

"Maybe while you're that far north you should take the time to check out that surgeon in Seattle."

"What? What?" she asked twice.

"Peyton, I love you. But we both know I don't

have nearly as much to offer you as that Seattle surgeon does. Or as Ted does, for that matter."

Peyton was stunned. *God, he's jealous. Of Ted. How ridiculous!* But ridiculous or not, it was plain as paint—Scott was licking his wounds and had been since the day Ted had descended on them, driving his fancy car, calling the clinic a dump and not good enough for Peyton, acting like the hotshot he thought he was.

Peyton thought that, of all the people she knew, Scott would know what a real pauper was.

She was quiet. She could try to soothe him, reassure him that Ted had nothing she wanted, that all his glitter meant nothing to her. She could go to him, be there in two or three hours, have a heart-to-heart with him about what things really mattered to her, and ask him to try to understand.

Or not.

"All right, Scott, everyone's entitled to be petty sometimes, so I'm going to just let that go. What I'm going to do is drive to Portland and see if I can help Ted's daughter. I might spend the night with my parents since I'm that close, and then I'm going to come back to Thunder Point where I happen to live at the moment. We're going to have a serious talk and get this issue completely resolved. When this crisis is behind me, we're going to talk our crisis to death. I'd do that right now, but I'm tired, I have hours of driving ahead, I have a lot of other things to worry about and, frankly, you really pissed me off.

But when our problem has been aired, we'll decide where we go from there."

"That sounds reasonable," he said.

"Tell me one thing, Scott," she said. "Are you sure you still love me?"

He sighed into the phone. "I don't think anything will ever change that."

"Then after we finally get this sorted out, you're going to feel really stupid."

"It won't be the first time," he said.

"I'll talk to you soon," she said, clicking off.

She sat for a moment. She was really too tired to allow her emotions to overwhelm her, but he was breaking her heart. Did he have so little faith in her? Did he not know her at all? Couldn't he look beyond the nice car or the ex-boyfriend with the even nicer car?

But the tears came, anyway. It just hurt so much that he was unsure of her.

She called the farm. "Mama? Hi. I'm on my way to Portland—I'm needed there. I've been driving, and I'm wondering—can I sneak into the house very late tonight and grab a few hours of sleep before going on to Portland? It will be midnight or so. I hope the dogs don't start barking, but I'll be as quiet as I can."

"Of course, my Babette. Don't worry about the dogs, they bark at the moon. Just come. What needs you in Portland?"

"One of Ted's kids is in trouble and called me for help. I'll tell you about it at breakfast. Thank you,

Mama. I'm sure I'll be very tired by the time I get there."

"Is there nowhere else for you to stop, darling?"

Like Thunder Point? Peyton thought. "No, Mama. I'm coming straight home."

Seventeen

When Peyton walked upstairs at the farmhouse, her mother met her in the hall. Corinne was wearing Paco's robe over her pajamas. She turned on the hall light and, frowning, looked Peyton up and down. "You're all right?" she asked.

"Just tired."

"Sleep, then. We'll talk in the morning."

Peyton hadn't even taken her suitcase out of the car. She stripped off her jeans and crawled into the bed that had been hers as a girl. It seemed that she'd closed her eyes for mere seconds when she was roused by the smell of coffee. She dragged herself out of bed, pulled on yesterday's clothes, ran her fingers through her hair and went down to the kitchen. Paco looked up and gave her a slight frown of concern. "Trouble?" he asked.

She knew he wouldn't want to talk about the details. Not at this time of the morning. He was all about getting out of the house. If she was around later when his work was done, they might sit on the porch and talk a little, but for now he would leave the details for Corinne to collect. "Nothing I can't handle, Papa."

Her mother put a bowl of oatmeal and a cup of strong coffee in front of her. Her father ate cereal, eggs, sausage. Around ten in the morning he would stop by the house to fill-up on toast and coffee, maybe some beans. And at one, lunch. At six, dinner. It took a lot of fuel to keep a farmer going.

Paco was done eating inside of ten minutes. He rose, rubbed his hands over his stomach and leaned down to give Peyton a kiss on the head. "You are the strong one," he said. Peyton knew he said some variation on that to every one of his children.

Corrine rinsed the dishes and brought her coffee to the table, sitting across from Peyton, silent and waiting. Peyton told the story of Krissy, and when she was done, all Corrine said was, "Fifteen. Holy Mother."

"Totally," Peyton said. "If that was your daughter, what would you do?"

She gave a helpless shrug. "We've had a slip or two in our vast family, not at fifteen that I can think of. My mother used to say, 'The first baby can come anytime, but after that they all take nine months.' Peyton, I'm surprised you'll go to help that fancy doctor. He hasn't often appreciated you."

"I'm not going for him. In fact, leaving it in his hands will be a challenge. He clearly expects me to handle it for him, no matter how long it takes or how much it costs me."

"I hope you've made up your mind how much you can take."

"I hope so, too."

Of course, her mother wanted to know all about Adele and the baby, wanted to hear about all of Lucas's family. They'd sent pictures almost daily to the entire Lacoumette family, but Corinne was hungry for gossip and details. They had a second cup of coffee.

"Mama, when did you know you loved Papa?"

"When my father told me I did," she said with a smile.

"Really?"

"I loved him before I knew him, like most brides. Then the truth came out. I found out what he was really like."

"Does he ever give you trouble?"

Corinne laughed. "Every day of my life. Peyton, please, tell me we're not talking about Ted."

She shook her head. "That was over a long time ago. Before I moved out. So sad. It makes me a little afraid that I'll think I'm in love again, and then it will slip away from me. That I'll see I was kidding myself. Again."

Corinne shook her head. "Peyton, it's not like you to play games with yourself. You, of all my children, have always known what you feel, what you want."

"I didn't with Ted," she said.

Corinne sighed. "Anyone could see you stayed much longer than you wanted to. You stayed for those children. Not because you loved them but because you *feared* for them. And with good reason, it seems. The next time you find yourself willing to accept a lie, be prepared to be disappointed. Paco can drive me crazy, but underneath everything, he is good. When I'm angry, I break his yolks. When he's angry, he grunts at his food and gives me his back in bed. When we fight, we keep score—he yields half the time and I yield *almost* half the time—it's a proven system."

"Mama." She laughed.

"He's stronger than I am. It's fitting he should carry a little more of the burden."

"Does he know this?"

"There is no question. Everything is going to be all right with your young doctor. He loves you. He looks at you in a way I haven't see a man look at you before. And he has a gentle strength. He enjoys people in an honest way. He's not afraid to give. He's not Basque, but otherwise he's acceptable." And then she grinned.

"He's been a little cranky lately," Peyton said.

"Oh? Then perhaps he has a mighty big problem. And so do you— Now, get yourself ready and get to the fancy doctor's house and get that behind you. I wish you good luck with that." She shook her head and *tsked*. "Such a terrible ordeal for that child. For everyone."

Peyton made it to Ted's house by just after nine in the morning. She called Ted's cell phone to announce her arrival, and the first thing he did was bitch about not being able to reach her because his number was blocked. She told him she was sorry, but she had no idea how to unblock it and told him he could call Krissy's number and ask to speak to Peyton if he needed something.

The next order of business was talking to Krissy. She was up, still in her pajamas, but already crying. For a little while it was just Krissy and Peyton, going over all the details again. Krissy said she knew right away that she was pregnant and had been terrified to tell her parents, which any girl would be.

After an hour listening to Krissy, Peyton made an appointment with a crisis counselor, who had been recommended by her sister-in-law Lori. She told Krissy to get cleaned up for an appointment in a couple of hours. Then she called Ted.

"Krissy has an appointment with a counselor at noon, Ted. You should take her."

"Listen, Peyton, I'm booked solid. Can you please take her?"

"It's the lunch hour, Ted! Someone can cover you."

"I can't, Peyton. But I'll come home early and get the details from you and Krissy then. Thanks for doing this."

"I should walk right out of here and leave you with whatever mess there is to clean up!"

"Please, Peyton. I won't ask anything more, I swear!"

"You're damn right, you won't!"

When she told Krissy, the girl just said, "I'd rather it be you, anyway."

"You understand this is private between you and the counselor, right? You can tell her anything and everything, and it's totally confidential."

"I know," she said.

"Have you been in counseling before?"

She shrugged. "Just at school. When I was younger. I don't think it was the same kind. We were sent to the counselor's office when we didn't behave."

"I bet that happened a lot," Peyton said. "Well, this kind is perfect for now—you're in a crisis. If you just open up a little, the counselor might have some ideas for you. She won't tell you what you have to do, but she might be able to help you cope with a very difficult situation."

Although she'd threatened not to, of course Peyton took Krissy to her appointment. She then sat in the waiting room. When Krissy finally came out, looking as if she'd been through the wringer all over again, the counselor asked Peyton to come into the office.

"You're a friend of the family, do I have that right?" the therapist, Margaret Kazerus, asked.

"Yes. I lived with Dr. Ramsdale for a couple of years and got to know the kids very well. Krissy called me, and I was surprised. I didn't think she liked or trusted me. We didn't get along that well."

"She tells me you said you could stay a couple of days, is that correct?"

"Right, again," she said.

"All right, then. I'm going to call Dr. Ramsdale. Unless you're planning to be responsible for Krissy in the long term, it's time to turn it over to the girl's parents. Do you know where the mother is?"

Peyton shook her head. "It's a joint custody situation. Ted and I had the kids three to four days a week. I left a couple of months ago. I work in a small town down the coast now, and I really can't stay any longer."

"That's fine… Is it Peyton?"

"Yes, Peyton Lacoumette. Is she going to be all right?"

"With the right support system and tools," she said, scribbling on a notepad. "I think it was very good of you to step in, Peyton. I understand you came a long way?"

"I was visiting my sister in San Francisco. It was a very long drive."

"Well, that was over and above. Whenever you feel comfortable leaving this in my hands, you can get back to your sister or your job. It's up to Krissy and her family now. I explained that to her."

"Thank you for seeing her. She scared me."

"I don't doubt it," the counselor said. "She's pretty unsteady right now." She stood behind her desk and extended her hand. "Thanks for finding her counseling, Peyton. It was a very good first step."

"Sure. Thank *you*."

Peyton took Krissy for a hamburger and listened to the story of her counseling experience. Then the poor exhausted thing went to her room for a nap. "Will you be here when I get up?" Krissy asked.

"I think I'll leave tomorrow. Are you going to school tomorrow?"

She shook her head. "Miss Kazerus wants another appointment tomorrow."

"Well, if your dad can't take you, I will, and then I have to leave. Once you're feeling a little better, I have to get back to work, honey."

"I know."

"You're going to be all right, you know."

Peyton rummaged around in the cupboards and refrigerator, looking for something for dinner. Typical of Ted, he hadn't mentioned dinner and was likely expecting her to round up something. She grabbed a pound of frozen ground turkey, fried it up and prepared to add beans, tomatoes and chili seasoning. She found biscuits in the refrigerator and got them out. While she was cooking, Pam and Nicholas came in from school.

"You're here," Pam said. "You came."

"Krissy asked me to come. I'm glad I did. How are you guys?"

"Okay," Nicholas said. "Is she real sick?"

"No, she's not sick, kiddo. Just upset. Hasn't anyone talked to you about what's making her upset?"

He shook his head, but Pam said, "She's pregnant."

"She can't be," her brother said.

"Never mind, Nicholas," Pam said. "Don't worry about it."

This family, Peyton thought. *How have they made it this long with no communication, no team effort?*

"How long will you stay?" Pam asked.

"I think I'll leave tomorrow. The longest I can stay is one more day, then I really have to get back to work. I think Krissy will feel a little better before I leave."

"I can't believe you came," Pam said again.

Peyton gave her hair a pat, a little stroke. "I'm throwing together some chili for your dinner. Does that sound okay?"

They both looked a little thunderstruck. But they both nodded. "Why don't you get started on homework?" she asked. And for the first time in Petyon's memory, they headed off with book bags toward their rooms. "I think Krissy is napping, so, please, don't wake her. She's had a hard day."

Chili done, biscuits ready for the oven, Peyton checked the time. Almost five and no Ted. Well, no surprise there. She poured herself a glass of wine and sat at the table. She texted Scott. She didn't call him, hadn't called him since that conversation the night before. But she didn't want to ignore him, knowing he'd wonder what was going on up here. Took Krissy to the counselor. I'm staying another day, I think, then maybe stopping off at the farm. Are you okay?

Before she received any response, Ted came in from the garage. He looked very unhappy. He was apparently no longer grateful. He glared at her, putting his bag on the counter.

Rather than talking, he fixed himself a drink. He

leaned against the breakfast bar and glared at her. "I'm required to be at counseling tomorrow," he said. "Is that your doing?"

"My doing? I have nothing to do with that, but it's a good idea."

"It's what you wanted all along, and now, it seems, I don't have a choice."

She raised her brows and looked at him. "Is that right?" she asked. "Well, I suppose you could refuse."

"No," he said. "I can't. She *threatened* me."

Peyton was frankly startled. "Who?"

"The counselor! Miss Kazerus!"

"How could she threaten you?" Peyton asked, confused.

"She said if one of Krissy's parents didn't show up with her tomorrow, she'd call the department of children's services. Olivia is out of town until tomorrow night. I offered you, but she said that wouldn't work. I explained my schedule, the critical demands of my patients, and she said I'd have to make a choice. Her mother should do this."

Wow, Peyton thought. *Right now Ted is slapping himself for not being out of town!* "I suppose you could skip it and let her make the call...."

"No, I can't do that. It would be too humiliating, as if my current situation isn't embarrassing enough."

Knowing he wouldn't get it, knowing he'd never understand what she was saying, she said it, anyway. "Ted, this isn't about *you.*"

"Did you suggest this? Be honest, Peyton. You've

been yammering about counseling for a long time. Did you tell the counselor to force me?"

She just looked at him for a long moment. She shook her head sadly. "I think I should be on my way," she said. "I made some chili for you and the kids—it appeared nothing was planned for dinner. I'll make sure Krissy is feeling better, and I'll just take off, drive down to the farm and stay with my mom and dad. I'll head home after that." Her phone chimed with an incoming text, and she ignored it. "I think you can take it from here."

"If you can manage, I'd appreciate it if you'd stay one more day," he said. "To make sure Krissy makes it through her next counseling session."

"All right," she said. "Then that's all the time I have."

He took a sip of his drink. "Can we have a discussion about us?"

"That ship has sailed, Ted. I'm ready to get home."

He took another sip. "Home?" he asked. "That place is home now?"

"It's working out. Would you like some chili with the kids?"

"I believe I'll make do with this drink for now," he said. And he left the kitchen and went to his office.

Peyton looked down at the text. It was from Scott. Is Ted behaving himself?

Surprisingly, Ted didn't bother Peyton any more that evening. He isolated himself in his office or the master bedroom. To his credit, he did check on

Krissy once, asking her how she was feeling. But Peyton had expected a full-court press regarding their relationship, and that didn't happen.

She, likewise, hid. She checked on each of the kids, then closed the guest room door where she talked on the phone a little, texted a little, read a little. At one point there was a knock at the door. "Come in," she said.

Pam peeked into the room, looking a little uncertain. Then she pushed the door open and came in. She was carrying a pair of leather-and-suede boots that Peyton had left behind because they'd gone missing.

"These are yours," she said.

"Yes, I see that," Peyton said, smiling. "I remember them fondly. I gave the credit to Krissy. It was you who took them?"

Pam nodded. "Sorry."

"They must be much too big for you."

"They were gonna fit pretty soon."

"By that time they would have been out of style."

"Don't be mad, okay?"

"Pam, I grew up with three younger sisters. You can't hold a candle to their thievery. They were in my stuff all the time, and it made me furious. Besides, I think I'm past being shocked by what you kids do. I was pretty ticked at losing these boots, but I'm done being mad now. I do think it's very mature of you to return them and apologize. Thank you."

"Will you come back now?" she asked.

"Why would you want me to?" Peyton asked.

Pam shrugged. "It's easier," she said.

"Ah. Well, little darling, I think you should prepare yourself to try a little harder, then. I found a
new job, a new little house all my own and some
new friends. Your dad and I decided our relationship
wasn't working, and we both moved on, no hard feelings." She gave her returned boots a pat and smiled.
"I think you know how to do the right thing. Why
don't you prove to your dad that he can depend on
you. That's a good place to start."

"I knew you wouldn't stay."

Peyton shook her head. "Did you also know you
were trying to force me to leave?"

"It wasn't that bad," Pam said.

"For who?" Peyton asked, very pleased to see Pam
blush slightly. "You can call or text me if you like.
We can keep in touch if you want to, but I'm afraid
it's time for me to leave. I'm starting over, too."

Peyton thought it was perhaps self-indulgent or
even self-flagellating on her part, but she chose to
stay at Ted's house until Krissy and Ted came home
from their counseling session. There was a bit of
generosity of spirit left in her because she did want
to comfort Krissy if necessary, encourage her a little
bit before leaving. She was quite sure she wouldn't
be back. Miss Kazerus was right—it was time for
Peyton to leave this family on their own. She was
an outsider.

She waited and waited and waited. She fully
expected Ted to drop Krissy at the house and go

straight back to his office. She wasn't sure he'd even come inside, and if he did, it would only be for one of two reasons—to say goodbye or ask her to stay and manage his home and family for him.

As the hours ticked by, Peyton hoped he'd at least taken Krissy out to lunch or something. Peyton's suitcase sat by the back door, ready for her departure. It was almost two, and they had been gone four hours when she finally heard the garage door rise. Krissy walked in first, Ted very close behind her. His hand was resting on his daughter's shoulder, and he looked wretched.

"Do you want to go lay down for a while?" Ted asked Krissy.

She nodded, but then in noticing Peyton's suitcase, she turned concerned eyes toward her. "If I take a nap, will you be here when I wake up?"

"I won't leave without saying goodbye," Peyton promised.

"Thanks," she said.

Ted came over to the kitchen table where Peyton waited and sat down. "You've been gone awhile," was all she dared to say.

He sat heavily. He rubbed his temples with a finger and thumb. "Jesus."

"Are you all right?" she asked.

He shook his head, pinching his eyes closed hard. She'd seen Ted in his worst moments, overpowered by enormous stress, and this expression he was wearing was completely new to her. Without looking at her, he spoke. "Krissy is going to spend a little time in a residential hospital. Hopefully, just a month."

"Residential?"

"My daughter is in serious trouble," he said.

Was Ted finally getting it? Of course she was in trouble. That's why Peyton was here.

"Maybe a different school after that. Maybe a boarding school next, but nearby so she can come home as often as she likes. I'm okay with her being here, but she might need more...." His words tapered off, and then his finger and thumb were on his eyes. His shoulders began to heave. And then he *cried!*

She reached out for the hand that rested on the table. "Ted?"

Although he concealed his tears with his fingers, she could see he was distraught. He gathered up his strength from within, gave a cough and a little huff. "Ah," he said. "Sorry." He cleared his throat and looked at her through red-rimmed eyes. "You can't imagine what I had to hear today. Do you know how Krissy got in this mess?" he asked.

"I assumed, the usual way."

"I hope it wasn't the usual way. My daughter has been in a lot of pain. Did it seem like that to you? Because I knew she could test my limits. I knew she could get in trouble. Fifteen-year-olds don't have much common sense most of the time. But Krissy hasn't been a normal teenaged girl. She was a girl with a plan. She was either going to have herself a baby or kill herself. And since boys her age are more than willing to cooperate with indiscriminant girls who are looking for sex, the baby idea won over the messy and painful suicide idea. And do you know *why*?"

Peyton, dumbfounded, just shook her head.

"Because no one loves her. Because in her whole life, she couldn't think of one person who really cared about her. And she thought if she had a baby, that baby would love her. She assumed this because she loves her mother and father…even though she was sure we didn't love her. And not just us—no one. Not an aunt or teacher or fellow student." He shook his head. "I thought she was popular. I thought she felt well liked and…well, and loved."

Peyton was not only *not* shocked by this revelation, she was disgusted that he was. "Teenagers are very fragile, Ted. They need a lot of consistency and support. All teenagers feel unloved and unaccepted from time to time in their peer groups, even the ones who are popular. Their maturity level is low and their insecurities very high."

"Enough to kill themselves?" he asked in a desperate whisper.

She made a sad face. "It's a growing problem."

He sighed deeply, trying to compose himself. "I can walk into an exam room, and I can read a patient in seconds. I know if they're lying, if they're terrified, if they just don't care. I can tell if they're exaggerating, dramatizing or if they're having symptoms they're not talking about because they don't want them to exist. If I can talk with them for ten minutes, we can almost always get on the same team. Hell, I don't even need the patient—I can look at the chart, the blood, the tests, and I know if they were misdiagnosed or if they need more than I can give them."

"You're known for that. You dazzled me with your perception. I think that's what I fell in love with—your sensitivity and brilliance."

"But my own daughter is in life-threatening danger, and I didn't see it."

Peyton chewed her lower lip for a moment. She knew it was risky, but she decided it was time to be brutally honest. "I didn't think you cared."

"I care," he said. "I love my kids." Then he shook his head. "I didn't see how to connect the dots, Peyton. What does making off with someone's sweater or deleting their TV shows have to do with desperation? I thought you were overreacting. I thought they were typical kids, missing curfew, changing plans without telling anyone, resisting authority."

"If you'd been here more, if you'd been the one whose personal property disappeared or whose shows were deleted, you might've asked yourself why they refused to follow the simplest rules, why they were acting out. They hated me because you loved me. They want their parents."

"Olivia…"

"Uh-uh," she said shaking her head. "You can try putting this off on Olivia, but that will only cost you valuable time. Right now, if you love them, you better figure out how to be a parent to them."

"When you were leaving me, you said I was emotionally unavailable." She nodded. "That's what the counselor said. She said my daughter didn't bring her problems to me because my door was closed. Is that true? That my door was closed?"

Peyton nodded. "The same way the door closes when you leave the patient in the exam room. You did your ten or fifteen minutes of assessment, gave them the protocol and the drugs and left. You don't have to live with them, hold them while they cry, sit up at night with them when they're scared—your job was done. You're done until they show up in the ER or make another appointment." She took a breath. "That's not how you parent. Parenting is full-time."

"I thought I was a full-time father. I took them to Disneyland."

She laughed at him. "*We* took them to Disneyland. They had a blast. You should have seen them. But you were on your laptop or cell phone most of the time."

He groaned.

"Listen, I understand you're programed to have a lot of little minions taking care of the grunt work. There's no other way you could have a practice as important and successful as you do—you need a lot of help. The thing is, you can hire babysitters and housekeepers and teachers—you can't do it all. You can't be aware of what's happening with your kids all the time, but you damn sure have to perfect a way of finding out as much as you can, or you're not only going to miss out, you're going to miss something really important. Like Krissy's desperation to be loved."

"Did you see it?"

"No. But then, the kids didn't reveal themselves to me—they pushed me away. They resented me so much. And when I tried to provide boundaries, you laughed me off. But, Ted, don't worry now. You can get some training. Now, while there's still time to help Krissy and time to keep from losing the other two."

"You have no idea what it was like to hear my daughter say those things," he said, his eyes growing watery again. "I had a mental image of seeing her dead."

"You must have been terrified."

"And guilty and ashamed and mortified. So filled with regret I couldn't even speak. I don't know what to do next. I don't think they know I love them."

"My mother always said there are only two things you have to tell your children. That you love them and you're so glad you have them. But she also said, if you don't make them do chores, you'll ruin them. They won't be able to live in the world. Her parenting philosophies are pretty simple, but she knows each one of her eight children down to the soles of our feet."

"Let's take the kids out to dinner tonight. Someplace they like."

"Ted, I can't do this for you. It has to be your family now."

"I understand. You're right. But before I have to go cold turkey, let's go out to dinner. We'll go early.

Then if you want to drive down to the farm, you won't get there too late."

She thought about it for a moment. It was Thursday. Right now she was desperate for the farm, if only to recover a little and get her bearings. "I'll hang around till Pam and Nicholas come home from school, until Krissy gets up from her nap. I want to tell the kids goodbye, but then I'm leaving. You take your kids out. Or even better, order something to be delivered. You guys have talking to do. I want to have a couple of days with my mom—she always sets me straight. And I want to get to Thunder Point by Sunday, so I'm ready to get back to work by Monday morning."

"Is that all it is? Work?"

"It's a good job, Ted. It's very satisfying."

"That doctor, is he a good doctor?"

She nodded. "He's amazing. He has to take care of a whole town with a wide variety of problems, and they don't have as many resources as a lot of people do. He can't just refer them all the time. You have no idea how they've come to depend on him." She smiled. "And he can't identify rashes at all. He has an online program to help him."

"Does he have children?"

She nodded. "Small children. They're four and five, and their mother is deceased."

Ted whistled. "Is he good at that, too?"

"Outstanding."

"What does he do that's so outstanding?"

"Well…he lets them make the dining-room table

into a fort with lots of blankets, and he gets in it with them. Sometimes he falls asleep there. If he has a babysitting problem, they come to the clinic and watch their movies or read books while he sees patients. Most of all, he talks to them and keeps them very close."

"And that's good?"

"It's the kind of stuff kids remember…sleeping in the fort, reading stories, digging holes on the beach, watching Dad at work…."

"I'm a fool. I blew it with you," Ted said.

"I don't know about that, Ted. I'm sorry about what Krissy's going through, what you're going through, but I think where you and I are concerned, we're in better places. You have a second chance with your family that you wouldn't have if someone was taking care of it for you. And I like the direction my life is going."

Eighteen

"What do you hear from Peyton?" Devon asked Scott during a quiet moment in the clinic. The last scheduled patient of the day had left, and it was just the two of them. Scott would stay a little longer while Devon rounded up their kids. "I thought she'd be back by now."

"She texted that she's spending a couple of nights with her folks at the farm," he said, not making eye contact.

"Texted?" Devon asked. "Have you talked to her?"

"We've talked a couple of times...."

"A couple of times?" Devon asked.

"She's been very busy with whatever Ted has her doing."

"Well, I don't think it was Ted, exactly. I got a pretty long email from her while she was sitting in the reception area of a counselor's office waiting for one of his screwed-up kids to finish a session.

She said it was a messy and complicated situation, and she'd explain later. So, what was the situation?"

"I have no idea," Scott said.

"How can you have no idea?"

He finally looked up. "I take it Ted's daughter, a fifteen-year-old, is pregnant. I assume Ted couldn't handle it. Beyond that, I didn't ask."

"Why didn't you ask?"

He sighed. "There needs to be more? If she had wanted me to know, she would have told me."

"Or maybe she wanted you to *ask!*"

"I'll ask when I see her," he said. "In fact, I'll try to arrange it so I can ask her when you're around, so you can get the answer, too."

"Wow, you're so irritable. You miss her, I guess."

"Of course I miss her," he said. Then he looked at Devon with earnest eyes. "Listen, I know you love Peyton. She's been amazing here and I hate to see her go, but I think we should be realistic. I don't think she's going to stay here."

"Oh? Really? Is she going to take that job in Seattle?"

"She hasn't said. But there's also San Francisco, near her sister. She and her sister are very close, and there's a new baby."

"What did she say to make you think she won't stay here?" Devon asked. "Because I kind of got the impression she was real happy here."

"I think this worked out for her for a while. But we know it's not the pay she deserves, and her talents exceed the needs of this little clinic."

"I've never heard her complain," Devon said. "You're acting weird. You're hiding something."

"I'm not hiding anything, don't be ridiculous. I think that if we're practical, we should accept that Peyton has bigger fish to fry."

"What fish? See, you're being very strange. I've gotten pretty close to Peyton, and she never mentioned any bigger fish to me."

Scott took a deep breath. "It's very reasonable that Peyton would be attracted to a high salary, and she can command one. It's not a crime to like nice things. I like nice things, too, but this is more my speed. This is where my heart is. I happen to like what I do. But Peyton grew up a poor farm girl. I'm sure she's striving for a lot more, and I don't blame her."

Devon was staring at him. Her mouth hung open. "Did you really just say that?"

"Say what? I just said a lot of things."

"Scott, Peyton isn't motivated by material wealth. And she's not a poor farm girl...."

He chuckled. "I guess that car is just a red herring...."

"That car of hers isn't that big a deal to her. She said she kind of regrets it. But forget about the damn car—she's thirty-five and in a high-end career field. She hasn't had anyone to spend her money on except her parents and nieces and nephews. She bought herself some nice things. But not because she's a poor farm girl!"

"I don't know about that...."

"Well, I do! Is that what you think? That Peyton

is just a poor girl who has wanted some rich stuff her whole life?"

"I admit, I considered that possibility."

"Well, I think you're very shortsighted. Maybe blind. I'm going to do you a big favor. I'm going to get the kids and take them out to my house. I'll get them fed."

"I have to take them with me to the game tonight. I'm the team doc, you know that. You're going with me, right? So if I'm needed for an injured player, there's someone for the kids?"

"Of course I am. But right now I think you should do yourself a favor and research a couple of things. You don't know your girlfriend. She knows you, but you don't know anything about her."

"What are you talking about?" he asked.

"Start by researching farms," she said, pointing at the computer. She pulled the strap of her purse over her shoulder. "Maybe Oregon farms."

"I've been to the farm, Devon."

"You went to the farm and still didn't see it? Remarkable. I'll see you at the house. If you have time, run by your house and grab some hoodies for the kids—it will probably be cold out there tonight."

"Sure," he said. "See you in a while."

"Google, Scott."

"I have some patient notes to look over."

"Suit yourself," she said. And then he thought he heard her mumble something that sounded like *idiot* as she went out the door.

Stubbornly, he sat at her desk, looking through

his notes on the computer rather than getting online. He'd keep the office open for a little while longer in case someone stopped by. He finished his charting, but it was too early to go over to Devon's to drive them all to the game....

So he looked up Oregon farms. *Whoa.* He read that the industry was worth over five *billion dollars? Okay, fine—divided by several thousand farmers, right?* Chief producer of Christmas trees, pears, berries, right up there with potatoes. Most of the farms were family owned.

He plugged in Lacoumette and came up with lots of references. Big family, involved in local and community services, business and politics. There was the winery—Uncle Sal, as he recalled. Lacoumette Farms? *Oh, boy.* It was one of the biggest farms in Oregon. So big that it would dramatically affect the agricultural economy if it collapsed.

Then there were articles about their product. Pears, potatoes, berries, wool. One of the most successful family-owned farms in the state, its profits were estimated in the millions.

But Peyton had told him how she grew up. They were all required to work very hard. Paco took them from the breast to the field. She worked through college. The house was not ostentatious——it was an ordinary farmhouse. Modest. It was built to accommodate a very large and ever-growing family, but it was far from upscale. The trucks he saw around the place were old and looked like hell. And now that he knew Paco and Corinne, he found it hard to believe they spoiled their kids, flung money at them. Their kids were forced to earn their way.

Damn, he thought. *She's right, Peyton's right. When we talk about this, I'm going to feel really stupid.*

He realized he'd been jealous of Ted's car, for Christ's sake. He wouldn't have one of those cars if it was forced on him! So, how was he going to explain thinking Peyton would be drawn to it? He'd been jealous of Ted, his tall good looks, his money, his car and all that diminished him and caused him to act like a fool.

This wasn't going to be easy to fix. Especially since he *was* a fool. And there was no excuse for it, either. If he thought about it for thirty seconds, he knew Peyton better than that. She was genuine and valued the things in life that were really important! She liked the feel of small children hugging her legs, cannoli delivered in a brown sack by a man who knew about her sweet tooth, a walk on the beach, a road trip with hours alone to talk.

He shut down the computer, locked the door and went to the house for hoodies. While he was there, he texted Peyton. I really miss you. I wish you could go to the football game tonight. There was no response, but then, why would there be? She hadn't been in touch too much, and he hadn't done too much to encourage her to reach out more.

He went to Devon's house where the kids were all eating their dinner. Devon was standing in the kitchen working her way through a hot dog. "Want one?" she asked.

He shook his head. "What do you have going on this weekend? Like from tomorrow morning to Sunday afternoon?"

She shrugged. "Same old stuff. House, shopping, kids, et cetera."

"No big social events?"

"No, why?"

"I might need a sitter. Overnight."

"Oh? What are you doing?"

"I think I better take a drive north. Up to the farm."

"You took my advice? You actually listened to me?"

"I didn't look into her. I looked at her, but not into her. I'm a schmuck."

"That's what I've been saying," Devon said. "I'll keep the kids. But you're going to owe me."

"I know. I'll owe you. I already owe you. But I think I'm in trouble here. And if I don't get her back, something inside me is going to die."

It was very rare that Peyton was the only one of the Lacoumette children at the table with her parents. Matt, the divorced brother who worked the farm and lived nearby, was the most frequent dinner guest. He took many meals at his mother's table because the cost was low, and though he wouldn't admit it, it comforted him. But Matt was not there this night, so it was just the three of them. Her father talked about potatoes and berries for a while, then he asked about that fancy doctor and his kids, so she told them everything.

Paco snorted and filled his mouth with more food. Corinne said, "Was there no other family?"

"Spread around. I met Ted's sister and brother-in-law, and it was obvious none of them were close. They didn't rely on each other for anything—why would Krissy rely on them during the scariest time of her life?"

"A family that works together comes together in the hard times," Paco pronounced.

"At least Ted takes it all very seriously now. I think he'll become a better father."

"Peyton, you're so sad," Corinne said. "Do you regret leaving Ted, after all?"

She shook her head. "I admired him so. I still admire him—he's the most wonderful doctor. But we haven't loved each other in a long time. It's just that..." She lowered her gaze to her plate and went quiet.

"What, darling?" Corinne asked.

She lifted her eyes. "If she was so in need of love, why couldn't she accept mine? I tried so hard."

"Oh, Peyton, people have troubles. We can't always help. Even when it's our own child, sometimes we aren't what they need."

"I don't have children," Peyton softly reminded her. "Maybe that's for the best."

"Pah! God has not spoken yet, that's all!"

"Well, I hope He sends me a text pretty soon, because I'm not getting any younger."

"My mother had her last child at forty-six," Paco said.

"I know. And I'm not doing that!"

Corinne patted her hand. "Nor should you, darling. I don't know what that woman was thinking. So, tomorrow we'll pull a little more out of the garden. I have some baking to do because next weekend there are a lot of family here. We'll can— I have bushels of tomatoes and other things in the cellar staying cool and fresh. You can take vegetables home to your friends. You can rest. After a night in a good bed, you'll be smiling again. Ted has a gift—a chance to manage his own family." She squeezed her hand. "He may not know it yet, but he's very lucky."

"He knows it, Mama. He could've been too late. And he was in time."

"I hope he thanked you for all you did."

"He did. Mama, did your children ever give you problems you couldn't help with?"

Corinne laughed. "More times than I could count. As recently as five minutes ago."

Peyton didn't even realize how emotionally drained she was until she turned in at eight. She checked her phone to make sure there were no messages. She texted Scott and told him she hoped he had had a good time at the game, that she was with her parents and would be back Sunday. She then texted Ted and said she hoped he was doing all right, that she had faith in him that he could make things work out in his family.

Of course, he could not text her back unless he borrowed a phone from one of the kids. But he could email her. She saw it as a good sign that he didn't. Perhaps he was busy with his children. And perhaps he was letting her go.

And then she slept the sleep of the emotionally depleted.

In the morning she worked in the garden with her mother, helped with lunch and after that she fled to the hayloft. And there, lying on her back, one ankle propped on a raised knee, she thought. *When I get home we'll talk about things, like trust and faith and true love. I hope I can get through to him because I love him. And I'm not going to give up without a fight.*

Scott saw the door to the Lacoumette house standing open, and good smells were wafting outside. It was a beautiful September afternoon. Peyton's car was parked in front, and he pulled up alongside it. He walked across the porch and stepped through the doorway. "Anyone home?" he called.

"In the kitchen," Corinne yelled.

He found Corinne at the stove and Peyton's brother George sitting at the workstation with a cup of coffee.

"Dr. Grant," Corinne said, wiping her hands on a towel. "We weren't expecting you!"

"I came on the spur of the moment. I'm sorry I didn't call ahead."

"It's all right, it's all right! George, go get your sister out of the hayloft."

"The hayloft?" Scott said. "Oh, she's working things out again? No, leave her there. But I have an idea—can you tell me where to find Paco?"

"I'll take you," George said. He stood and drained his cup and put it in the sink. "He's probably watching the harvester—the potatoes are coming in. I'm so glad I don't have potatoes. Dirty work. Come with me."

As he was following George out of the back of the house, he heard Corinne say she'd set a place for him for dinner. She had not asked him what he was doing here and on the drive out to the fields, George didn't, either. In fact, George didn't have much to say at all. He remarked on the weather, said again he was glad his crop just had to be sheared and he didn't have to harvest so much, especially the delicate fruits of pears and berries. He just liked to eat them.

Paco was leaning against the front of his old pickup truck, arms crossed over his broad chest, one leg crossed in front of the other. He watched two enormous pieces of farm equipment moving slowly down the rows of potatoes, spitting them out into trucks.

"There you go," George said.

When Scott got out, George sped away. Scott had expected him to get out, maybe make a little small talk with his father, give Scott some time to amp up his courage.

"Dr. Grant," Paco said. "You hungry again?"

He laughed. "Yes, sir. Something pretty wonderful seems to be happening in that kitchen."

"Good, good. You look well enough for a man looking for his girlfriend's father."

Well, he's straight to the point. "Right now Peyton isn't very happy with me. I'll have some penance to pay."

"Don't worry too much. She's a forgiving girl."

"Your farm does very well, Mr. Lacoumette. You have a true gift."

"It's a good farm most days."

"It's one of the biggest farms in the state. I looked it up on the internet."

"Pah, that internet. It should be illegal. It knows too damn much."

"It would be a very helpful tool for a farmer."

"It is. It is. We use it. But it knows too damn much. A man has no secrets anymore. So, you planning to rob me?"

"Yes, sir, I am. If Peyton forgives me for being a fool, I want to ask her to marry me. And that's a lot to ask, believe me. I have children. I have a crazy life sometimes. Sometimes I have no sense."

"Peyton knows children and crazy. She grew up here. But I don't know. You're not Basque. What are you?"

He laughed a little. "Everything," he said.

"At least there are no feuds," Paco said. "Intermarry enough and the feuds all die away. So, what do you have to offer her? Or did you just come to examine her dowry?"

"She has a dowry?" Scott asked.

Paco turned to face him. "Look at me! Do I look like a rich man?" He turned the pockets on his worn overalls inside out. "I have no money." Then he gestured to the fields where those huge harvesters that cost about a billion each chugged along. "My wealth is in the ground! In the stock! In the orchard." Then he paused meaningfully and said, "In my children. That's the dowry—she is worth a king's ransom to me."

"I don't have much. A clinic that's small and takes every cent to run. But I love her, Mr. Lacoumette."

"Well, let's talk about what you have. Do you have a strong heart? Are you a man of your word? Are you faithful and willing to work for your family? Do you have a generous spirit that's willing to help people?"

"Yes, sir," he said.

"And are you willing to dance for your family?" he asked softly. "Because life is not only work, you know."

"Yes, sir."

"Then, perhaps you'll do. I leave that to my daughter. And I warn you, she has made a mistake or two."

"She won't make a mistake with me, sir."

"She's stubborn—it's terrible at times. She's also very softhearted. I see her with the children and with the animals, and she has trouble being firm with them. She has a difficult nature when she wants to be right, but I admit she gets that from her mother. But she's not delicate, that's an advantage. You might have trying days with her, son. She will not be easy to tame."

"I have no desire to tame her, sir. I admire her."

"Just as well, because you wouldn't likely win that one."

"How did you meet your wife, sir?" Scott asked.

"Ah, her father forced her on me. I wanted to send to the old country for a woman—I wanted a good Basque wife! Not that skinny thing."

"But Mrs. Lacoumette is Basque," Scott said.

"I said *good* Basque! That skinny American thing wasn't what I had in mind at all." Then he grinned and said, "But she's one helluva woman, eh?"

"Yes," Scott said, laughing. "You don't say those things to her, do you?"

"What? I'm poor! I'm not stupid!"

"Thank you, sir," he said, shaking his hand. "I'm going to go find Peyton."

"I'll drive you. I want to get you there before you lose your nerve. Get in."

Scott got in the passenger side, and Paco tore out of the field and down a dirt road that cut across a meadow, went through the orchard and bounced along beside a corral. There were no seat belts. Scott hung on for dear life. "I know you're poor as a church mouse, but did you ever think about a new truck?"

"Why? This one runs fine!"

"How's your spine holding up?"

"Strong as an ox!" Paco pulled up to the house. "Go find her. If she says yes, we'll open a bottle of sack!"

Scott took a deep breath before climbing up the ladder that led to the loft. When he was all the way to the top, he saw her. She was lying on a hay bale, one leg dangling off and the other bent at the knee and propped up. She was twirling a piece of hay in one hand, looking at it distractedly.

"Peyton."

She jumped at the sound of her name and fell off the bale, rolled over and sat up, hair and straw in her face. "What are you doing here?"

"I came to talk to you. To apologize. I made some very dumb assumptions about you that weren't just all wrong, they were offensive. Can you forgive me?" He climbed up into the loft and took a step closer.

"This is a sacred place, Dr. Grant. Any lies you tell will send you straight to hell."

"I'm not going to lie. I'm really sorry. And embarrassed. I don't know why I acted like I did. I'm not that guy, I'm really not. I don't give a shit what Ted drives, and I know you aren't the kind of girl who's fooled by that stuff. I think I was afraid Ted would find a way to get you back."

She considered him for a moment. "If you'd been honest with me, we could've talked about it."

"I know that now. I won't make that mistake again. But, Peyton, you're different on the outside than you are on the inside."

"Is that so?" she asked indignantly.

"It is so. You like nice things, and you look so... so *sophisticated*. Even in jeans," he said, his eyes running over her. "Especially in jeans."

"Excuse me, but how is that misleading?"

"Well, it shouldn't be," Scott said. "But I was afraid you were attracted to Ted's money."

"I don't think Ted actually has money," she said. "I think he has *things*—and they cost a lot. In fact, it costs Ted a lot to live."

"Then there was your car...."

"Pah," she said, sounding so much like her father. "It's a car, Scott! And I'm not all that happy with it, anyway!"

"You're not?"

"Buyer's remorse," she said with a shrug. "I missed the money the second I let it go. Now I'm going to be driving it till I'm ninety, so I'm going to have to make peace with it."

"All that, and then you answered his call for help," Scott said. He sat down on the floor, circling his knees with his arms. "I was intimidated by everything—the car, the ex-boyfriend, the job offer in Seattle. I didn't think any woman in her right mind would choose me over all that."

"Well...I haven't. *Yet.* And I didn't answer Ted's call for help, I answered his daughter's. I told you that. I thought she was suicidal."

"Holy Jesus," he said.

"She's getting help now. If you hadn't been a complete ass, I would have explained all that. It wasn't hard for me to ignore Ted's pleas for help, but I couldn't walk away from a young girl in trouble."

"I'm sorry. I have no excuse. But there's been research out of Stanford that being in love actually causes brain damage."

"Does that mean recovery requires you stop being in love?"

"The opposite," he said. "It requires you make a promise. A bond. I love you, Peyton. I don't want to live without you. I don't think Jenny and Will want to live without you, either. I want you to marry me. No matter what you say, I think I'm going to love you forever."

"Well," she said, considering. "There are terms."

"Name 'em."

"Well, for starters, you're going to have to learn to communicate. If you'd asked questions or opened a dialogue, you might not have to do so much apologizing."

"I agree to that. Absolutely."

"Next, after we're married, I want to be an associate in the clinic. We can make it strong if we're partners. As long as we have enough, the income doesn't matter as much as the work we can do."

"I want that, too. And I agree."

"And I want another child."

His mouth fell open.

She put a hand up. "I know you might be scared, given what happened to Serena. But that won't happen to me. And I think when people love each other and make a bond, it's good for them to make a child if they can. That might be very old-world thinking, but I promise not to surprise you with eight of them. I just… I really want to feel our baby move inside me. I want to watch it grow."

He crawled over to her and pulled her into his arms. "I'm not afraid. I'd like that."

"And finally, you have to promise to be fearless with me, with everything that concerns me. You have to suck it up and stare our problems in the eye. There will be problems. I'll usually be right, of course…."

He grinned. "Your father mentioned that might be the case."

"He did? That old bull—he's the one who has to always be right!"

"Really? He said if I took you off his hands, we'd open a bottle of sack to celebrate."

"That's his special stock, sent to him years ago by a relative in the Balearic Islands in Spain. He must be rooting for you."

"He offered me a dowry. Of course, it was only you, but—"

She slugged him. "*Only* me?"

"God, you hit hard! I was about to say, but you're all I want."

"Better."

"I thought you were a poor farm kid."

"So did I," she said with a laugh. "Farmers are very careful—one bad year can be a disaster, two bad years can be the end. They're superstitious— they don't brag about their success. You know what Papa said when he saw my fancy car? He said, can you live in it? Will it make baby cars? Is there a point to it?"

"Your father is wise. And he's been very successful."

"Don't tell him that. 'Do I look rich? My wealth is in the ground, hanging from the trees,'" she mimicked. "Poor Mouth Paco—he could buy and sell Ted five times over."

Scott ran a finger along her jaw. "His wealth is in his family. And my wealth will be in my wife and children. Marry me, Peyton. Belong to me. I'm not worth a damn without you."

* * * * *

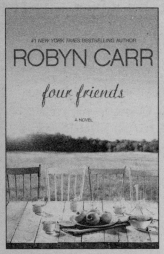

REQUEST YOUR
FREE BOOKS!

2 FREE NOVELS
FROM THE ROMANCE COLLECTION
PLUS 2 FREE GIFTS!

YES! Please send me 2 FREE novels from the Romance Collection and my 2 FREE gifts (gifts are worth about $10). After receiving them, if I don't wish to receive any more books, I can return the shipping statement marked "cancel." If I don't cancel, I will receive 4 brand-new novels every month and be billed just $6.24 per book in the U.S. or $6.74 per book in Canada. That's a savings of at least 22% off the cover price. It's quite a bargain! Shipping and handling is just 50¢ per book in the U.S. and 75¢ per book in Canada.* I understand that accepting the 2 free books and gifts places me under no obligation to buy anything. I can always return a shipment and cancel at any time. Even if I never buy another book, the two free books and gifts are mine to keep forever.

194/394 MDN F4XY

Name _____ (PLEASE PRINT)

Address _____ Apt. #

City _____ State/Prov. _____ Zip/Postal Code

Signature (if under 18, a parent or guardian must sign)

Mail to the **Harlequin® Reader Service:**
IN U.S.A.: P.O. Box 1867, Buffalo, NY 14240-1867
IN CANADA: P.O. Box 609, Fort Erie, Ontario L2A 5X3

Want to try two free books from another line?
Call 1-800-873-8635 or visit www.ReaderService.com.

* Terms and prices subject to change without notice. Prices do not include applicable taxes. Sales tax applicable in N.Y. Canadian residents will be charged applicable taxes. Offer not valid in Quebec. This offer is limited to one order per household. Not valid for current subscribers to the Romance Collection or the Romance/Suspense Collection. All orders subject to credit approval. Credit or debit balances in a customer's account(s) may be offset by any other outstanding balance owed by or to the customer. Please allow 4 to 6 weeks for delivery. Offer available while quantities last.

Your Privacy—The Harlequin® Reader Service is committed to protecting your privacy. Our Privacy Policy is available online at www.ReaderService.com or upon request from the Harlequin Reader Service.

We make a portion of our mailing list available to reputable third parties that offer products we believe may interest you. If you prefer that we not exchange your name with third parties, or if you wish to clarify or modify your communication preferences, please visit us at www.ReaderService.com/consumerschoice or write to us at Harlequin Reader Service Preference Service, P.O. Box 9062, Buffalo, NY 14269. Include your complete name and address.

ROM13R

ROBYN CARR

32942	HARVEST MOON	___ $7.99 U.S.	___ $9.99 CAN.
32931	WILD MAN CREEK	___ $7.99 U.S.	___ $9.99 CAN.
32899	JUST OVER THE MOUNTAIN	___ $7.99 U.S.	___ $9.99 CAN.
32898	DOWN BY THE RIVER	___ $7.99 U.S.	___ $9.99 CAN.
32897	DEEP IN THE VALLEY	___ $7.99 U.S.	___ $9.99 CAN.
32870	A SUMMER IN SONOMA	___ $7.99 U.S.	___ $9.99 CAN.
32868	THE HOUSE ON OLIVE STREET	___ $7.99 U.S.	___ $9.99 CAN.
32768	MOONLIGHT ROAD	___ $7.99 U.S.	___ $9.99 CAN.
31599	THE CHANCE	___ $7.99 U.S.	___ $8.99 CAN.
31582	TEMPTATION RIDGE	___ $7.99 U.S.	___ $8.99 CAN.
31571	SECOND CHANCE PASS	___ $7.99 U.S.	___ $8.99 CAN.
31513	A VIRGIN RIVER CHRISTMAS	___ $7.99 U.S.	___ $8.99 CAN.
31459	THE HERO	___ $7.99 U.S.	___ $8.99 CAN.
31452	THE NEWCOMER	___ $7.99 U.S.	___ $9.99 CAN.
31447	THE WANDERER	___ $7.99 U.S.	___ $9.99 CAN.
31428	WHISPERING ROCK	___ $7.99 U.S.	___ $9.99 CAN.
31419	SHELTER MOUNTAIN	___ $7.99 U.S.	___ $9.99 CAN.
31415	VIRGIN RIVER	___ $7.99 U.S.	___ $9.99 CAN.
31385	MY KIND OF CHRISTMAS	___ $7.99 U.S.	___ $9.99 CAN.
31300	HIDDEN SUMMIT	___ $7.99 U.S.	___ $9.99 CAN.
31271	BRING ME HOME FOR CHRISTMAS	___ $7.99 U.S.	___ $9.99 CAN.

(limited quantities available)

TOTAL AMOUNT	$ _____
POSTAGE & HANDLING	$ _____
($1.00 for 1 book, 50¢ for each additional)	
APPLICABLE TAXES*	$ _____
TOTAL PAYABLE	$ _____

(check or money order—please do not send cash)

To order, complete this form and send it, along with a check or money order for the total above, payable to Harlequin MIRA, to: **In the U.S.:** 3010 Walden Avenue, P.O. Box 9077, Buffalo, NY 14269-9077; **In Canada:** P.O. Box 636, Fort Erie, Ontario, L2A 5X3.

Name: _____

Address: _____ City: _____

State/Prov.: _____ Zip/Postal Code: _____

Account Number (if applicable): _____

075 CSAS

*New York residents remit applicable sales taxes.
*Canadian residents remit applicable GST and provincial taxes.

HARLEQUIN® MIRA®
www.Harlequin.com

MRC0714BL